Miss February

Book One of the Calendar Girl Duet

Karen Cimms

Lone Sparrow Press

Diane Lane Stone, my forever friend.
Thank you.

Cover Designer: Garrett Cimms

Line Editing: Lisa Poisso, lisapoisso.com

Proofreading: Lori Ryser

ISBN: (Print) 978-0-9974867-8-0

ISBN: (eBook)

Pained eyes. Pink lips.
Silly boys only look at hips.
Subtle lies. Midnight cries.
Men drink her words in greedy sips.

—n.a. denmon

CHAPTER ONE

Rain

The bell chimed over the door, just loud enough for me to hear over the pulse of running water as I scrubbed scorched clam chowder from an aluminum stock pot.

"Can you get that?" my mother called from the office where she'd disappeared after the lunch rush to work on payroll for the week. "If I have to add these numbers one more time—"

I flicked off the faucet and dried my hands on the apron I wore over my cutoffs. "Got it."

I didn't normally work Saturdays, but when my mother called at seven a. m., desperate for an extra pair of hands, I'd rolled out of bed and brushed my teeth. I hurriedly twisted my hair into a long messy braid and snatched up my five-year-old, who was still wearing her favorite pink and purple dinosaur pajamas. At least I didn't have a long commute, given I lived above the luncheonette. I hadn't even washed my face, let alone put on makeup. A cardinal sin in my book, but at our luncheonette, I was chief cook, baker, and pot scrubber. My presence wasn't usually required behind the counter—which meant no makeup, no big deal. Unlike my night job, bartending, where I'd learned that playing up my assets meant more tips in my jar at the end of the night, even if they were often accompanied by a slap on the ass or a lewd remark.

Hey, it paid the bills, and I had a kid to raise.

I stepped out of the kitchen to see two large hands resting on top of the glass bakery case. Their owner was bent over, studying the last of the week's cookies and cupcakes.

"Can I help you?"

He straightened, and the first thing I noticed was his Pearl Jam Vitalogy T-shirt. And that he was tall—like six foot three at least. He had a great pair of arms. Strong, well-defined. Like he worked hard rather than worked out. Dark-blond hair brushed the tops of his shoulders.

He pointed to the bottom shelf of the display case. "Those cupcakes look amazing."

Of course they did. I made them. "They are amazing." One should never be modest about baked goods.

He pushed his mirrored sunglasses atop his head, revealing a pair of blue-green eyes that rivaled pictures I'd seen of the waters in the Caribbean. They were framed by long, thick lashes beneath full, dark eyebrows, giving him a serious look, even when he smiled. His chiseled nose, mouth and jaw could probably cut glass. Despite a face that could've graced the cover of GQ, he looked like he'd be far more comfortable posing for Field & Stream or Popular Mechanics.

"The sign on the door said you're closing soon. Is it too late to order something to go?"

I blinked to break the spell he'd somehow cast. "No problem. What can I get you?"

He scanned the menu board over my head. "I'm starving. What's good?"

"Everything, but if you're hungry, how about a Rainmaker?"

His smile widened and he gave me a flirty look. "I don't know. It's too nice out today to chance rain. But just in case I want to risk it, what's a Rainmaker?"

"It's a twelve-inch sub with roast beef, provolone, and a sliced-up hard-boiled egg, topped with lettuce, tomato, onion, and Russian dressing."

"I hope that comes with a side of napkins."

"Absolutely."

"Sounds unusual, but I'm game."

I pulled a roll from the bread bin, sliced it lengthwise, and opened it on the stainless steel work counter, then began layering on thin slices of roast beef.

He continued to read the menu board. "Do you have any salads?"

"We're out of macaroni salad, but we have coleslaw and potato salad. I think we might have a little pasta salad left."

"Nah. Just greens and veggies—plain—if you have it."

This was a big guy. Lean, but well built. I didn't picture him as the side salad type.

"Is that for you, or do you have a pet rabbit?"

He had a nice laugh. It kind of rose up out of his chest in a low rumble. He hooked a thumb toward the parking lot. "No. My fiancée."

I felt a blip of disappointment. Why, I had no idea. I'd never seen this guy before. Besides, I had a boyfriend—sort of.

"She barely eats since we got engaged. She wants to make sure she'll fit into her dress. I'm afraid she might disappear if she doesn't eat a few carbs now and then."

I gave him an extra squirt of dressing before folding his sandwich and cutting it in half. "We have some spring mix. I can toss in some peppers and onions."

"That would be great. But no onions. She won't eat them." The way he was grinning, I guessed he was happy that his fiancée wouldn't be eating onions. I was about to point out that he hadn't asked me to leave the onions off his sandwich, but I wasn't the one who'd be kissing him. Which was a shame. His lips looked very kissable.

I finished wrapping the sandwich and set it next to the register. Then I filled a to-go container with lettuce and slices of green pepper.

"Do you think she might like a hard-boiled egg with this? Or any meat or cheese? You know, a chef salad?"

He shook his head. "Nope. Just the lettuce and peppers."

"Dressing?"

"Nope." He shrugged and laughed. "What can I tell you? She's a rabbit."

He pulled a bottle of root beer and a bottle of water from the cooler and set them on the counter. I began ringing him up.

"Wait! I want some of those cupcakes." He scanned the case again. "Give me three of the chocolate ones. And what are those there? The ones with the tan icing and the toasted marshmallows?"

"S'mores. Chocolate cake with marshmallow cream inside and graham cracker buttercream on top."

He tilted his head back. "I think I've just died and gone to heaven. Three of those too, please."

I carefully placed the cupcakes into a box, sealed it, and tied it with red and white string. We weren't a bakery, but I treated my baked goods as if we were.

"Are you going to eat all six of these?"

The grin he flashed made my toes curl. Lucky rabbit. "Damn straight."

"That'll be $21.75."

He reached for his wallet and his T-shirt rode up, exposing a sliver of tan skin. I had to drag my eyes up where they belonged.

He handed me two bills. I counted out his change and dropped it into his hand. "Thanks," I said, closing the drawer. "I hope you enjoy your sandwich and your cupcakes." I stepped out from behind the counter so that I could lock up behind him. "And that your girlfriend enjoys her . . . lettuce."

He smiled again. "I'm sure we will."

I'd barely closed and locked the door when my mother popped her head out of the office. "Oh my god! He's adorable. Who was that?"

"I dunno. I never saw him before."

"I hope he'll be back."

"Why? You interested in younger men now?"

"If they look like that, hell yeah."

I faked a shiver. I adored my mother. But once she got over my father's death, she'd lost her filters. Or maybe she never had any, and I'd just never noticed.

She pointed her chin toward the door. "He's back," she said and disappeared into her office.

"Is something wrong?" I asked, opening the door.

"Yeah, actually. You gave me change for forty. I only gave you thirty."

"Are you sure? I could've sworn you gave me two twenties."

"Positive. I only had one twenty and the rest are tens."

If I hadn't been staring at that strip of skin above his waist, I might have been paying closer attention.

He held out his hand to give me the extra money, and when our hands touched, a spark shot through me. Like static electricity, only stronger. Startled, I pulled away. The bill floated to the ground. I shook the sting out of my hand. "That was weird."

He bent and scooped up the money. "What was?"

"Didn't you feel that?"

"Feel what?"

From this close, his eyes were mesmerizing. I glanced down, breaking the gaze, expecting to find the answer sitting in the palm of my hand. "That shock. You didn't feel it?"

He shook his head. "No. Not really."

It was the strangest thing. I didn't know much about science, but I thought the only time you could get a shock from touching someone was in the winter.

"Just me, I guess." I held up the ten. "Thanks for being honest. Not everyone would do that."

He smiled again, and it seemed as if the air temperature around us climbed at least ten degrees.

"Well, I'm one of the good guys." He touched two fingers to his head and tipped an imaginary hat. "Ma'am."

I bit back a laugh. He was cute and corny. "Thank you kindly, stranger."

I stepped inside as he crossed the parking lot toward a black pickup with Pennsylvania plates. A dark-haired girl sat in the front seat, her head down, and I assumed she was busy with her phone. She didn't look up when he opened the door to the truck.

He hesitated, looked down at his hand, then back toward me. Had he felt something after all? It looked as if he might come back, but he didn't. He settled his glasses on his nose, slid into the driver's seat, and pulled away.

The surface of my palm was warm and it tingled. I expected to see a mark, but there was nothing. Nothing but my empty hand.

CHAPTER TWO

Rain

"Now do mine, Mama."

Izzy sat on the edge of the bathroom counter and waved my mascara wand in her chubby little hand, eyes closed, face tipped up, waiting. I placed a kiss on the tip of her perfect little nose instead.

"You're so pretty you don't need mascara."

Her eyes popped open. "But you're beautiful, Mama, and you need it."

I looked at my image in the mirror. Smudged, smoky black eyeliner around ice-blue eyes; several thick coats of mascara; penciled eyebrows; lined lips. Blond hair bleached even lighter, curled into soft waves falling to the middle of my back.

I had my mother to thank for my body. Although I was a bit taller, we had the same long legs and narrow waists. And my friend Diane insisted Mom and I must've been standing in line with both hands out when the good Lord was passing out boobs—and then greedily come back for more.

Beautiful? It was an illusion. A disguise. It was the armor I wore to protect the fifteen-year-old hiding inside, the girl I was before my daddy died and I let my life spiral out of control.

I leaned in and applied a layer of lip gloss over my pale nude lipstick.

"Pucker up," I said to Izzy, making a kissy face. "I think all you need tonight is a touch of lip gloss. What do you say?"

Her little head bobbed, curls the color of corn silk bouncing. I lightly touched the wand to her lips. Two small dots, top and bottom. "Now what do we do?"

She pressed her lips together and moved them side to side.

"Perfect!"

I plucked her off the counter and set her on the floor. "Your suitcase packed?"

I probably had the only five-year-old in New Jersey who could pack her own suitcase, but between staying with my mom a couple nights a week and weekends with Jeff's parents, or with Jeff when he wasn't away at school, Izzy knew what she needed to bring. And since she'd begun packing it herself, Mom no longer had to make extra trips back to my apartment to grab whatever I'd forgotten to throw in the suitcase.

She zipped out of the bathroom and into the bedroom, returning with the daisy-covered suitcase on wheels Jeff's parents had given her last Christmas.

"Do you remember the plan?"

The way she huffed and rolled her eyes, you would've thought she was fifteen instead of five. "Jeff is picking me up and taking me to his new house and tomorrow he's bringing me to Gramma and Grampa's for dinner and that's where you'll pick me up."

"Iz, what did I tell you?"

Her lower lip popped out and her little brow furrowed. "But I don't like calling him Daddy. His friends laugh at me."

I dropped to my knees and brought my face closer to hers. "They're not laughing at you, pumpkin. They're laughing because they don't understand how great it is to be a daddy. Honestly? I bet they're jealous."

The look she gave me said she saw right through me. Jeff was an ass, but he had been the most popular ass in high school, and I hadn't exactly been thinking straight back then. He'd broken up with me about a minute after I told him I was pregnant. He left for college before Izzy was born. Over the past few years, he hadn't really spent much time with her other than an occasional weekend when he visited his parents, and I imagined it was only because they insisted.

When he graduated and got a job and a place of his own, he'd said he would take her twice a month but that didn't last long. We were down to once a month now, and those visits, according to Izzy, featured a bunch of guys hanging around Jeff's living room, watching sports, both Saturday and Sunday.

When Jeff knocked a short time later, Izzy dragged herself off the sofa and trudged toward the door like she was heading for a firing squad. She pulled it open and Jeff's lean, lanky frame filled the doorway.

"Hey, kiddo, you ready to roll?" The hint of impatience in his voice had me wanting to kick him right in the nuts.

She looked at me, her eyes pleading. My daughter would rather sit on the floor in my mother's office and color, instead of spend a weekend with her father.

"Iz, go pick out a bottle of nail polish so that Daddy can paint your nails this weekend."

Her little mouth dropped. "Really?"

"Rain—"

"Go on. Make sure you find something good."

When she scampered from the room, I addressed the sperm donor.

"Listen to me. You need to spend time with her. Not park her in front of the TV in your room to watch cartoons while you and your buddies—"

Jeff pushed off the door frame and strolled into my living room. "Don't lecture me—"

He was lucky I wasn't doing far worse. "I'm not lecturing. I'm advocating. That's my kid, and she doesn't exactly look forward to weekends with her father. Jesus, Jeff. You see her for what? Thirty hours a month? And half of that time she's probably asleep."

He brushed his hair from his forehead as his eyes drifted from my mouth, down the column of my throat, and landed on my breasts.

"Eyes up here!" I snapped.

He did as I asked, but I still wanted to smack the smirk off his face.

"Tell your buddies to stay home this week and do something with her. She deserves it. I'm not asking for me." I lowered my voice so that there was no chance she would hear me, and took a step closer. "She's your daughter. Make the next few hours about her. Could you do that, please?"

He huffed and rolled his eyes, and if Izzy hadn't appeared behind me, chances were good he'd be lying on my deck, clutching his nut sack. God, he brought out the worst in me. How the hell half of his DNA had helped create this exquisite little person was a mystery to me. I took a deep cleansing breath to steady myself.

Izzy excitedly held up five bottles of nail polish—one for each finger on each hand of course—from light pink to deep red, including my favorite Victoria's Secret pink. "I'm ready," she announced. At least now she sounded like she meant it.

I squatted beside her, and she wrapped her arms around my neck. "Hugs and kisses, punkin. Now you be good for Daddy, okay? You're going to have so much fun this weekend." I cocked my head up toward her father. "Right, Daddy?"

He gave me a sour look as he chewed on the side of his mouth, but when he smiled at Izzy, at least it was genuine.

He snatched up her suitcase. "You bet. But I don't know how to put on nail polish."

She tucked her little hand in his and heaved a great sigh. "Oh, Daddy. I guess I'll just have to teach you."

CHAPTER THREE

Rain

It was busier than usual for a Saturday night. Most of the stools along the bar were filled, as were most of the tables in the back room. A cute older couple had been in earlier, nursing their one drink each and pouring quarters into the ancient jukebox, but they'd left. Now, instead of Lady Antebellum and Miranda Lambert, I was serenaded by the crack of pool balls coming from the back room, and assorted screams and cackles from the other side of the bar.

I stifled a yawn. I should've taken a nap this afternoon when I'd had the chance. I'd tried. I even set Izzy up in front of the television and lay down on the sofa beside her, but I couldn't stop thinking about the guy who'd come into the luncheonette and what happened when he'd touched my hand.

The sensation had faded, but the experience remained vivid. The only person who might've understood what had happened or could explain it, was my dad. But he'd been gone for almost six years.

Like him, I've always been a bit psychic. Nothing like Miss Cleo or that chick from Long Island. Simple things. Guessing middle names, figuring out what card someone's hiding behind their back or what number they might be thinking of. Useless stuff, really.

My dad? He had a real gift. He knew when to schedule a picnic or a trip to the shore and when to stay home. If the phone rang, he knew who was calling before any of us answered it. (Although that was an easy one. It was almost always Diane, my best friend since kindergarten.)

He knew when the Giants or the Nets were going to win, and he often dreamed the winning lottery numbers. But he never played. He wouldn't use his gift to help himself. He said it wouldn't be right.

The only time he ever pursued one of his visions, or whatever you want to call them, was when he met my mother. He swore from the moment they met that she was the one. He just had to win her over. And he did. I'd never seen two people so in love. They used to embarrass the hell out of me, but at least I grew up knowing what love was supposed to look like.

But there was more, and that's probably what had me feeling so unsettled.

I was pretty young, maybe eight or nine, when I remember hearing my parents talking about Dad's new boss. He said the guy was going around the warehouse introducing himself to everyone, and he shook my father's hand. That night, I overhead my dad telling my mother that the moment their hands touched, he knew the guy would be dead within six months, and he was.

I had been so freaked out, I was afraid to let my father hold my hand for weeks after that.

I put down the rag that I'd been using to wipe down the bar and stared at the spot on my hand. Was that it? The guy hadn't looked sick. Far from it. But you never know, right? A chill settled over me, and I tried to shake it off. I was giving myself far too much credit.

What I could do was nothing more than a party trick. I couldn't predict anyone's illness or death.

And I damn sure wouldn't want to either.

"Something wrong with your hand?"

My head snapped up, and my hand flew to my chest. "Preston. You scared the shit out of me. What're you doing here?"

"Scared you? I walked in the door and said 'hello' three times. You've been staring at your hand for the past minute at least. You got a splinter or something?"

I wiped my palm against my thigh like I had something to hide. "No. Just thinking. Tired." I lifted up on my toes and leaned across the scarred mahogany bar, meeting Preston's lips and inhaling his warm, woodsy scent.

Preston Jamison was the most pulled-together man I had ever seen: close-cropped, sandy hair, a handsome face, and a mouth full of perfect teeth to go with his perfect smile. He was wearing some expensive-looking shirt and a pair of khakis, and though he wasn't wearing one of those expensive suits of his, he still stood out among the bulk of our clientele in their grease-covered Carhartts and smelly T-shirts.

We'd been seeing each other for several weeks. Nothing serious, but I did like him. Besides, I didn't have time for anything serious anyway.

"How's my girl?"

"Busy." I nodded toward the peals of laughter coming from the dining area. "It's women's league night."

"Sounds like they won."

I hoisted a tray of drinks for the bawdy bowlers. "That, or they're really good losers."

When I'd finished passing out drinks and collecting empties, I returned to my spot behind the bar, just as my best friend's fiancé and his racing crew burst through the door arguing about chains or belts or some other nonsense that must've gone wrong on their modified stock car that night. They planted themselves around Preston, drawing him into their little world, while I grabbed a handful of Buds from the cooler.

"So has Rain figured out your middle name yet?" Wally asked Preston.

"Wally." I gave him the stink eye. I didn't want Preston thinking I was some nutcase, which was how most people responded when they found out I considered myself to be a somewhat psychic.

"What's this?" Preston looked amused, a look he often wore around Wally and the guys, as if they're there for his entertainment.

"Rain's psychic. She knows things."

I strolled over to the end of the bar where a thin, bearded man sat wearing a worn and faded Caterpillar cap pulled low over his eyes and grabbed his empty mug. I slipped it under the spout and pulled the tap handle.

"Yep. I had to channel all my psychic ability to know Fish needed a refill."

"That and the empty glass," Preston pointed out.

I winked at him. "Exactly."

"C'mon, Rain," Wally said. "Tell him his middle name."

"I can't always do it." I scanned the perimeter of the rectangular bar. Everyone's glasses were full, and no one seemed to be in need of anything.

"She's got a record going," Wally's brother, Bobby, said, adding his two cents. "Twenty-seven in a row. No misses."

Preston set down his bottle. "Oh, this I've got to see. Get over here, sweet cheeks."

I glared at him, but given the wild way he was grinning at me, I couldn't help but crack a smile. "Okay, but I'll warn you. I'm not feeling it tonight, so no promises. Give me something that's yours. Your keys, wallet, something you've touched or held."

He dipped into the pocket of his slacks and pulled out the keys to his Corvette.

"Now give me the first initial of your middle name."

"That doesn't seem fair, to give you hints."

"Stop whining and give her the initial," Wally demanded.

"Fine," Preston said. "It's F."

Palming the keys, I closed my eyes and tried to empty my mind. Narrowing my focus, I paired vowels with his name: Fa, Fe, Fi, Fo, Fu. I giggled. I did it again. Fi stood out. This was a tough one. I wasn't feeling a typical boy's name.

I opened my eyes, and I immediately wanted to wipe the smirk off his face.

"It's not Frederick or Francis. It's a family name."

I squeezed the keys and closed my eyes again. Jamison was Scottish or Irish in origin. There was a buzzing—no, a fizzing. Fizz. Fitz. Fitzpatrick. I squeezed harder.

Got it!

Opening my eyes, I smiled and handed Preston his keys.

"Well?" He returned his keys to his pocket.

"Well, you tell me, Mr. Preston Fitzgerald Jamison."

His jaw dropped. Bingo!

"How'd you do that?" he asked.

"Because she's psychic!" Wally crowed, slapping Preston on the back so hard I thought his head would roll off.

I left Wally and the boys to regale Preston with tales of my supernatural accomplishments while I filled mugs, mixed drinks, and made my rounds.

By the time I'd rung up the last of the lady bowlers, it was closing time.

"Zamykamy!" Irena clapped her hands and shouted, as if the few remaining customers had already wasted enough of her time. "Czas się zbierać!"

"C'mon, boys. You heard the lady. Time to go," I hollered, translating Irena's Polish into something they'd understand.

Preston nursed the last of his drink while I settled up with Fish.

"You comin' home with me tonight, sweetheart?" Fish asked, slurring his words and steadying himself on the back of his stool.

"Not tonight," I said, like I told him every time he asked. "I don't think your wife would like that."

"Screw 'er!"

"That's your job, babe."

Wally and the crew rose from their stools and shuffled toward the door.

"You guys okay to drive?" I knew damn well Fish wasn't, which meant he'd leave his car like always, and Wally, Bobby, or Dennis would drop him off at home.

"Zamykamy! Zamykamy" Irena called from the kitchen door.

After a few more minutes, I herded everyone out the door except for Preston. I clicked the lock behind them.

"Have a drink with me," he said.

"I'm drinking club soda."

"C'mon. I'm buying."

I laughed, but still, I gave in. "Tequila?"

He gave me a slow, sexy smile. "How about a body shot?"

"How about a glass?" I suggested with a frown, in spite of the crazy little thrill that ran through me.

"Okay, but just this once." He winked.

I poured us each a shot of tequila and set out the saltshaker and two wedges of lime. He grabbed a wedge, put it between his teeth, and waggled his eyebrows.

Okay, rich boy.

I picked up his hand and licked along the inside of his wrist, then sprinkled it with salt. I licked the salt, took my shot, then stood on my toes while he leaned forward. I bit down and sucked on the lime in his mouth, shivering as my lips brushed his before I pulled back. I tucked a wedge between my teeth, and waited.

He took my arm in both hands and ran his tongue from my wrist to the inside of my elbow, his eyes never leaving mine. Then he sprinkled it with salt and licked it again, much slower this time, leaving a trail of goosebumps in his wake. He tossed back the tequila, and after he bit his lime, he tugged it from my mouth, spit it out onto the bar, and with his hand against the back of my head, pulled me forward and kissed me.

It was just the right amount of tequila, citrus, and tongue.

When he let go, I actually swayed.

"You have to be anywhere right away?" he asked, his voice low and throaty. "I wouldn't mind spending a little time with you."

My voice deserted me after that kiss, and that was with two feet of mahogany between us.

I swallowed hard. "I think that can be arranged."

CHAPTER FOUR

Rain

The minute we stepped into my apartment and the door closed, Preston had me up against the wall. He cupped the back of my head with his hand as his mouth crushed mine. My lips parted and his tongue found mine, teasing, circling. He dragged his lips over my jaw and down my neck, where he planted wet, open-mouthed kisses along my collarbone and over the swell of my breasts. He seemed hell bent on working out the week's frustration on me.

"Bedroom," he murmured against my skin as he walked me through the living room to the bedroom, where we tumbled onto my unmade bed, our lips still touching. He covered my body with his, and my arms circled his back, my hands finding their way under his shirt.

He moved his thigh between mine, and I felt his hardness pressing against my hip. His hand crept under my shirt, pushing it up. His mouth closed hot and wet over my nipple, his teeth capturing it through the thin lace of my bra.

I tugged at his belt buckle, but we were too close for me to get it undone. He rolled away, jerked it open, and tugged off his pants. His eyes held me in place, scorching me as he undid each button. The shirt hit the floor next. He hooked his fingers into my leggings, and slid them off in one smooth motion, taking my panties with them. A condom wrapper crinkled and tore. Seconds later, he was sinking into me.

Foreplay consisted of the heat we'd exchanged at Blondie's, and the two minutes it had taken us to get from my front door into my bedroom. And considering the size of my apartment, two minutes was a generous estimate.

It was fast and frenzied, and over just about the time I was getting started.

Preston rolled off me, climbed out of bed and crossed the hall to the bathroom. Then he lay back down, looped an arm around me, and tucked me into his side.

"Rough week?" I asked, unused to the uncharacteristic swiftness.

His sigh grazed my forehead. "You have no idea."

"Want to talk about it?"

"Nope." He pressed his lips to my hair and held them there. "I just want to lie here and enjoy you."

Maybe it hadn't been the most amazing night of lovemaking we'd ever had, but it was nice cuddling up against him.

He nodded toward Izzy's single bed tucked under the eaves. "It still freaks me out to no end to see your daughter's bed there. All those stuffed animals watching us."

I couldn't help laughing. Izzy and I shared a bedroom, but it was more her room than mine. Her artwork covered the walls, and most of her books and toys were tucked onto a shelf in the corner. And of course there were the voyeuristic stuffed animals gawking at us whenever Preston and I had sex.

"I can't afford anything bigger, rich boy. You know that. I couldn't even afford this place if my mother didn't own the building. We don't all have massive townhouses and Manhattan apartments with more bedrooms than people."

"I'm going to bring you to my penthouse one of these days. We'll spend the whole weekend in New York. Go to the theater. Eat at my favorite restaurant."

I'd heard this before. A few times, actually. But so far it hadn't happened. The idea both excited and scared me. I was a low-budget girl. I wasn't too sure I'd fit in with the life Preston lived. I drove a twelve-year-old Ford Escort wagon with a wonky trunk latch, four mismatched tires, and only three hubcaps.

"You promise?" I said, but only because I assumed he expected a response.

He turned off the light on the nightstand and pulled the covers up over my shoulder, then dropped a sweet kiss on my forehead. "I promise. Now go to sleep."

***

I woke to an empty bed and a note on my pillow. Preston, as usual, was gone. I could count on one finger how many times he'd stayed the whole night. I didn't know if he had a dog he'd never mentioned, or an early morning racquetball session, or if he was going to church since it was Sunday.

Didn't want to wake you. You're so beautiful when you sleep. Even when you snore.

He'd signed the note with a neat, bold "P."

I rolled onto my side, wrapping my arms around the pillow beside me, breathing in the lingering scent of Preston's cologne.

We'd never discussed what was going on between us. I was okay with casual dating, and the sex was great. It was the perfect situation, really. I was a single mother working multiple jobs. Maybe a part-time romance was all I could manage right now.

Taking care of myself and Izzy was number one. I'd experienced first-hand what my mother went through when she lost the love of her life, and I didn't ever want to be in a position where I couldn't function or would let my daughter down.

My friends were off finishing college or starting careers, having fun. And I'd been working my ass off.

I didn't regret it, but losing myself in the arms of someone I cared for and who cared about me?

Of course I wanted that. Someday. Why wouldn't I?

CHAPTER FIVE

Rain

I sat across from my daughter at our kitchen table, watching her drag her fork through a plate of pasta covered with her favorite marinara, her elbow on the table and her head resting in her hand.

"What's wrong, Iz? You don't like your spaghetti? You need to try and eat a little more."

"I can't. My froat hurts."

She'd come home from preschool that afternoon with a runny nose and a cough, so I'd taken the night off to stay home with her. Her cheeks were pink, and when I pressed my lips to her forehead, it was warmer than it should be.

"Would an ice pop help your throat?"

"I fink so," she answered mournfully. My poor little pumpkin.

I'd just finished settling her on the couch with her blanket, Harvey the bunny, and an ice pop when Preston called.

"You're home. I was worried Irena might have locked you in the walk-in freezer."

"Me?" I snorted. "Never. I'm her best bartender—although you might need to worry. Is she in a mood?"

"I didn't stay to find out. When I saw you weren't working, I bought a six-pack and got the hell out of there."

"We don't sell six-packs of Molson."

"I didn't say I was going to drink it. Now tell me why I'm sitting outside Blondie's in my car, missing you."

My heart did a little somersault.

"My daughter came home from school sick, and my mother isn't feeling well either, so I called off. I don't like leaving Izzy with anyone but my mother if she's not feeling well."

"Poor kid. Do you need anything? I can run to the store for you."

I tried to picture Preston Fitzgerald Jamison III wandering around ShopRite or Rite Aid, looking for pediatric cough syrup or another box of popsicles. It was downright comical. I had to wonder if he'd ever set foot in a grocery store. He probably had people for that kind of thing. It was hard not to laugh.

"You know, I don't really need anything for Izzy. But if you could grab me a box of tampons, that would be great."

There was nothing but silence, and I thought he'd hung up. But then I heard him take a breath, and I couldn't hold it in any longer. I burst out laughing.

He waited until I got myself under control. "I'll get them. I was just trying to figure out where."

I had to dab at the mascara running under my eyes. "You're so full of shit. Fortunately, I don't need any tampons today."

"Good to know. Can I come over?"

I stopped laughing. Izzy had never met anyone I dated, other than her father. And he didn't count.

"I don't know. My daughter—"

"I'd love to meet her. I love kids, Rain. I want a house full of them some day, and I'd like nothing more than to spend the evening with you and your daughter. I mean it."

I glanced over at Izzy curled up in her blanket with Harvey, sucking on her ice pop. She'd be going to bed soon. What harm would it be for Preston to come over and spend a few minutes with her before she went to sleep? If things kept going the way they were, it was only a matter of time before she met him anyway. I had feelings for him, and it was foolish to try and convince myself otherwise.

Maybe it was time Preston met the real love of my life.

***

Preston arrived about a half hour later, bearing gifts: a small bouquet of flowers, a coloring book and crayons, and a can of chicken noodle soup. Unfortunately, Izzy had already fallen asleep, and I'd carried her to bed just before he arrived.

"Look at you," he said, following me into the kitchen and pressing himself against me while I filled a glass with water for Izzy's flowers. Judging by the hardness pressing against my ass, I knew what we'd be doing if my daughter wasn't asleep in the other room. His hand slipped under my tank top and over my bare stomach. "If you aren't the prettiest nurse I've ever seen. Remind me to get sick some time soon."

"There'll be no nursing anyone but Izzy tonight, just so you know."

He spun me around and twisted a lock of my hair between his fingers. "I know. And I respect that. This thing with you means more to me than just sex, Rain. Even if that's how you see it."

It wasn't how I saw it. At least not anymore.

He hooked his fingers into the waistband of my jeans and pulled me closer. His eyes searched mine, waiting for an answer, and then dropped to my lips.

"It's not." I swallowed. "It's not how I see it."

The corner of his mouth quirked up, and he looked almost smug. "Good, because I'm developing real feelings for you. Serious feelings." He leaned back. "In fact, let me prove it to you."

"Preston," I whispered. "I can't. Not with Izzy here."

I hadn't noticed his hand reaching across the counter for the bag he'd brought in with him until it crinkled.

"Get your head out of the gutter," he scolded as he handed me the bag. "I brought you a gift too."

My cheeks reddened. Then to make it worse, my hands shook as I pulled a box from the bag he'd handed me.

When I saw what it was, I burst out laughing.

"Tampons? I was kidding."

"I know. But I wanted you to know that you mean this much to me. Enough for me to stand in line at the grocery store holding a box of tampons. If that isn't love, then I don't know what you'd call it."

Love? The rich boy had bought me tampons, and I was wacky enough to find it the most endearing gift I'd ever received. I chewed on my bottom lip to keep my grin from stretching all the way to my ears.

Tampons. Who'd have thought?

CHAPTER SIX

Rain

For someone who claimed he had feelings for me, Preston didn't show up the next day or the day after that. I got a text saying he'd been working late. He offered to call me later after I got off of work, but I had caught Izzy's cold and all I wanted to do was to fall into bed.

Preston: Saturday then? Dinner?

Me: Definitely.

Lying on the couch, blowing my nose, and coughing gave me plenty of time to think. And what I thought about, was the comment he'd made when he bought me that box of tampons.

If that isn't love, then I don't know what you'd call it.

Was he trying to tell me he loved me?

I didn't have much experience on that front. Jeff had said he loved me, but I'd bet anything that hundreds if not thousands of teenage boys said the same thing if it got them laid. If Jeff ever had loved me, he fell out of love the moment he learned I was pregnant.

And what about me? Was I in love with Preston? I know I'd never loved Jeff, even if I'd told him I did. It was like responding to a sneeze:

I love you.

I love you too.

Gesundheit.

I had nothing to measure my feelings against.

Preston was sexy and attractive, confident and successful. He was attentive and generous. I may not have truly loved him yet, but I was pretty well on my way.

With that in mind, I decided I would cook for Preston Saturday instead of going out like he'd suggested. Izzy was spending the weekend with Jeff's parents, so it would be perfect. He was probably sick of restaurants, anyway, after client dinners and lunches out several times a week, eating food with names I couldn't even pronounce. What he needed was a decent, home-cooked meal—good old American comfort food. My specialty. Served wearing the pink-and-black lace bra and panties I'd just bought. Also my specialty.

I'd show him plenty of comfort.

***

The table was set, the Cornish game hens with wild rice and chestnut stuffing tented in a warm oven to keep them from going dry. The glazed carrots would need to be reheated and the salad dressed.

I'd shaved my legs, curled my hair, and put a dab of perfume on all my pulse points, including the backs of my knees and my ankles. I shimmied into the low-cut, sleeveless black dress I'd borrowed from my mother, leaving my legs bare. I had the perfect strappy sandals to go with the dress, but the extra four inches would have made me almost as tall as Preston, so I opted to remain barefoot. It's not like I was going anywhere.

At seven o'clock, I popped a John Mayer album into my CD player and lit the candles.

At 7:20, I turned off the oven, since the game hens were getting dry, and wrapped the foil around them tightly so they wouldn't turn to shoe leather. I checked my cell phone. The last message I'd received from Preston on Thursday said he would pick me up at seven.

I refrained from texting him. He wasn't that late. Besides, he'd had a busy week and might still be working.

At seven forty-five, I turned off the music and poured myself a glass of chardonnay. At eight thirty, I blew out the candles and poured another glass of wine.

After the third glass, I grabbed my phone.

Me: I thought we had plans tonight.

It was a silly thing to write, because the message above that said he would see me Saturday. At seven.

The little dots on the screen began to bounce. Then they stopped. I waited about fifteen minutes, then tried to call him. The call went straight to voicemail.

I didn't know whether to be angry or worried, although I was leaning heavily toward anger. I stormed into the bedroom, yanked the borrowed dress over my head, and slipped into an oversized sweatshirt and a pair of leggings. Then I pulled my hair into a messy bun atop my head and began cleaning up my ruined dinner. I wanted to toss the entire mess into the garbage, but I couldn't afford to be that dramatic.

I was picking the last of the meat off the carcass—at least I could make chicken salad for dinner tomorrow night—when my phone chimed. I was tempted to let it go, but who was I kidding?

Preston: Are you still up?

Me: No.

Preston: Funny. Then why are your lights on?

I should've ignored him, let him see how it felt. But I couldn't.

I opened my front door to find him leaning against the doorjamb.

"I'm tired, Preston. You shouldn't have come."

"We had plans."

"Five hours ago. And now I'm tired. I don't feel like talking to you right now."

I tried to close the door, but he pushed it open and stepped inside.

I was so not in the mood for this. "Preston!"

"I've had a bad night, Rain, and this isn't helping." He closed the door with a quiet click.

"Yeah? Well, so did I. I wanted to surprise you with dinner, and now it's ruined."

He looked at my sad kitchen table: the two place settings, the melted candles. Even the flowers were drooping.

I should've cleared it all away. Not even told him I'd made dinner. Let him think I'd forgotten we had a date.

I felt so stupid.

He rested his hands on my upper arms and tried to pull me toward him, but I resisted.

"I'm sorry, baby. I really am."

"You could've at least called. Or texted me."

"I know. It was just . . . a bad time."

"Yeah, well. Shit happens."

Since I wasn't budging, he stepped toward me and wrapped me in his arms, then rubbed his hand up and down my back. "Can we talk?"

"I told you, I don't feel like talking right now."

He let out a long, familiar sigh, the kind I used when I was trying to reason with a five-year-old.

"Rain, please. It's important. I need you hear me out."

I broke away from his embrace and stalked all of two feet to my couch, where I dropped heavily onto the cushions and glared at him.

"Go ahead. Talk." I probably shouldn't have mixed wine with disappointment. It made me cranky.

Instead of sitting beside me, Preston paced, if you could call taking five steps in either direction pacing. He gripped the back of his neck with both hands. Then he scrubbed a hand over the scruff on his face. Preston never did scruff. He also didn't do wrinkles, yet his shirt looked as if he'd slept in it. Even one of the front tails was untucked.

Maybe he really had had a bad day.

He stopped and faced me. "When we met, I was seeing someone."

Oh my god. He was like Jesus, only instead of turning water into wine, he was turning the wine in my stomach to bile.

The pacing started again. "This is difficult for me, Rain."

My brain was going a hundred miles an hour, but I said nothing. And I had a sick feeling that I wasn't going to like whatever he had to say either.

He sank down onto the couch beside me and lifted my hand, running his fingers over my palm, then clasping it tightly in his own.

"Suzanne and I have dated since high school. Off and on. Mostly on." The grip on my hand grew tighter. "It was mostly over when I met you. But it's been . . . complicated."

A shard of glass had somehow become lodged in my throat, but I forced the words out anyway.

"And now you're back together, is that what you're saying?"

"No." He shook his head. "Not exactly."

I tried to remove my hand, but his hold was too strong. He leaned forward until his face was just inches from mine.

For a split second, I wanted to head-butt him. I could always blame the wine.

"I'm in love with you, Rain. I am. But I've been with Suzanne since high school. Our families are friends. We move in the same circles. Belong to the same clubs."

Circles. He was talking about social circles and clubs. My circle consisted of my daughter, my mother, and Diane. And clubs? I didn't even belong to Sam's Club. I should've known better than to fall for someone so far out of my league it was a surprise we resided in the same area code.

My eyes prickled and burned, but there was no way I was going to cry in front of him, which meant he had to go. Now.

"Look, Preston. I get it. We're from two different worlds. No biggie." I tried to stand, but he pressed me against the sofa.

"I'm not finished." His voice was demanding and authoritative.

I'm sure he talked to lots of people like that, but not to me. I wasn't one of his fucking employees. I pushed harder, but he only held on tighter.

"Well, I am."

"Don't do this." He rested his forehead against mine. "Would you just hear me out?"

"What's there to say? After all your talk the other night about being my boyfriend, you already have a girlfriend. Obviously, it was just sex, right?"

I really needed him to go.

"It wasn't just sex, and you damn well know it. You almost introduced me to your kid, for chrissakes."

"Yeah, well. My bad."

He plowed on, ignoring my sarcasm and my efforts to get away from him.

"Suzanne's mother died tonight. That's where I was. Like I said, I've known her family for a long time. I was there to support her. As a friend. That's it. I've been trying to break it off. Gently. But it's been hard with all the shit that's been going on. Her mother had some real aggressive form of breast cancer, and it didn't respond to treatment." His grip loosened and he leaned back against the cushions. "I didn't have the heart to end it when her mother was dying."

Emotions bombarded me. The strongest was sadness for a girl who had just lost her mother, which diluted some of my anger and the embarrassment of being lied to. I knew how it felt to lose a parent. It sucked.

"I'll make this right, Rain, I promise. I'm just going to need a little time." He ran a finger under my chin and lifted my face to his. "You understand, don't you?"

Sadly, I did. "Yeah, sure."

He stood. "I probably won't be around for the next week or so. I promised to go with her when they make arrangements, and of course there's the wake and services."

I looked down as I pushed myself off the sofa, desperate to hide the surprise and hurt that had to be marching across my face. "You're leaving?"

"Yeah, I told her I was just going to run to my place for some clothes and then I'd be back. She probably shouldn't be alone tonight. She's pretty upset."

He was staying with her. The man I stupidly fell in love with was leaving to spend the night with his on-again, off-again girlfriend. I pressed a hand against my churning stomach while I walked him to the door. How was I supposed to respond to that?

He kissed my forehead. "Thank you for being so understanding. You're a good girl, Rain. The best."

After locking the door behind him, I couldn't help but wonder.

The best what?

CHAPTER SEVEN

Rain

Suzanne needed him, and he still didn't have the heart to tell her it was over. At least that's what Preston said. Considering he spent most of his free time with her, leaving me with the occasional weeknight or two, it was clearly very much not over, and I wasn't sure if it would ever be over. If I brought it up, he told me it was "complicated," reminded me of the loss she'd suffered, and praised me for my compassion and understanding.

I might not have liked it, but I did understand. I'd been devastated when my dad died, so as much as I hated sharing Preston, I understood how badly Suzanne needed his support. His dedication to her and her family just showed how kind he was and how much he cared about his friends.

So I was patient.

And according to Diane, pretty fucking stupid.

"What do you mean, he's dating someone else?"

"You know, for a little girl, you have a big mouth," I pointed out as I wiped down the luncheonette tables after the noon rush. "I don't think they heard you down at the gas station on the corner. You want to repeat that?"

"I just don't understand why."

"I told you. Her mother just died."

She shook her head. "No, why are you dating a loser who has a girlfriend?"

I was going to point out that Suzanne wasn't really his girlfriend, but if he'd never actually broken it off, then she was. Technically.

"Look. I care about him, and other than this one thing, I'm happier than I've been in a long time. Isn't that enough?"

"No, it isn't. And that one thing is fucking huge. Don't you think you deserve someone all to yourself?"

"I'm not ready to be in a serious relationship." At least that's what I'd been trying to convince myself. "I have Izzy to think about. I don't have time to be worrying about some guy full time."

"I've known you all your life. Don't bullshit me."

"I'm not. Besides, you said you liked him."

"That was before I knew he was a Bluebeard."

I shoved a stack of napkins into the metal holder and slammed it shut. "A pirate?"

She rolled her eyes. "That was Blackbeard. Bluebeard was the one who killed all his wives."

"So now he's a murderer?"

She pulled me into the booth alongside her.

"Rain, what are you doing?"

"I'm trying to work. Other than that, I'm having a little fun, that's all."

Her eyes connected with mine, but it was the frown tugging at the corners of her mouth that told me just how disappointed she was with me. I hated that she felt that way.

"Is he coming to the wedding?" she asked.

"Oh, now it's okay to invite him to your wedding?" I was being bitchy, but I couldn't help it. I was tired of having to defend myself.

Diane kept glaring at me, waiting.

"He's going to be out of town that weekend."

She swirled the straw in her Diet Coke. "Do you believe that?"

"Yes, why wouldn't I?"

"Did you think maybe he told you that as an excuse not to come, so that no one sees you together and reports back to the girlfriend? Think about it, Rain. When you see him, it's at your place or at Blondie's. If he does take you out, it's to some dark, out of the way place none of his hoity-toity friends would go. I never expected you to turn into someone who would let some guy hide your light under a bushel."

Tears prickled at the back of my eyes. I struggled to speak, but the words just wouldn't come.

"I'm getting you a date for the wedding."

"I already have a date. Wally's brother. Isn't Bobby supposed to be my date?"

I was Diane's maid of honor, while Bobby was Wally's best man.

"He's your escort, not your date," she said patiently. "He's married, remember? Or are you only interested in men who are unavailable?"

The wedding was less than a week away. Even if I wanted a date, it was too late to find someone at this point. So I lied. "To be honest, I'll have a better time by myself. I can dance with all the good-looking, unattached men. I can mingle. Actually, I prefer it."

Given the sour look on her face—and the fact we'd been friends so long—she didn't believe me.

"Are you going to keep seeing Preston?"

I fixed my face in an evil glare. "Diane."

"Rain," she said, mimicking me.

I grabbed my rag and climbed out of the booth.

"I'll think about it, okay?"

I didn't need to be psychic to know she didn't believe me that time either.

CHAPTER EIGHT

Rain

A week later, I watched as my best friend married the man of her dreams and started her happily ever after. The wedding had been beautiful and the reception first-class all the way. The day was perfect—for them. For me, it was another reminder that I was alone—more or less. Other than the sporadic attention of the lead singer in the band, who was a bigger flirt than I was, I'd spent most of the evening as a wallflower. I danced briefly with Bobby when the wedding party was introduced, but his wife, Janelle, cut in quickly. After dinner I danced with one of Diane's cousins. George was several inches shorter than me and breathed heavily against my breasts the entire time. As soon as the song ended, I excused myself and made a mad dash for the ladies' room, where I ran into the bride.

"How come all of my bridesmaids are wearing the exact same dress, yet you're the only one showing cleavage?" Diane asked as we stood side by side in front of a row of sinks.

I looked down at my lavender-swathed breasts and back at my reflection. The girls did look exceptionally perky. "Lucky, I guess."

She smirked while I dragged a wet paper towel over my neck and chest.

"Having fun?" she asked, nodding at my chest. "Other than dancing with Georgie."

Grabbing another paper towel, I shivered. "I can still feel his breath on me. And not in a good way."

"Aw, Rain. That's not nice. The poor guy has asthma."

I glared at her reflection. "Then why are you laughing?"

"Because he's a pain in the ass, and the look on your face out there was priceless." She gathered her full skirts in her hand and took a step toward the door. "I've got to get back out there. Wally's eyeing the dessert table, and if I'm gone too long, he might start on the wedding cake without me. If my cousin asks again, just call him Georgie Porgie. I guarantee, he'll leave you alone."

"You should have printed that on the invitations to warn all the single ladies. I'm not the only one he's tried to seduce with his heavy breathing tonight."

I heard her laughter even after the door had swung shut. I tossed the paper towel in the trash, then leaned closer to the mirror and scrutinized my forehead. There had to be a big "L" stamped on there somewhere.

My loser status was confirmed a few minutes later when I stepped out of the restroom, feeling sorry for myself, and walked right smack into a broad chest in a black suit.

"Whoa!" Two strong hands wrapped around my upper arms to keep me from tipping over. "I'm sorry. I didn't see you. You okay?"

I knew it was him before I even looked up. That strange rush of electricity. I brushed the hair off my face and raised my chin. I'd never forget those eyes, but it was the vibration from his hands against my arms that told me I was right.

I greeted him like we were long lost friends. "Hey, it's you."

He arched an eyebrow and cocked his head. Guess I wasn't as unforgettable.

"Have we met?"

I tilted my head and fluttered my lashes. "Steve, right?" Why I was lying, I had no idea.

Chuckling, he released me. The loss of his warmth on my bare arms was significant.

"Sorry, no. I'm Chase." He held out his hand, so I took it. I was prepared for the vibration this time, which was as sharp and warm—and tingly—as it was that day at the shop. "And you must be . . . a bridesmaid?"

"Maid of honor actually."

"There you are." I glanced over my shoulder to see a tall, slim brunette heading toward us. "They're getting reading to cut the cake."

Must be the rabbit fiancée. She was speaking to him but flashing daggers at me.

I took a step back. "Sorry for running into you like that." Another step. "Enjoy the cake." I pushed the bathroom door open with my back, even though I'd just come from there, and then I did something even dumber. I fucking saluted, and then let the room swallow me up. As the door swung closed, Chase looked amused. The rabbit just looked confused.

***

I stayed in the ladies' room so long, I missed the cutting of the cake. The band was playing and the lights had been turned down by the time I picked my way to the bar and ordered another vodka martini—I'd lost count as to whether I'd had four or five or maybe even six—and then hung back and watched couples swaying on the dance floor, including Chase and his stunning fiancée.

Why I was feeling jealous of a woman I'd seen for mere seconds, I hadn't a clue. Chase could be an abusive jackass for all I knew. Scratch that. I did know. I didn't understand the vibrations coming off him, but I'd swear on a stack of Bibles that he was a good man.

Lucky rabbit.

Yep. Definitely feeling sorry for myself, and alcohol wasn't helping. When Preston told me he couldn't make it, I should've just asked someone else. It would've been better than hovering by the bar, trying to avoid cousin Georgie.

And to make matters worse, I had no way to get home. My only alternatives were to catch a ride with my mother and her date or go in the limo with Diane and Wally and have them drop me off on the way to their hotel.

I rubbed my forehead. Maybe the "L" was invisible.

I was about to order my fifth, sixth, or seventh martini when the bandleader called for all the single women to step out onto the floor for the bouquet toss.

Oh hell no, I grabbed my evening bag and ducked out. Diane would understand. It was an unwritten rule among besties. Act like a jerk at your BFF's wedding, and she has to forgive you. At least that's what I was telling myself, although with Diane, I might have to do some groveling.

I was almost to the lobby when my bag began to vibrate. I fished out my phone.

Preston: Trip a bust. Miss you. Wedding over yet?

I hadn't seen him in over a week and wasn't sure how to answer. A smart, sober girl would have told him I couldn't possibly see him that night, but I was neither smart nor sober. I opted to make him jealous instead.

Me: Just caught me. Wedding over. Heading 4 drinks with guys in band.

My phone rang two seconds later.

"That's not even funny," he said when I answered.

"It wasn't meant to be."

"Have you been drinking?"

"It's a wedding. Of course I've been drinking."

"I'll be there in fifteen."

He must be pretty sure of himself, expecting me to jump because he suddenly wanted to see me. It pissed me off that he was right, and that he knew damn well that in fifteen minutes, I'd be standing in front of the Marriott, holding my shoes and waiting.

I was also twirling my panties on the end of my finger when he pulled up.

Suzanne might be winning the battle, but the war wasn't over—and I was very good in the trenches.

***

I woke the next morning with a hangover the size of New Jersey and Preston lying beside me. Since he rarely stayed over, I panicked, as if I were the one hiding something.

"Preston." I shook him. "You fell asleep."

He made a face. "And I was still asleep too."

"It's morning! Wake up!"

"Damn it, Rain. I know."

"Shouldn't you be somewhere?" I asked pointedly.

"I have nowhere else to be but here with you." He rolled onto his back. When I didn't respond, he peered at me through one sleepy lid.

"Seriously?" I asked.

He nodded. "It's over. I told you it would happen. She finally gave me the boot."

Finally. Despite my hangover, I climbed on top of him, grateful that I'd started on the pill, and showed him just how glad I was.

When the fog cleared a little later, I tried to remember if I'd misheard him. Because if he had been the one trying to break things off, why had Suzanne been the one to end it?

CHAPTER NINE

Rain

One of my biggest talents was the ability to smile no matter what was happening in my life, but it had to be clear to anyone who saw me Monday at the luncheonette that my smile was bigger and brighter than usual.

"What's going on with you?" my mother asked. "I haven't seen you this happy since . . . I can't remember. Maybe not since before . . ." Her eyes clouded over. She was thinking of my father.

"I'm happy." I hugged her, and she squeezed me back.

"I'm guessing you met someone at the wedding. Was it the lead singer in the band? I saw him eyeing you. What was his name? Ben?"

I shook my head, grinning. "I didn't go home with him."

She furrowed her brow and tapped on her chin. I could see her mentally ticking off every available man she'd noticed at the wedding.

Her eyes met mine. "Diane's cousin?" she asked incredulously.

"Ew. No."

Her face went blank, then fell. "Oh, Rain. Not Preston?"

My happiness quotient dropped a couple degrees. The problem with treating your mother like a friend, was telling her things you'd later wish you hadn't. Like Preston's relationship with Suzanne.

"Why would you say that? It's over with him and . . . you know. They broke up. We spent the day together yesterday. I let him meet Izzy, and he took us to Flat Rock. It was wonderful. Can't you just be happy for me?"

"Oh, sweetheart. I don't want to see you hurt anymore, and it seems this man has some kind of control over you." She sighed deeply. "Please be careful."

"I'm not playing in traffic, Ma, okay? I know what I'm doing. I love him. He loves me. I don't see the problem."

"You're not playing in traffic. You're letting someone play with your heart. I think that might be worse."

I dumped ten pounds of potatoes into a large stock pot filled with water and hoisted it onto the stove. "Whatever."

I was determined to remain happy, and if it meant avoiding her negativity the rest of the day, then so be it. I kept busy in the kitchen while she worked the front.

When we closed at two, I raced to the drugstore to pick up a few things for Preston so he could stay over on nights Izzy was at my mother's. I got him a toothbrush, and after sniffing several men's deodorants, I picked one that reminded me of him. It wasn't what he usually wore—his probably came from a fancy department store—but it was close enough. I bought a razor and shaving cream, shampoo, and a few other things he might need. It set me back forty bucks, but hopefully I'd make it back in tips, especially since the payment for Izzy's preschool was due soon. I rushed home and straightened up the apartment, then picked Izzy up, gave her dinner, and took her to my mother's.

I hadn't heard from Preston all day, which wasn't unusual. Before I left for Blondie's, I sent him a text.

Me: See you tonight?

Blondie's was busy for a Monday. I checked my phone several times, but there were no messages.

By closing time, I still hadn't heard from him. I fired off a text before I pulled out of the lot.

Me: Everything OK?

I didn't hear from him overnight. When I got to work at six, I made Izzy's breakfast and gave her some crayons and paper to entertain herself until the bus came.

The next few hours were hectic, and I was able to keep my mind occupied slicing lunch meat, making soup, and smiling only when I absolutely had to.

Around ten, as I prepared for the lunch rush, a huge bouquet of red roses was delivered for me. I wanted to squeal, but instead, I snuck up to my apartment, where I set the vase in the center of my small kitchen table and tore open the card.

There were only two words: I'm sorry.

He hadn't even signed his name. Just the letter P. It wasn't even written in his handwriting.

I dropped into a chair and stared at the card in my hands until the words became blurry. An invisible string wove its way around my spine, wrapping itself tightly around my guts and through my chest, while I tried to convince myself I was overreacting.

It could have simply meant that he was sorry he hadn't called me yesterday. Or that he'd been really busy. But it didn't. I knew one thing with absolute certainty: he'd gone back to Suzanne.

I pushed myself away from the table and made it to the kitchen sink in time to lose what little I'd put in my stomach. I wiped my face and rested my head against the cool Formica countertop.

My life was a freaking roller coaster ride. Some days I just wanted to let go and fly off into space, away from all the heartbreak and disappointment; maybe find some peace and comfort with the man who'd loved me first and best—my dad.

I took a few deep breaths of what air remained in the room. I rinsed out my mouth and smoothed my apron. I wanted to call Diane, but she was on her honeymoon. She would have reamed me out at first, but afterward, she'd have hugged me and cried with me. It had only been two days, but I missed her.

When I heard someone coming up the back steps, I wiped my eyes, dropped the card into the trash under the sink, and opened the door.

"Are you all right?" my mother asked. "What's wrong?"

I forced a smile. "Nothing. Preston sent me flowers. Isn't that sweet? I didn't want anything to happen to them, so I brought them up here. Let's go. I have lunch meat to cut yet, and if I don't get to it soon, we're going to get slammed."

She wasn't buying it. "You sure you're all right?"

"I think I'm coming down with something. When we're done with lunch, if you don't mind, I may lie down for a while."

"Go lie down now. If you're getting sick, you shouldn't be around food anyway. I'll pick up Izzy after school and keep her until later if you want."

She knew I wasn't sick. I nodded.

"Thanks, Mom."

I closed the door and waited until her footsteps faded before I slid to the floor and buried my face in my hands.

CHAPTER TEN

Rain

I heard nothing from Preston for three weeks. But instead of listening to my mother or Diane remind me that they had warned me, I pretended I was fine. I even agreed to a blind date Diane set up with a guy she worked with.

What a nightmare.

The guy was cute. And he seemed nice. Funny too. But when he took me to a club where a bunch of his friends were hanging out, I began to feel like I was some sort of conquest. When I overheard him ask a buddy if he thought I could pass for one of the Victoria's Secret models, I knew he was only interested in me because he wanted to make his friends jealous.

Maybe I should've been flattered, but I didn't want anyone that needy.

When word spread through Blondie's that I was unattached (as if I hadn't been the only one actually attached in that relationship), one of the staties brought his brother around to meet me. He was a state trooper too and just about as sweet a guy as I'd ever met—maybe a little too sweet, especially after he rushed home the night we met to get his accordion.

After Irena locked up, about a half dozen troopers remained, including Brian, who led me into the back room to play for me. He was puppy-dog adorable and a great catch, but I just didn't see how it could work. First of all, I hated the accordion, and I struggled not to laugh at his earnest playing, especially when I could hear his buddies cackling in the bar.

But he was so sweet that when he asked me out, I agreed. He took me to dinner the following week at a very nice restaurant, where he was attentive and well-behaved—a real gentleman. At the end of the night, he gave me a sweet, chaste kiss. Although I didn't feel any kind of spark or chemistry with him, I agreed to go out with him again the following week for dinner and a movie. He was a nice guy.

And nice guys didn't cheat or lie about their supposed ex-girlfriends.

I was living my life backward. I already had a kid, and now I was working my way back to the type of dating everyone else did back in high school while I was drinking and screwing around.

Late Thursday, after his shift, Brian came in with his brother and some of the other troopers. He wasn't much of a drinker, and I wondered how much time he spent practicing that awful accordion.

I was a little self-conscious about how I was dressed, but he seemed unfazed. I was wearing low-slung, skintight leggings and a crop top that showed off my new belly button piercing. Brian just smiled whenever I looked his way, nursed his beer, and took turns at the pool table in the back with his buddies.

It was a little after eleven when Preston walked in. I ignored him, wishing my heart would do the same, and dipped into the kitchen under the guise of getting ice. Let Lynette, the new bartender, or Irena wait on him. Better yet, let him take the hint and just turn around and go.

I was still in the kitchen ten minutes later when he came in after me.

"You can't be in here," I said, forcing the words out.

"I don't care. I had to see you."

I shook my head. "I don't think so. You need to go."

"Please, Rain." He reached for me, but I stepped back. Unfortunately, I was right up against the walk-in freezer with no place to go. He grabbed me about the waist and pulled me to him. I pushed against his chest, but he wouldn't budge.

"Please don't." I begged. "You made your choice. I'm done. I can't do this anymore."

He ignored me and alternated between kissing my neck and whispering in my ear. "I'm sorry. I love you. I'm so unhappy without you." He planted desperate kisses on my neck. "Don't push me away."

I wanted to put my arms around him and scratch his eyes out at the same time. And I hated myself for it.

"I love you, Rain, you know that. I need you."

I hated how much I wanted to hear those words, how badly I needed to hear him say them to me. And I hated how my arms slipped so easily around his neck.

I'd become nothing more than a marionette, and he held the strings. I wanted to ask if he was still with Suzanne, but what would it matter? Even if he said he wasn't, who knew what tomorrow or next week would bring?

So I didn't say anything. I just let him kiss me.

The kitchen door swung open, and Brian stood in the doorway. His eyes traveled from me to Preston and back again. When our eyes connected, it felt like he'd already begun to hate me.

"I assume tomorrow's off."

I pulled away, although Preston kept one arm around my waist. I pushed on his hand, but he held firm.

"Brian, I'm sorry. I—"

He held up his hand to silence me. "Forget it, Rain." The door swung closed behind him.

I jerked away from Preston and followed Brian back into the bar. He and the other troopers were already settling up with Lynette. He headed for the parking lot as soon as he saw me, and each of his buddies gave me a long, hard stare before they left.

I didn't need to be psychic to know there was a big fat traffic ticket in my future. I spun on my heels. "Why are you here?"

"I told you. I missed you." Preston actually had the nerve to look shocked that I was questioning him. "And I also had news. Good news."

I narrowed my eyes. I didn't want to hear anything he had to say.

"Not interested." I pushed past him and scooted back behind the bar. He wouldn't dare follow me. Irena would skin him alive.

That didn't stop him from following me along the outside. When he went one way, I went the other. I began to feel like a duck in one of those arcade games on the boardwalk in Seaside Heights.

"Will you stay still?" he shouted "I'm trying to talk to you."

I couldn't decide if I was angrier at him or myself. Since I preferred it to be him, I crossed my arms in front of me and glared at him.

"Talk. You have ten seconds."

"A few weeks ago I nominated you for one of the most beautiful bartenders in New Jersey, and you won."

He'd lost his damn mind. "What are you talking about?"

"It's a calendar to raise money for kids with cancer. I sent them a few pictures of you. Once they got a look at your photos, they sent someone here to see you in person. I got an email tonight saying you were chosen to be Miss February."

I wasn't sure what to say or even what to think. Turned out, at that moment, it didn't matter.

"Go!" Irena yelled, her eyes magnified to twice their normal size behind the thick lenses of her glasses. "You go!"

At first I wasn't sure if she meant Preston, me, or the both of us. But when she took my arm and propelled me toward the door, I knew she meant business. Irena measured everything in dollars, and I'd probably just cost her at least a hundred bucks when the state troopers walked out.

I stormed into the kitchen, grabbed my things, and pushed past Preston and out to my car. I unlocked the door and got in, while he slid in on the other side.

"Talk to me."

"No!" I cried. "You do the talking. I don't have anything to say."

He talked. But everything he said, I'd heard before. He and Suzanne had been dating since high school. Their families had always been close. They belonged to the same club. Suzanne had become even closer to Preston's mother since her own mother died, and not having a daughter of her own, Mrs. Jamison adored her. Everyone expected them to get married—everyone but Preston, or so he said.

"That last night I saw you, I stopped to visit my parents on the way home, and Suzanne was there. She was crying and telling my mother we'd broken up. Then I had the two of them ganging up on me . . ."

The expectant look on his face told me he seriously expected me to feel bad for him.

"I'm sorry." I couldn't hold back on the sarcasm. "I'm pretty sure I saw a pair of balls hanging behind your dick."

"C'mon, Rain," he chided. "Don't be so crude."

I snorted. He had no problem with me serving boob shots for bigger tips or apparently nominating me to pose half naked for a calendar—but he drew the line at being crude.

"Get out of my car." He didn't move, so I said it again. Louder. "Get out! Now!" When the bastard still didn't budge, I grabbed my purse and jumped out, slamming the door so hard, I was surprised my three hubcaps didn't fall off.

"It's six miles home, Rain," he yelled after me. "Are you seriously planning to walk?"

There was only one answer to that. I just hoped it wasn't too dark for him to see the one-finger salute I gave him.

I walked for about five minutes, before Preston pulled up alongside me in his Corvette.

"Get in."

I kept walking.

"Just get in, and I'll bring you back to your car and leave you alone."

I kept walking.

"I promise."

I turned, opened the door, and dropped down into the seat, staring straight ahead. As soon as he took a breath to speak again, I opened the door to get out.

"Fine. I'll take you back to your fucking car."

I wanted to remind him that he had no right to be angry, but I didn't want to open the door to any type of conversation. As he slowed down next to my car, I jumped out and was in my car with both doors locked before he could park. I nearly hit him as he climbed out of the Corvette, but I finished backing out and headed for home.

As I suspected, he wasn't far behind, and by the time I stepped out of my car behind the luncheonette, he was already waiting for me.

"You don't listen very well, do you?" I snarled.

"I don't want to lose you," he said, his voice thick. "I love you. Why don't you believe me?" He grabbed hold of me and held me tight against him. He smelled of sandalwood and citrus and a scent that was singularly his own.

"I can't believe you, because you're in love with someone else."

"I'm not. And you know it won't last."

"It has lasted, Preston. Since high school. You said it yourself." I tried pulling away.

"I'll break up with her—I will. It's just complicated."

This was ridiculous, and I was an idiot for listening. Now it was his turn.

"Do you expect me to live my life in the shadows for you? To never be seen in public together? To go to every party and wedding I'm invited to alone, because you don't want to risk someone seeing us together?"

"Of course not."

"Then when you've got it all figured out, you let me know. Now step aside and let me pass. I don't want to do this anymore. I hurt a really nice guy tonight because of you, and that makes me feel like crap. That's not me. I'm not even sure who I am anymore, thanks to you."

"Please let me come in."

"Just go."

I pulled away, and this time he let me. When I looked out the apartment window a few minutes later, his car was still there but I didn't see him. Not long after I turned off the porch light, the engine of the Vette fired up, and he squealed out of the parking lot.

I sent my mother a text and told her I'd pick Izzy up in the morning. Then I poured myself a glass of wine and took a long, hot bath. I plugged my phone in to charge before I went to sleep and discovered a message.

Preston: You know you're the only one for me.

My fingers flew over the keys.

Me: I'm not the one you need to be telling that to then.

CHAPTER ELEVEN

Rain

The next morning there was another delivery of red roses. I held my breath, ready for the worst, although I'd already done that.

Preston: It's over. You're all mine. Big dinner tonight. Pick you up at seven. Dress up.

Although it wasn't lost on me that he had written "you're all mine" rather than "I'm all yours," I was cautiously optimistic.

My mother, much less so. She even threatened to refuse to babysit, but when I told her I'd call a neighborhood teenager, she caved. No one was good enough to watch her granddaughter. There were times I was sure that included me.

Other than Jeff's senior prom and Diane's wedding, I'd never been somewhere that I had to really dress up. I owned nothing fancier than my bridesmaid's dress. Most of my clothing allowance, such as it was, I spent on skimpy outfits for the bar. At the luncheonette, I wore T-shirts and jeans. I deserved a splurge on something special, and it had to be a knock-your-socks-off kind of outfit.

As soon as the lunch rush ebbed, I zipped off to the mall, where I found the sexiest, barely-there cocktail dress on sale at Victoria's Secret. Once Preston got a look at me, he wouldn't even remember Suzanne's name.

When Preston arrived to pick me up later, I met him at the door already wearing the long wool coat I'd borrowed from my mother. Why not build a little suspense? There was nothing wrong with making him wait until we got to the restaurant to see what I was wearing. I thought I was playing it cool. But when we pulled into the gates of the Bernardsville Country Club, I had a hard time finding my words. Preston's BMW followed the curve of the long, winding road until an enormous white brick building flooded with about a million lights came into view.

"Your club?" I started to panic. "Why didn't you tell me this is where we were going?" I tugged on the sleeves of my coat. "I'm not sure I'm dressed properly."

"Nonsense," he said, leaning over and kissing me. "You look beautiful."

My door opened just as he stepped out on his side.

"Preston," I called after him, but the door slammed shut.

The valet held out his hand. I took it against my better judgment and let him help me onto the sidewalk.

"I thought we were going to a restaurant," I whispered as Preston escorted me up the steps.

Most of the women I could see ahead of me were wearing gowns, although some wore cocktail-length dresses under their fur coats.

I gripped his sleeve. "I mean it. I think you should take me home. You can come back."

"Don't be silly. I can't wait to show you off."

That was what I was afraid of. I clung to him tightly as we walked into the stately mansion. The lobby was the grandest room I'd ever seen. Large squares of black and white marble covered the floor. The ceiling soared to an impressive, multicolored dome. Two curving staircases covered in plush red carpet led to the second floor. Straight ahead was a ballroom where elegant couples mingled, conversing softly.

Preston slipped off his overcoat and handed it to the woman in the coat room. I nearly choked when I saw he was wearing a tuxedo.

"Preston, really, I think this is a mistake."

"Give me your coat."

I shook my head. "I'm cold. I'll keep it on."

He lowered his voice. "Rain. People are beginning to stare." He smiled at the two couples waiting behind us, then returned his focus to me. "Give me your coat, please."

I took a deep breath and slowly unbuttoned the long black wool coat.

"Oh my," someone said from somewhere behind me.

I smiled up at Preston and shrugged.

He looked a bit shocked but to his credit, he recovered quickly.

"You should have told me we were going to your club."

The dress I had found on the clearance rack was barely suitable for a restaurant and probably more appropriate for a rave. It was dark brown with a deep V-neck that displayed more cleavage than this club had probably ever seen before. The halter style showed off the constellation tattooed on my left shoulder. Since I was wearing five-inch heels, I was taller than Preston, something I'm sure he wasn't too happy about. My skirt was quite short and I wasn't wearing pantyhose. Thank god I'd had enough sense to wear panties.

"Wow," he said.

I grabbed the sleeve of his tuxedo. "If you want to take me home, I understand."

"No way." With his hand against the small of my back, he moved me across the foyer and toward the bar. "Besides, I need a drink."

I couldn't have attracted any more attention if I'd been completely naked, which was exactly how most of the men were looking at me. Preston introduced me to several people. Friends I assumed, although all of the couples at our table, he explained, were clients. Fortunately, the men launched into a discussion about some building Preston was designing for them, so I wasn't forced to make small talk with their wives or girlfriends. Chances were pretty good we had nothing in common anyway.

Several waiters appeared, setting the first course in front of all eight of us at the table in unison. I was impressed until I realized that whatever sat in the middle of my plate had tentacles. I didn't consider myself a fussy eater, but there was no way in hell I was eating that.

Preston lifted his knife and fork and was about to cut into what he'd been served, when he noticed I hadn't moved. "What's wrong?"

I leaned closer so that I could speak without anyone else hearing me. "This looks like a baby octopus."

He snickered. "Yep. Pretty sure it is. Don't you like octopus?"

"Um, no."

"Would you like to switch?"

"Do you like octopus?"

"I could take it or leave it, but if you won't eat it, I'll trade with you."

I couldn't imagine "taking or leaving" octopus. I wish the waiter would come back, take mine, and leave with it.

"What did you get?"

Preston poked at the food on his plate. "I believe this is the smoked salmon with sturgeon and trout roe served on a potato pancake and topped with crème fraîche."

"Isn't roe fish eggs?" I whispered.

"Yes," he whispered back.

"No thanks."

"Should I call the waiter over and get you something else?"

And draw more attention to myself? "No. I'm fine. I'll just skip this course."

He kept insisting on flagging down the waiter, but I insisted that he not. He eventually settled in and ate his fish eggs.

The second course wasn't any more promising than the first. It was a combination of cod, mussels, cockles, calamari, and shitake mushrooms.

Here I'd been worried about not knowing which fork to use. The way things were going, I might not use any of them.

"Aren't you hungry?" the woman sitting across from me asked. I'd already forgotten her name, but I had noticed that her face hardly moved when she spoke. I was starving, actually, but so far all I'd eaten was a dinner roll.

"Not really. I had a big lunch." That was a lie. I'd skipped lunch so that I could go dress shopping.

"You don't like that either?" Preston asked quietly.

I shook my head. "Did you choose my meal for me?" I asked, surprised that he'd gone so far out of the box.

He cleared his throat and reached for the crystal glass filled with ice water and took a sip. Of course he hadn't chosen my dinner. He hadn't chosen it because he didn't know until today that he was bringing me. The knowledge that this was most likely Suzanne's meal, made it even less palatable.

By the time the third course was served, I was certain the man next to me could hear my stomach growling. My plate held three baby carrots, a sliced beet, porcini mushrooms, and some type of meat on a thin bone and chunks of something fried, nestled on a bed of polenta and drizzled with a white cream sauce. The same dish was set down in front of Preston.

I might get to use my knife and fork after all. I sliced into the meat, but nothing about it looked familiar. "What is this?" I asked Preston, poking it with my knife.

I waited while he finished chewing the bite he'd just put into his mouth. "Braised rabbit. It's delicious. And those," he pointed to the crispy fried rounds, "are sweetbreads."

"Sweetbreads?"

"Offal. Organ meat. It's a delicacy."

"Sounds awful."

The man beside me laughed. Apparently, I'd spoken much louder than I'd intended. Keeping my eyes on my plate, I cut off a chunk of carrot and popped it into my mouth and chewed. It was the tastiest carrot I'd ever eaten. I hated beets, but I ate them as well. Then I ate whatever polenta I could scrape out that hadn't touched the rabbit or the sweetbreads.

"Please let me ask the waiter to bring you something else."

"I'm fine. Like I said, I had a big lunch. I'm saving room for dessert."

When dinner was mostly over, the twelve-piece orchestra that had been quietly tuning up began to play.

Preston held out his hand. "Dance?"

"I'd love to." I was rising from my chair when an older gentleman stepped in front of me, escorting an elegant-looking woman. The man addressed the three men sitting at our table. "William, Edwin, Charles, I hope you and your lovely wives are enjoying yourselves this evening."

They bantered back and forth for a few moments while Preston stood stiffly at my side. When the small talk died down, the man fixed a sharp gaze on me and held out his hand. "Since my son has forgotten his manners this evening, allow me to introduce myself. I'm Preston F. Jamison II. This is my wife, Gwendolyn."

I wanted to sink into the floor. Preston's parents carried themselves so regally, I had a strange desire to curtsey. I held out a shaky hand. "It's a pleasure to meet you sir. I'm Rain."

He leaned closer, as if he hadn't quite heard me. "Excuse me? Rain?"

"Yes, sir."

"What a delightful name. I hope that doesn't mean you're sad and depressing to be around."

I glanced at Preston, expecting him to respond, but he said nothing. His body language, however, spoke volumes. His shoulders were back, his nostrils flared, his chin raised, his eyes hard. The only movement was the barely noticeable flicker along his jaw. He and daddy mustn't get along very well.

It was important that Preston's parents liked me, so despite the nervous fluttering in my stomach, I turned on the barroom charm. "No, sir. I certainly hope not."

Mr. Jamison let go of my hand, and I held it out toward his mother. She glanced down as if she wasn't quite sure what to do with it. At least she didn't keep me hanging too long before giving it a limp bob up and down.

"It's nice to meet you, Mrs. Jamison."

Preston resembled his mother. It was obvious in the way she held her head, especially when her nostrils flared before she spoke.

"Yes. Thank you."

Before I could dwell on how badly this version of Meet the Parents was going, Mr. Jamison placed his hand on my elbow and pointed me toward the dance floor.

"My dear, would you do me the honor? I'm sure Preston wouldn't mind if his old man has a go at you first."

The two of them exchanged looks, and I thought Preston's jaw might actually crack, but still, he said nothing. Tension swirled around us—so dark and heavy, it weighed on my skin. Despite that, Mr. Jamison was all smiles as he led me away from Preston and his mother.

With his hand against the bare skin of my lower back, he swung me out onto the dance floor like he was a celebrity guest on Dancing with the Stars. Although this wasn't my kind of dancing, the way Preston's father moved us about the floor had me feeling like a pro.

He pulled me close, his mouth hovering above my ear. "So tell me, how did you and Preston meet?"

"He came into the bar where I work a few months ago."

"I see. And what, exactly, do you do at this bar?"

It could've just been nerves, but I wasn't sure I cared for his tone.

"I'm a bartender."

He twirled me out and pulled me back in. The man had serious moves. "Is it a club of some sort? I think if I'd seen you tending bar at one of Preston's regular haunts, I surely would've recognized you."

The idea of Blondie's being a club was so ridiculous, I couldn't help laughing. "No. Definitely not a club. Just a regular old neighborhood bar." So that he understood I was more than just a bartender, I also told him about the luncheonette.

"So you cook too? An admirable quality in a woman."

I caught a glimpse of Preston's mother talking animatedly with him on the edge of the dance floor. It was difficult to picture her standing in a kitchen, let alone in front of a stove flipping pancakes.

"I bake too," I blurted out. I loved baking, and I was good at it, but trying to talk myself up from bartender to baker, didn't sound all that impressive, even to my ears. "And we cater." I should just stop talking.

"I promise you then, the next time we need a bartending baking caterer for one of our functions, you will be the first person we call. You'll have to contact my secretary and give her your rates. Do you charge by the hour?"

He was mocking me. Despite his charming smile and polished manners, he was easy to read. He disliked me. As far as he was concerned, I didn't belong there. At least not on the dance floor. My place was behind the bar or better yet, in the kitchen where no one would see me.

And he sure as hell didn't want me dating his son.

As if I'd somehow summoned him, Preston tapped his father on the shoulder.

"You've monopolized my girl long enough," he said, although his eyes were focused on mine. "It my turn now." He practically wrenched my hand away from his father and stepped between us.

"Of course. Thank you for the dance, Rain. And don't forget, please contact my secretary. Preston will give you the number."

Preston twirled us away before I could respond and didn't stop until we were practically on the other side of the dance floor.

"What was that about?" he asked. "What number?"

I debated telling him his father was a jackass, although chances were pretty good he already knew.

"He wanted me to leave my information with his secretary so he can call me next time he needs a bartender."

His hand tightened over mine. "I'm sorry. He's a controlling son of a bitch. He shouldn't have said something like that to you. You can't help it you're only a bartender."

Gee, thanks. That doesn't make me feel bad at all.

I was about to excuse myself, when one of Preston's friends cut in and asked me to dance. Before Preston could turn him away, I accepted. I needed a minute away from him before I said something not likely heard on the dance floor in a country club before.

Once the first guy opened the gate, Preston's friends spilled out onto the floor, cutting in—repeatedly—until I got tired of being passed around like a hot potato. I excused myself and made a beeline for the ladies' room.

I opened the door to find a beautifully appointed room decorated in salmon, cream, and gold. There was an ornate love seat with carved wooden accents and a matching wing chair. A coffee table with the same carved legs held a huge arrangement of fresh flowers. A woman in a white uniform stood beside a fancy wooden chair. Her eyes widened when she saw me, but her features quickly smoothed back into place. I bet not too many women dressed like me walked through those doors.

Oddly, the only thing missing were toilets. Sensing my confusion, the attendant motioned toward a hallway to the right. I gave her a nod and a smile. How rich did you have to be before you expected someone on standby in case you ran out of toilet paper?

The bathroom facilities were as nice as the room leading to them. There was a long peach-colored granite countertop with four sinks, and directly across from that were four separate stalls with louvered doors. I slipped into the last stall.

Here I was, perched on the edge of the toilet, locked in a stall in the most elegant restroom I'd ever seen, wishing for a window. Better yet, a time machine.

What the hell had I been thinking, wearing a dress like this? Everywhere I'd looked, people had been staring. Preston had seemed amused, right up until the time his father had asked me to dance.

I tugged a few sheets of toilet paper off the roll and blew my nose. I was giving myself a pep talk, when the door to the ladies' room opened. From the ring of the laughter, it sounded as if two or three women had entered.

"Oh my god, I almost died when they walked in. Could you imagine what poor Suzanne would say if she saw Preston with that Barbie doll wannabe?"

Barbie doll?

"Well, I'm certainly not going to tell her." The second girl had a British accent.

"I might not tell her, but there's nothing stopping me from posting a picture of them dancing on my Facebook page." She giggled. "You know, by accident."

A gasp was followed by a snicker. "You wouldn't!"

The first girl spoke again, but her words were mangled, like she was applying lipstick. "Suzanne's a bitch. Do you think I care if she finds out what Preston is up to?"

The door opened and a third person joined them.

"Well? What do you think?" the Brit asked.

"About what?" A different voice this time.

"Preston."

Someone tsked. "I think he's lost his mind, that's what I think."

"Did you see she has a tattoo on her shoulder? So tacky."

"I bet she has a tramp stamp."

They all laughed.

Fuck this! I tossed the tissue into the toilet and ran my hands over the front of my dress. The moment I flushed the toilet, the giggling stopped. I threw my shoulders back, unlocked the door, and stepped out. It wouldn't be the first time I'd gotten into a fight in a ladies' room.

Three sets of eyes widened at my reflection as I stepped out behind them. One of the girls, a brunette, had been so startled by my sudden appearance, she dragged her lipstick outside of her lip line causing a blood-red smear.

"Hello, ladies." Ignoring the thrum of my pulse beating in my ears, I turned on the faucet, and even though I hadn't used the bathroom, I washed my hands. No reason for the gossips to think I didn't wash my hands after peeing. The three women shuffled closer to one another, as if they were afraid I might bite. Smart move. I dried my hands on a linen towel and dropped it into a basket on the counter.

With a hand parked on my hip, I hoped to display a confidence I didn't feel. "I couldn't help overhearing your little gossip fest. While I have every right to be as big a bitch as you three, I'll pass. Being rude and intolerant doesn't come as easy for me as it may for you. But let me say this: I don't know you, and you don't know me. No matter what happens between me and Preston, I'd like it to stay that way." I took a few steps past them, but then turned back. "And whoever made that crack about my tattoo, it's in memory of my dad. So just shut your fucking mouth."

Okay. So maybe I was a little rude, but they had it coming.

I didn't have my purse, so I couldn't tip the attendant. I mumbled an apology, and stepped into the hallway. Even the staff would be talking about me by the end of the night.

Instead of returning to the table, I walked in the other direction, past the men's room, and around the corner. I slumped against the wall in the empty corridor, trying to talk myself into the strength and composure I needed to walk back into that room, especially now that I knew for certain what people were saying about me.

It shouldn't have bothered me. I'd never been one to care about what people thought. My reputation was exaggerated, and in many cases, downright false. Usually, I didn't let it bother me. But this time, I couldn't help wondering if Preston might be thinking the same thing.

Footsteps echoed from around the corner. As they grew closer, I stepped further into the shadows, hoping whoever they belonged to would be searching for a restroom and not heading my way. I needed a few more minutes before I'd be able to plaster a smile on my face and pretend everything was fine.

A door opened. Two men were speaking in low tones until a familiar voice interrupted.

"Have either of you seen my date?" Preston asked.

"I'd ask how you're doing, but judging by the Playmate of the Month I saw hanging off your arm, I'm going to say pretty bloody fantastic."

Another man laughed. "And judging from the way your father has stationed himself at the bar, throwing back Macallan, I'm guessing you're pushing all the old man's buttons tonight."

I recognized the low rumble of Preston's chuckle. "Could be. No harm in shaking him up a bit."

"So where did you find her, and are there any more like her at home?"

"Like I'd tell you."

"What's the deal with you and Suzanne?"

"There is no deal. I just needed a break."

Someone snickered. "Hey, if I could find a piece like that, I'd try to talk Leslie into a break too."

They laughed. I couldn't tell if Preston had laughed as well, but it still hurt.

"If you see Rain, will you let her know I'm looking for her?"

"Rain, huh? I'll let her know as soon as she's done screaming my name."

More laughter. "If she sees you coming, she'll be screaming all right."

"Shut the fuck up," Preston said. His voice was more playful than serious. "Just point her in my direction and keep your hands to yourself."

I waited until after the last footstep disappeared, and then I waited a few minutes more. By the time I returned to our table, the waiters were preparing to serve dessert.

Preston stood and pulled out my chair. The other men at the table stood as well. It was like being in a movie, only now I knew that when the cameras weren't rolling, these clowns were just like every other guy I'd ever met. Rich or poor, they all thought with their dicks.

"Are you okay? You were gone for a long time."

There was genuine concern in his eyes, which surprised me, given the conversation in the hallway a short time ago. As soon as I sat, he returned to his seat and slipped an arm around my shoulders.

"I'm fine. Seems I got a little lost there for a while. I won't make that mistake again."

His eyebrows creased, but before he could respond, I picked up my evening bag. "On second thought, I'm getting a headache." I rose and the men rose with me. I wanted to sit back down again, and then stand, to see if they did as well, but I wasn't in the mood for games. Especially since I was the one being played.

"It was nice meeting you all," I said to the couples seated around our table, then to Preston I added, "I'm going to call a cab and head home."

He tossed his napkin onto the table. "Don't be ridiculous. We'll both go."

I rested my hand against his chest. "Don't be silly. Besides. I think your break is about over." I took the shortest route, which was right through the middle of the dance floor, my heels clacking angrily to the rhythm of the drums. I reached the exit just as Preston's hand curled around my arm.

"What's going on? What happened?"

I tried to shake him off, but he wasn't having it. "I want to go home. This was a huge mistake."

He led me to the coat check and handed the attendant our tickets. Clearly, I hadn't thought this through. Had he let me go, I would've stormed out without my mother's good coat, and I sure as hell was never coming back here. After the girl handed us our coats, Preston stuffed a five into the brandy snifter on the counter.

I stuck out my hand. "Give me five dollars." He didn't ask why, he just ruffled through the bills in his wallet.

"I don't have another five. What do you need it for?"

"What do you have?"

He opened his wallet wider, and when I saw a fifty, I grabbed it.

"Where are you going?"

I didn't answer. And he didn't follow. Probably because he knew there was no other way for me to leave. I slipped into the ladies' room, handed the bill to the attendant, and left before she could answer. At least one person might have something nice to say about me.

On the drive home, neither of us spoke for the longest time. I stared out my window. Angry and embarrassed, I also felt like I'd let him down.

"It's not your fault, you know," he said after a while. "I should have been more specific."

So it wasn't just me—he was also embarrassed.

"Maybe. To be fair, you said to dress up. You didn't say dress like a tramp."

"You don't look like a tramp."

I glared at him. "Oh no? I think there were several women I passed in the hall who thought I was there to jump out of a cake."

"It wasn't that bad."

"C'mon, Preston. Your mother was mortified." And hey, I was pretty mortified myself. "And your father—"

Tension rolled off him in waves. "Don't worry about my father. I told you. He's a controlling jackass who thinks he can run my life."

"They're right, Preston. You and me—we come from different worlds. I heard you talking with your friends. So you and Suzanne are just on a break, huh? Did you bring me tonight just to piss off your father? If that's the case, well done—you did it."

The car swerved hard to the right. I gripped the door handle, and for a moment, I thought we were going over. We traveled along the gravel until we skidded to a stop on the side of the highway.

Preston stared straight ahead, his hands tight on the steering wheel. "That's not true. It's over. I told you that. I didn't want to discuss my relationship with Suzanne or with you with those guys. It's none of their business." It was dark when he turned to me, not even a streetlight to illuminate his face, but his words were sincere. "I only care about what you think. I did break up with Suzanne. I told you that. If you never want to go back to the club, you don't have to. And if my parents won't accept you for you, then to hell with them."

Brave words, but I imagined they'd be hard to live up to. I didn't want to come between him and his parents. As for the country club, that was an experience I wouldn't want to revisit anytime soon—if ever.

He ran his hand along the side of my face and held it so that I was looking at him.

"Do you believe me? I'd do anything for you."

I wasn't sure I believed him, but I was willing to try. "Anything?"

He nodded somberly.

"There's a McDonald's about a mile up the road. After trying to get me to eat tentacles and organ meat, the least you can do is buy me a Happy Meal."

CHAPTER TWELVE

Rain

It wasn't unusual at all for me to dress in skimpy outfits when I was tending bar, but the getup I wore today had me squirming. And while I really was excited to have been chosen Miss February—once I got over the shock—and I didn't have a problem posing half naked, especially for a good cause, I didn't want to get frostbite in the process.

"Can you turn the air conditioner down a little?" I asked, trying hard to keep from shivering. "It's really cold in here."

"Not if we're going to keep your nipples erect," the photographer's assistant answered without even looking at me. "We usually use ice, but we can't get your top wet."

You'd think a long-sleeved turtleneck would have kept me warmer, but it was cropped to allow the bottom half of my breasts to be visible, which meant my back and stomach were also exposed. The matching red lace V-thong panties weren't doing much to warm my lower half either.

My nipples were erect, all right, and so was my skin. Tiny goose bumps populated my legs and stomach.

The assistant finished fiddling with the lights and turned her attention to me, a quivering mass of flesh perched on the bar at Blondie's.

"I guess Antoine or I can pinch your nipples. That usually works."

She had to be fucking kidding.

Reading my mind or perhaps the horrified look on my face, she continued. "Antoine is gay, so it's no big deal. It's no different for him than changing the f-stop on his camera." She adjusted the bandanna covering her black-and-purple hair. "And I'm a lesbian, so at least I know what I'm doing. But you're totally not my type." She pointed her finger at me and waved it up and down. "Bleached hair, fake nails, fake boobs—not my thing."

If this calendar hadn't been raising money for sick kids, I'd have taken my real boobs and my fake everything else and walked the hell out of there.

"My boobs are not fake," I said, trying to sound indignant while my teeth chattered.

That seemed to perk her up. "They're real? And they stay up like that?" She took a step toward me. "Can I touch them?"

"No, you can't touch them! I'll touch my own boobs, thank you very much."

I folded my arms, crossed my legs, and glared at her. I'd gone from feeling like a still life of a bowl of fruit to the prize sheep in a petting zoo.

"Hey, if autoeroticism is your thing and you can keep those babies erect, go for it," she said, dangling a pair of long-stemmed cherries in front of my face. "Just have them up and ready to go when Antoine is ready. We can't be waiting on your nipples."

She waved the fruit in front of me. "Now open your mouth and stick out your tongue."

***

Preston called late the night of the calendar shoot. I was already asleep and had been for at least two hours.

"How'd it go?"

"Fine," I whispered. "Just hoping I didn't catch pneumonia." I crawled out of bed and down the hall into the living room so I wouldn't wake Izzy. "They had the AC turned so low I could almost see my breath."

"You're kidding! Irena was okay with that?"

"She wasn't there. I have a key, so she didn't need to come in until she had to start getting ready for the lunch crowd. We started at seven, and by the time she came in, I'd talked them into letting me pinch my own nipples so they could turn the AC off." I tried to muffle a yawn.

After a long silence, Preston spoke.

"What?"

"What what?"

"What the hell are you talking about? Pinching your own nipples."

I giggled. "The AC was to keep my nipples erect during the shoot. But after I offered to pinch my own, and they stayed erect, they stopped trying to flash freeze me."

"I've never noticed a problem with your nipples."

"Preach. But I guess they were worried I'd ruin the shot or something. They even offered to pinch them for me, but I turned that shit down." I tugged an afghan from the back of the sofa and pulled it over me. "I don't let just anybody touch the girls."

His laughter rumbled soft and low.

"And even though I refused to let him take matters into his own hands, so to speak, the photographer said he might have other work for me."

"What kind of work?"

"I'm not sure. I'm okay with sexy photos, but I'm not doing porn, if that's what you're asking."

"Hey, you never know. With your looks and that killer body, you could make a fortune."

He probably meant that as a compliment, but I couldn't help feeling disappointed that he would be okay with me doing those kinds of photos. But like I always did when someone mentioned my obvious (and maybe only) positive attribute, I played along.

"Yeah, who knows? Maybe he could get me on the cover of Juggs."

When he laughed, my heart slipped from my chest into my stomach. When he finally got it out of his system, he cleared his throat.

"Hey, babe, listen. Something's come up at work, and I'm heading to South Carolina first thing in the morning."

I fluffed one of the sofa cushions and tucked it under my head so I could lie down. "How long will you be gone?"

"A few weeks at least. For now. I'm sorry. I don't really have a choice. The old man's been coming down hard on me lately, and this is a big project."

I didn't have the guts to ask if he's father's recent behavior had anything to do with me. I didn't have to. Preston rarely spoke about his parents. Remembering how they'd reacted to me when we met, and how insulting his father had been, I didn't push him either.

"Will you be able to come home on weekends?"

He was silent so long, I assumed he was trying to decide how to answer me. "I'm not sure. Maybe not right away. I'll see what I can do, okay?"

I pulled the afghan tighter and wrapped my arms around myself.

"Okay. Have a good trip."

"I love you."

My throat was thick with emotion, and I had to force the words out.

"Love you too. G'night."

CHAPTER THIRTEEN

Rain

In late October, Irena threw a big bash at Blondie's to celebrate the release of the Most Beautiful Bartenders of New Jersey calendar. She must have been counting on the exposure to make her some big money. She even set up a free buffet.

Preston had flown up from South Carolina for the event. He'd even contacted Antoine, the photographer, and ordered a life-size copy of my photograph from the calendar. Irena hung it on the wall where anyone entering the bar would see it right away.

I'd refused to wear the outfit from the calendar shoot to the party, but I did wear a short, tight red dress in keeping with the theme. Lynette had made me a white satin sash with Miss February written in red glitter. For an additional five-dollar donation, I posed in front of my photo for anyone who wanted to take a selfie with me.

Surprisingly, even though I'd known most of these people my whole life, there were plenty who wanted my picture. But better than that, we sold out of all of the calendars Irena had ordered, which thrilled me, because the money was going to St. Jude's.

Preston sidled up to me when there was a lull in the picture taking. "Having fun?"

"I am, but I'm exhausted." I leaned against him and rubbed my cheek. "I can't imagine being a real celebrity and doing this stuff all the time. My face hurts from smiling. And if one more person asks me to hold a cherry in my teeth, I might bite them."

He pressed his lips against my ear, and his words flowed over me like warm honey. "Well, if you insist, I'll let you bite me later."

"Since this whole thing was your idea, I might just do that."

"What would you do for me if I told you I made a ten-thousand-dollar dona-tion to St. Jude's in your honor?"

My jaw almost landed on my chest. "Are you serious?"

"Of course I am. I'm proud of you." His hand swept the bar, encompassing the crowd and ending at the half-naked picture of me. "This is amazing. All of these people are here for you, Rain. They all bought calendars, and you've helped raise a lot of money. I wanted to do my part too."

Before I could fully digest Preston's generous donation and his comment about being proud of me for doing little more than taking off my clothes, Antoine appeared.

"Have you given any thought to my offer?" he asked.

Seemed like everyone wanted me to take off my clothes these days.

"Not really. It's been kinda crazy here tonight."

"What offer?" Preston asked.

"I'd like to work with her more. I have a lot of clients who would be interested in a beautiful woman like Rain, and that body . . ." He kissed the tips of his fingers. "Incroyable!"

Preston slipped his arm around my shoulders and winked at me. "I agree. Will you be paying her?"

Antoine straightened and glared at Preston as if he'd just been insulted, but honestly, I had wondered that myself.

"Of course. What do you take me for?"

"And you'll let her pinch her own nipples?" Preston laughed, but Antoine looked slightly miffed.

I was feeling a bit miffed myself.

"Preston, please."

"C'mon. I'm just joking. I think it's a great idea. You can make a little extra cash. Why not?"

"Can I think about it, Antoine? If it's tasteful, I might be interested, but I really want a little time to make a decision."

"Absolutely." He dug his card out of his shirt pocket. "Call me. If you're interested, I can probably have some work for you in early January."

With no purse and no pockets, I tucked the card under the strap of my bra as Antoine headed back to his assistant, who was following Lynette around like a lost puppy. So much for her dislike of fake boobs. I knew for a fact that Lynette's had been bought and paid for by her last boyfriend.

Preston stood beside me, taking a careful stab at one of the cocktail meatballs on his plate.

I wasn't used to the attention and the constant references to my body was getting uncomfortable. I would never be celebrated for my mind, but a little respect, especially from the man who kept proclaiming he loved me, would've been nice. "Would you mind not bringing up my nipples as a topic of conversation? It kinda creeps me out."

He popped the meatball in his mouth and pushed it to the side so he could answer.

"You're kidding, right? I said I was joking."

"Still. I don't discuss your body parts with anyone, and I'd like it if you did the same."

The apology I'd hoped for didn't materialize. Instead, he blinked once or twice, and then burst out laughing. "Good one, Rain. I thought you were serious there for a second."

I turned with a flounce and came face to face with my own perky breasts and erect nipples.

"Who are you pointing at?" I snapped, then I stalked off toward the pool room, where my 2-D image could no longer mock me.

CHAPTER FOURTEEN

Rain

The calendar was a huge hit. It sold out everywhere and also raised the most money of any other calendar the Beautiful Bartender organization sponsored. Thanks to Preston's ten-thousand-dollar donation, of course.

Over the next several months, Preston was home less and less; sometimes only once or twice a month. He spent the holidays at his family's home in Palm Beach. My Christmas present had been delivered by courier: the latest iPhone and a MacBook Air. I didn't like accepting expensive gifts from him, but this time, I agreed since I was also frustrated with my cheap-ass phone, and I didn't own a computer. But I'd accepted the gifts under one condition—that he allow me to put the phone in my name and pay for the monthly service myself. He fought me on that, never understanding why I wouldn't allow him to buy me things, but he finally relented when he realized it was that, or I'd stick with my old flip phone. I think knowing we'd never be able to Skype if he didn't give in, finally had him seeing it my way.

When Preston was able to get home, sometimes only for a day or two, I'd take the night off from Blondie's, have Izzy stay with my mom, and we'd spend most of the time holed up in my apartment. Even though it was over with Suzanne, it still felt like I was some kind of secret that needed to be locked away. Preston's father was to blame for our current situation. He was the one sending him to South Carolina and Palm Beach. For as much as Preston railed against him, his father pulled the strings, and he did whatever the old man wanted.

Oddly, I was mostly content. Maybe I didn't really want a serious relationship. Why else was I willing to settle for someone who made few demands on my time or how I lived my life? I hated to think that might be the case, but I was seriously beginning to wonder if I either didn't want more or didn't believe I deserved it.

If I had the money, I would invest in some heavy-duty psychotherapy. I bet if I asked, Preston would've even agreed to pay for it.

For now, sitting on Diane's deck, drinking margaritas and watching the sun dip behind the pole barn was therapy enough.

I licked a drop of salt from my bottom lip and stretched until my toes gripped the top rail of the deck, enjoying the warm night air. Summer wouldn't officially begin for weeks, but it was already off to a great start.

"I think we should declare every Sunday Margarita Night," I proclaimed.

"As long as you mix 'em." Diane refilled her glass from the nearly empty pitcher. "I think next week we should switch to frozen margaritas. It'll be warm enough." She rubbed a sliver of lime around the rim of my glass and dipped it in the saucer of kosher salt on the table between us, then filled it to the rim. Squinting at the quarter-inch of pale green liquid remaining, she lifted the pitcher to her lips, tilted her head, and drank until it was empty.

She blinked at me, her pretty blue eyes rimmed in pink from a few too many cocktails. "Should we mix up another batch?"

"Nah. I have to drive home. Besides"—I swiveled my foot toward her—"I think the salt is making my ankles swell."

She stretched one of her legs up next to mine—which wasn't easy, given my legs are several inches longer than hers—compared our ankles, and then knocked my foot off the railing with a grunt.

I inched my chair beyond her reach and put my feet back on the railing. The sun was completely behind the barn now, and the sky had turned that magical shade of blue between dusk and nightfall.

On a clear evening like this, when the stars would sparkle overhead, I felt closest to my dad. Somewhere, high above, I knew he was watching over me. Always.

Other than the sound of a bug zapper hanging in a nearby tree, it was quiet. Unusually quiet.

"Where's Wally? I thought after last night's crushing defeat that he, Bobby, and Dennis would be out in the barn, tearing that damn car apart trying to get ready for next week."

She made a face. "Oh, they will. They went to a mud hop. They're drowning their sorrows in mud and beer, watching idiots in jacked-up jeeps with giant tires tear their transmissions apart." She dragged a nacho through the last of the guacamole. "They'll be at it again tomorrow night, trust me. He finally found a mechanic to replace Davy, so he figured they could afford to take a night off." She licked her fingers. "I told him not to get any bright ideas. That money pit on wheels costs us enough as it is. I'll be damned if he's going to start racing in mud too."

The track was bad enough. I couldn't imagine finding joy getting sucked into a mud pit.

"Sounds horrible."

"You're telling me. I went once. Two minutes into the first run, I was covered from head to toe."

"Boys and their toys."

"Tell me about it."

A mosquito landed on my wrist, and I flicked it off. "So who's the new mechanic?"

She made a show of fanning herself. "Oh. My. God. What a hottie! Tall, built like he was carved out of stone. Dirty blond hair he wears pulled back into a ponytail. He's quiet, serious. I don't think I've ever seen him smile, to be honest, but I gotta tell you, one look and he could incinerate your panties."

"Diane!"

She laughed. "Hey, I'm married, not dead. Wally told me to stop bringing drinks and snacks up to the barn when they're working. I figure he's on to me."

"Since when do you schlep drinks and snacks up to the barn?"

"Exactly."

"I'm trying to picture this smoldering hottie you're describing, and I'm pretty sure Wally hasn't brought anyone like that into Blondie's. In fact, he doesn't sound like anyone from around here."

"That's because he just moved here. Wally knows him from the track and they hit it off. He was a pretty highly ranked driver, but he wrecked last year. Wally said it was so bad, they couldn't believe it when he climbed out of the car on his own. Nothing but cuts and bruises, although that was it for him. He gave up racing."

"Who could blame him?"

She shook her head. "Not me. I'd kill Wally myself before I'd let him kill himself behind the wheel."

I snorted. "That makes no sense, but I get it." I stared into the remnants of my glass. How was it already half empty? "I think I might be drunk."

"Yeah, me too."

"So this guy went from a track rock star to mechanic?"

"Pretty much. You know Dylan Holgate?"

I grimaced. "Lorraine's husband? I didn't know he raced."

"Not him. It's his brother, Chase. Wally says he bought half of Dylan's Sunoco station."

Given my intense dislike for Lorraine Moynihan, which went all the way back to tenth grade, I didn't frequent her husband's gas station. Likewise, neither she nor Dylan ever came into Blondie's or my mother's restaurant. Lorraine probably wouldn't let her husband within ten feet of me, especially after what had happened back in high school.

"I still hate that bitch," Diane muttered, as if she were suddenly the one with psychic powers and could read my mind. "And Skanky Stankevich."

Callie Stankevich, or Skanky as we used to call her, had been Lorraine's best friend in high school. They were seniors when Diane and I were sophomores. Callie hadn't taken it very well when Jeff, her boyfriend of three years, had dumped her for me.

"I still can't believe those two besmirched my high school record." Diane said, slurring her words.

I laughed so hard I almost fell out of my chair. "Besmirched? I think both our records were besmirched long before Lorraine and Skanky got us suspended."

"Maybe yours was, but I'd never been caught before. I thought my mother was going to kill me. Although even now, the feel of my fist connecting with Lorraine's cheek . . ." She curled her hand and held it up as if it were a prize. "Those were the good old days."

"You are drunk. That was only six years ago. But I'll never forget how you came to my aid," I said. "For barely clearing five feet, you're pretty scrappy."

"Damn straight. Lorraine called you a whore. She had it coming."

We'd been in the girls room after school, where I was checking the piercing I'd just gotten on my tongue—I still can't believe I'd done that. Diane was sitting on the sink watching when Lorraine, Callie, and two of their friends had come in.

I don't remember who said what to who, but it got ugly fast. Unfortunately, since I'd already been in trouble several times that year, the principal believed them and not us, and Diane and I got suspended for fighting. Turned out my high school record was pretty much toast, anyway. By the end of the summer, I was knocked up, and Jeff and I were through.

I leaned back and took in the night sky. Venus was shining brightly. Either the conversation or the alcohol was making me melancholy.

"You ever regret some of the things we did back then?"

"Nah. You?"

"Nope. I wouldn't trade Izzy for anything. And yanking out a handful of Skanky's frizzy brown hair was worth the three-day suspension."

Diane's chuckle was pure evil. "Totally worth it."

She raised her plastic glass in a drunken toast, clumsily hitting the rim of mine, and sloshing much of what was left of my margarita onto my hand.

"Here's to my partner in crime. May we keep kicking ass and taking no prisoners."

I giggled. "Damn straight."

She drained her glass and tossed it off the deck.

"A-fucking-men."

CHAPTER FIFTEEN

Chase

The first time I saw Rain Storm in the pit at the racetrack, it was love at first sight.

Okay. That's a lie. It was lust—pure, unadulterated lust. Rain is the kind of woman a guy looks at and thinks, Yeah, I want to hit that. Not that I'm some kind of pervert or anything. I just know how men think. And any guy who says he doesn't think like that when he looks at a woman like Rain is either lying or gay.

Case closed.

But if I'm being honest, it was her laugh that hooked me. She has a great laugh. Musical. Like notes ascending the scale. It's just so damn sexy.

It was early in the season, and I was going over the engine of the Jackson brothers' number 57 when I heard her laugh. At first, I thought somebody had brought their kid into the pit. When I looked up, my heart did one of those things like at the carnival—you know, the strongman's game? You hit the base with a mallet, and the little puck flies up the tower and hits a bell at the top, then drops back down again. That's exactly what it felt like.

She was tall, with these tight jean cut-offs, a low-cut top, and a pair of black cowboy boots. She was soft in all the right places and hard and firm where it mattered. Her hair was that white blond you know has to be bleached, and it was scraped back into a ponytail and looped through the back of a baseball cap. I couldn't see her eyes—she was wearing huge, dark sunglasses—but she was beautiful, and she had this wide, pouty mouth that just about made me want to cry.

If I were enough of a Neanderthal to believe in such a thing as a woman who was asking for it, I would've said there she was, standing right in front of me.

Truth was, all she would've had to do was crook her little finger, and I'd have dropped my torque wrench right there to follow her wherever she wanted me to go—on my hands and knees, if she'd asked.

Too bad she was hanging off the arm of some other guy.

No one bothered to introduce us, so after she and her friend left, I asked Wally about her. He smiled, and I was pretty sure I could read his mind too.

"That's Rain," he said. "Rain Storm."

I laughed. "What is she? A stripper?"

He shook his head. "No, but she could be."

"I'll say." I was having a hard time watching the sway of her hips as she walked away.

"I think her parents were either trying to be cute, or they were hippies. Can't really remember. Her mom owns a luncheonette near the industrial park. She works there during the day and then at Blondie's a couple nights a week."

"Is that a strip club?"

He clapped me on the shoulder and laughed. "I think somebody needs to get laid. Naw, it's just a neighborhood bar. Used to be more of a shot and beer joint, but since Rain started working there, it kept getting busier, as you can imagine. Now it's quite a popular little hot spot. She tends bar."

Familiarity tugged at me, and if she was the girl I remembered from the sandwich place—the one who'd made those awesome cupcakes—this clown was all wrong for her.

Rain and her friend disappeared into the crowd. Heads turned as she passed.

"What's his story? He doesn't look like the kind of guy you usually see in the pits."

"Who, Preston?"

I snorted. "Preston?" He even had a clown name.

"Hey, don't diss my man. That's his name painted across the side panel."

I'd been working on the car since the beginning of the season, but I'd never paid any attention to whose name was painted where. I leaned back to read the side of the car: Jamison Architectural Associates Inc.

"He's an architect?"

"I guess," he shrugged. "All I know is that he's loaded. I just thanked him for the check and told Moose where to paint his name and how big to make the letters. I don't know that anyone who sees it around here will ever need an architect, but if he wants to put up some green for the show, who am I to judge? Personally, I think Rain put him up to it." His smile slipped a little. "She's a good girl, a real sweetheart—a heart as big as those tits. I've known her for a long time. She and my wife have been best friends since they were in diapers. Let's just say she hasn't had it easy. And with Preston, I think she's just looking to get hurt again."

"Why's that?"

"Diane says he's got a longtime on-again, off-again girlfriend. It's supposed to be over, but Diane thinks he's just shining Rain on."

I was stunned. "Seriously? Gotta wonder what she must look like."

"I saw her once. She couldn't hold a candle to Rain. Actually kind of mousy-looking."

"Next to her, I imagine most women would look kind of mousy."

"Maybe—but then again, I'm married to a redheaded spitfire, so I'm good."

Right. Wally's wedding. I'd taken Jennifer. Trying not to look as if I'd just been kicked in the nuts, I flipped my wrench in the air and caught it.

"Yeah, you're a lucky man."

I could no longer see Rain, but still I stared off in the direction she had headed. "So, Blondie's, huh?"

Wally nodded. "Why? You suddenly a little thirsty?"

"Man. You have no idea."

CHAPTER SIXTEEN

Chase

I got into the habit of stopping at Blondie's for a beer on my way home. It was a small neighborhood bar located next to the municipal airport. The blue-collar clientele was about a sixty-forty mix of men to women, and the owner looked nothing like you might expect. She had short gray hair, and wore squeaky, rubber-soled shoes, and thick-lensed glasses. When she wasn't simply abrupt, she could be downright rude.

No wonder she hired attractive bartenders.

Rain wasn't working the first few times I was in. The first night she was, I ended up sitting at the wrong end of the bar, and the old lady waited on me. Still, it gave me a chance to check out Rain without appearing obvious. She was definitely the girl from the sandwich shop and the same one I'd run into outside the bathroom at Wally's wedding.

She was even more beautiful than I remembered, as well as a bona fide flirt. She smiled and fawned all over her customers, and they practically drooled whenever she walked past.

They probably went through a lot of napkins in this place.

On Wednesday, I went straight to Wally's after work to tune up the car for Saturday. It was almost eight thirty by the time we finished. When Wally suggested we grab a beer, I told him I was going to pass since I hadn't had a chance to grab dinner.

"C'mon. I'll buy you a beer. If we get there before nine, the kitchen should still be open."

"Is the food any good?"

"What do you care?" He gripped me by the shoulder and gave me a friendly shake and a wink. "I think your favorite bartender's working tonight."

When Wally and Bobby and I walked into Blondie's fifteen minutes later, it was like an episode of Cheers. Cries of "Walter!" and "Wally!" went up around the room, and Wally waved like royalty greeting the masses. I trailed behind him and Bobby to a seat on the far end of the bar.

"Evening, gentlemen." Rain flashed a smile that I could feel all the way down into my boots. "Bud, Bud—and you?" Her perfectly shaped eyebrows formed a question.

"Heineken."

"Oh, a big spender." She winked, then grabbed a bottle from the cooler and opened it before filling two glasses from the tap for Wally and Bobby.

Wally wrapped his big mitt around his glass. "Rain, sweetheart, this is my friend Chase. He's on the pit crew now."

She held out her hand, showing long, slender fingers and bright pink nails. She clasped my hand a bit longer than I expected. When she did, I could have sworn she not only looked into my eyes but deep inside of me.

She narrowed her gaze a bit, then shook it off and released my hand slowly.

"Nice to meet you, Chase. So you're new around here."

It sounded like she was telling me instead of asking me. I nodded. "A couple months."

"You know Dylan Holgate?" Wally asked her. "Owns the Sunoco? Chase is his brother. They're partners now."

"Right." She nodded. "I don't really know Dylan, but I remember Lorraine from high school."

The way her smile faltered, I got the distinct impression she wasn't a fan of Lorraine's. My brother's wife was an acquired taste, one I had to admit I hadn't developed yet—but hey, if my brother was happy, that was all that mattered. I hadn't been too lucky in that department, so I wasn't one to talk.

"Sweetheart," Wally said. "Chase hasn't had dinner yet. Is the kitchen still open?"

The clock hanging on the wall near the restroom must've been on bar time and showed it was a little past nine. According to my watch, it was ten till.

"Not really, but I can make you something. What would you like?"

"I don't want you to go to any trouble," I said, even though I was starving.

"It's no trouble. Irena's probably closed the grill down already, but I can probably whip you up a cheeseburger real quick in the frying pan. That okay?"

"If it's no trouble."

She touched my hand. Again, she lingered—not that I minded. "No trouble at all."

As I waited, the owner stuck her head out of the kitchen and glared at me. I hoped she paid Rain well, because without her, I couldn't imagine the place would still be in business.

"How's your hamburger?" Wally asked a little later. Rain was on the other side of the bar, waiting on customers who'd just walked in.

"Delicious." I was actually a little surprised. She'd added sautéed mushrooms and onions, melted some Swiss cheese on top, and then hit it with a little barbecue sauce.

"See anything else you like?" he asked.

I smiled as I chewed, pushing the food to one side of my mouth so I could speak. "Definitely."

"Listen, Diane's having a surprise birthday party for Rain on Friday at the house. You should come."

"What about her boyfriend?"

He shook his head. "Not coming. Although it killed Diane to invite him, he said he couldn't make it. Come. What've you got to lose?"

"I don't know. I'm not much for parties these days."

"C'mon . . . If nothing else, you get a free meal. Diane, her mom, and Rain's mom have been cooking like crazy all week."

"Yeah, but a birthday party? That's kind of weird. I don't really know her to go out and get her a present, and I'll look like a jerk if I don't get something."

Wally shook his head. "That's not my area of expertise. How about I ask Diane and see what she says? If she says you should get her a present, I'll just tell her to pick something up she thinks Rain will like. Okay?"

I wanted to see her again, so this was a no-brainer. I nodded.

"How much would you want to spend?"

I shrugged. "I don't know. A hundred?"

"Jesus. You'll scare the shit out of her! She'll think you're some kind of psycho. A hundred! How about twenty?"

"Yeah, whatever. I don't know. Whatever Diane thinks is best."

"Then you'll come?"

For another chance to spend time with Rain? I smiled as I reached for my beer. "I wouldn't miss it."

CHAPTER SEVENTEEN

Rain

I swore up and down that I was surprised, but I wasn't. If there were ever a time I was certain I was psychic, it was times like this. I felt bad, especially knowing all the trouble Diane went through, but I'd known for two weeks that something was up.

After I arrived and everyone jumped out and shouted "Surprise!" at me, I scanned the room for Preston. My disappointment was probably obvious to everyone, but I tried hard to keep smiling through the gifts and the cake. The party was a special gesture, and I was disappointed in myself for not being more enthusiastic.

Diane would've invited him, although she wouldn't have wanted to. I wasn't going to ask, though, because it would've hurt too much to hear her tell me he couldn't make it.

He'd finally finished the project in South Carolina and was home now—at least until his father found another project for him to manage. I had a feeling things were back on with Suzanne again, but I refused to bring it up. He had taken me to dinner last night to some French restaurant just over the state line in Pennsylvania. I had to let him order for me, since I only had a year of high school French, and none of that included what one might order in a fancy restaurant. At least he didn't try to get me to eat octopus or snails this time.

I'd assumed dinner was my gift, but when we got back to my apartment, he gave me a heart-shaped diamond pendant. He said he'd wanted to give it to me when I was naked so it would be the only thing I was wearing.

I'm sure it was expensive, but I felt cheap when he fastened it around my neck and it fell between my bare breasts. Despite no evidence even suggesting it, I couldn't help feeling like the other woman. Call it intuition or my hit-or-miss sixth sense, something nagged at me.

Worried I was about to be swallowed up by some sort of melancholy, I slipped outside the first chance I got. It had rained earlier, but now the moon was playing hide-and-seek with the clouds as they passed. The sky was an inky black, and a handful of stars winked down at me. I fingered my necklace, raised my face, and closed my eyes, thinking about my dad. A smattering of raindrops from the tree above me kissed my face.

"Don't cry, Daddy," I whispered. "I'll be okay."

The grass rustled nearby. I opened my eyes to see Chase slipping into the shadows.

"Too late," I called. "I saw you."

He turned back. "Sorry. I saw you sitting here alone, and I thought I'd come out and see if you were okay." He hesitated. "I'll leave you to . . . whatever it was you were doing."

I shook my head and patted the spot on the retaining wall next to me.

"It's okay. I was just talking to my dad."

He sat beside me and stretched his long legs out next to mine. "How long?"

A smiled tugged at the corner of my mouth. Finally. Someone who didn't make me feel even a little crazy for talking to the stars.

"Almost eight years."

"I'm sorry."

"I miss him every day, but I have good memories. He was a great dad."

He handed me a bottle of Heineken. "I don't know what you drink, so I just brought you one of these."

"Tequila, but this is fine."

"I'll have to remember that."

I laughed since he'd given me a bottle of tequila as a birthday present.

"Oh, yeah." A slow smile crept over his face after I reminded him. "I forgot."

"You liar." I playfully bumped him with my shoulder. "Who bought it? Diane?" Of course she had—and she was probably watching us from somewhere in the house. "Did she send you out here after me?"

He shook his head. "Absolutely not. I came on my own."

"I think you're still lying."

"I swear! Don't you think if she'd sent me out, she'd at least have made sure I brought the right drink?"

He had a point. He also had a great smile. He seemed pretty serious for the most part, but when he smiled, his eyes sparkled as if he were lit from the inside.

"So what's your story?" I asked. "I'm sure you've already heard all my ugly secrets and way more than I'm comfortable with anyone knowing."

He shrugged. "Not much to tell. I'm twenty-seven. I grew up outside of Allentown. I moved here a couple months ago to work with my brother. Like I said, not much to tell."

"Oh, there's more," I assured him, wondering what had happened with the rabbit, and if she'd moved here with him. "You're just not talking." I stood up and faced him. "Can I have your hand?"

He looked confused but held out his left hand.

I shook my head. "No, the right one."

He transferred his beer to the other hand, wiped it on his jeans, and held out his right hand. In spite of the cold, wet bottle, his hand was still warm. I put my hand in his as if we were going to shake hands and felt it again—a low-voltage vibration. I'd felt it the first time, when he'd come into the luncheonette, and at the wedding when he'd touched my arms, and again when we shook hands at Blondie's last week.

I still had no idea what I was feeling. Again, I remembered my dad's fateful declaration about his boss all those years ago, and how he'd known he was going to die just by shaking his hand.

"Are you feeling okay?" I asked.

He smiled. "You mean right now, while you're holding my hand? Yeah, actually, I feel pretty good."

I shook my head. "I mean health wise. Are you healthy?"

"Why? What did you have in mind?"

It seemed he wasn't going to take me seriously.

"Nothing."

I reached for the other hand. He finished his beer, set the bottle on the ground in front of him, and held it out to me. I held both of them, closed my eyes and concentrated.

"Has anyone ever told you they felt some type of electricity when they touched you?" I asked after a while, opening my eyes.

"Actually, yes." He laughed when I made a face.

"I'm a little psychic," I said. "My dad was extremely gifted, and I heard him say once that he shook someone's hand and knew the guy was going to die soon."

"Jesus." He pulled his hands away as if he were the one feeling the shock. "That's one hell of a party trick you got going there."

I shook my head. "I'm not saying I feel that. I don't know what I'm feeling, but I'm feeling something. A vibration. It's faint, but it's definitely there." I sized him up. He looked healthy. "Still . . . I'd feel better if you got a checkup."

"Oh, you would, would you?"

"I'm not crazy." I sounded exactly like someone who was crazy. "It's a deep gut feeling. I just know things. I also usually know when someone is lying to me." Given that I was involved with someone who lied, or at least bent the truth to suit him, I probably should revisit my earlier declaration about not being crazy. "Sometimes I just know what's going to happen before it happens—sometimes just seconds before, so it's not like it does much good, but still. Don't tell Diane, but I knew about this party, although I wish I could've been surprised."

I cocked my head. "I know! I'll prove I'm psychic. I can guess your middle name."

He ducked his head and chuckled. "I doubt it."

"Seriously. What's your last name again?"

"Holgate."

"Okay, Chase Holgate. What's your middle initial?"

He shook his head and laughed. "Too easy. You have to figure it out on your own."

I narrowed my eyes. "Challenge accepted."

"Oh, and one other thing." The corners of his mouth turned up. "If you don't guess my middle name, I get to give you a birthday kiss."

"I'm very good," I warned.

"So am I."

I bit down on my bottom lip to keep from smiling while the rest of me got all warm and tingly, and he wasn't even touching me this time. Given my relationship with Preston, it came as a bit of a surprise. Chase was extremely attractive—and probably could incinerate a pair of panties if he wanted—but he was a bit rough around the edges, especially compared with Preston.

"Deal," I said. I couldn't remember the last time I'd missed a name. "Will you tell me if I guess the right initial first?"

He shook his head.

"C'mon!"

"Nope. Stakes are too high."

I stared at him for a little while, but nothing was coming to me. Not even a letter.

"Give me your hands again."

That had never worked before, but I was really struggling. He smiled and extended his hands. I held onto him for a while, but still I got nothing, although the vibration grew stronger. I tilted my head up to the night sky and tried to focus.

"Hey! No cheating. Your dad can't help."

I'd been sad thinking of another birthday without my father, but that made me laugh. After a few more moments, I gave up.

"You win." I let go of his hands and offered up my cheek.

"Oh no." He gave a deep laugh as he stood, towering over me. "I get to kiss you, and not on the cheek."

"You know I'm seeing someone," I reminded him, although I was sure he must already know. I wasn't about to lead him on.

"I know," he assured me, "for now."

My traitorous body was buzzing. "You have a lot of faith in yourself, don't you?"

"I just know my strengths and my weaknesses."

He put his hand against the small of my back and pulled me closer. Then with his right hand resting on the back of my head and tangled in my hair, he tilted my face toward him. His kiss was gentle at first, but he slowly applied more pressure, and I could feel myself yielding. He pulled back a fraction of an inch, hesitated, and then kissed me again. And I let him. I didn't owe him more than one kiss, but I let him kiss me—and to my surprise, I kissed him back.

When I finally pulled away, he didn't try to stop me.

"I . . . um . . ." I wasn't quite sure what I was going to say.

"Um . . ." he replied teasingly.

"Okay," I said finally. "You're a very good kisser."

He grinned. "Thank you. You should keep that in mind."

He leaned forward, and I thought he was going to kiss me again. Instead, he whispered in my ear. "I don't have a middle name."

I gasped. "That's not fair! You lied to me."

"No, I didn't. And you gave up. You didn't figure out there was no name."

"That sounds like a technicality."

"A win's a win." He grinned. "Want to kiss me again?"

It surprised me how much I wanted to say yes, but I didn't. I just laughed. "No, you cheater."

His smile faded as his features darkened. "No, not a cheater. I'm what they call a good guy. We're the ones who finish last."

There was sadness in his voice. It was the part of the story he wasn't telling. But before I could surmise anything more, he headed toward the street.

"I have work in the morning, so please make my apologies," he called, walking backward. "Happy birthday, Rain. I hope this next year is your best one yet."

A few minutes later, the silent night was filled with the throaty roar of his bike as he disappeared into the night.

And as strange as it was, it felt as if he'd taken a little part of me with him.

CHAPTER EIGHTEEN

Chase

It may not have been the hardest thing I've ever done, but it sure as hell wasn't easy walking away from Rain after that kiss. I'll admit, when I saw her at the track I thought she was just a really hot piece of ass, and I believed that after all the shit I'd been through in the past six months, I deserved a good fuck with no strings attached. Given a choice, she's who I would've chosen.

But in the short time I'd known her, I no longer saw the hard candy shell. She was more than sex on a stick, with her bleached-blond hair, beautiful face, inch-long fingernails, and body that just wouldn't quit. I'd caught a glimpse of her softer side. The girl sitting outside alone the night of her party, crying quietly under the trees, had seemed innocent and vulnerable. And the few times I'd seen her since, at Blondie's or at Wally's, I'd caught her watching me like she really was concerned about my health or something.

It made me want to get to know her, not just nail her, although I sure as hell wouldn't be averse to that either.

We'd finished up working on the car early Thursday, and the crew and I headed to Blondie's. I hadn't eaten, so a burger and some of Irena's homemade pierogis washed down with a couple Heinekens was just what I needed. I couldn't get over how good the food was for such a little hole in the wall.

I was about to settle up with Lynette and head home when Rain and Preston walked in. I sat back down and ordered another beer. Other than that night at the track, I'd never seen the two of them together, and I was curious what it was about him that kept her hanging on, especially if there were even a remote chance that he was two-timing her.

It didn't take long for me to wonder if she was a glutton for punishment, because from where I sat, he was a first-class jerk. They'd taken two stools near the door, directly across from us. Rain saw Wally and waved, but I was partially blocked by the display of bottles in the center of the bar. Either she didn't see me, or she was ignoring me. I fancied that she was thinking about kissing me. I was probably kidding myself, but the kiss we'd shared had gotten me through some lonely nights.

She seemed unusually subdued, and it was clear after only a minute or two that her boyfriend had been drinking. He was loud and boisterous, and although I couldn't hear what she ordered, I heard him insist on pouring his own. Lynette handed Rain a glass of club soda with a twist of lime, then set a shot glass and a bottle of Jameson in front of him. Even though the spelling was different, it wouldn't have surprised me to learn some distant relative of his owned the distillery.

He whispered something to Rain and nuzzled her neck. I had to look away. I had no right to feel anything, let alone jealousy. But for as much as I tried to remain focused on Wally's discussion of the merits of Hoosiers over Goodyears, I couldn't help zeroing in on what was going on across from me.

Rain seemed tense and irritable and growing more so. Preston kept grabbing her. At one point, he held her around the waist and stuck his shot glass into her cleavage. When he reached for the bottle of whiskey, she pulled it out and slammed it on the bar.

"C'mon, babe." He picked it up and tried to put it back.

Fish and one of his buddies started egging her on.

"Go ahead, Rain! I bet that's not the only place he sticks his face."

Fish burst out laughing while the drunk beside him clapped him on the back, then yelled, "If he's no good, I'm an excellent linguist."

He stuck his tongue out like he was Gene Simmons. I wanted to yank it right the fuck out of his head.

Rain usually had a snappy comeback, but not tonight. Tonight she seemed defeated. Preston pulled her out of her chair, stood her in front of him, and slipped the glass between her breasts again. She seemed miserable, but for some reason, she appeared willing to let the jackass have his boob shot. At least until she looked away. When her eyes met mine, I could feel her embarrassment from across the bar.

"No!" She yanked the glass away. "I said I don't want to. Isn't that good enough?"

"Aw, c'mon, babe. What's got into you?" He made like he was going to bury his face in her cleavage, glass or no, but she pushed him away. "What the fuck is your problem?"

Fish let out a wild catcall. Rain shot him a threatening look.

"Just stop," she said to Preston, trying to keep her voice low.

"C'mon, please?" He raised the glass above his head, and though he spoke to her, he did it for the benefit of everyone in the barroom. "Let me do a boob shot, and I'll buy a round for the house."

The place erupted in cheers.

Rain snatched her purse off the bar. "Fuck you, Preston! You want to do boob shots, bring your girlfriend in and put her on display."

She spun toward the door.

He called after her. "Your tits are nicer!" When the door slammed shut behind her, he added loudly, "Fuck you. You can walk home."

"I'll fuck her," Fish yelled, and the place erupted with more cheers, especially when Preston lifted his filled shot glass and toasted the bastard before throwing it back.

The only person who wasn't enjoying the show, besides me, was Wally. He gripped my shoulder.

"You look like you're ready to kill somebody." He spoke low enough so that only I could hear him. "He's drunk. I've never seen him like this before."

I shook my head. "I gotta go, or I'm gonna end up kicking the shit out of him."

Wally gave my back a couple pats. "Good idea."

Preston was in no hurry to go after Rain. Although he hadn't gotten his way, he ordered a round for the bar anyway. He was everybody's fucking hero.

I picked up my helmet and threw a twenty on the bar.

Preston was talking to Lynette as I passed. "She can wait until I'm good and ready, or she can walk her ass home."

I was almost to the door when he reached out and grabbed my arm. He was stockier than me, but I had several inches on him, plus I was fast. I also wasn't drunk.

"Where you going?" His speech was slurred. "I'm buyin', motorhead, dincha hear?"

"Yeah, I heard. No, thanks." I yanked my arm from his grasp.

"Eh, fuck you too," I heard as the door closed behind me.

There was no sign of Rain near the apple-green Corvette I assumed was Preston's. I was climbing onto my bike, when I caught sight of someone walking about half a block away. When she passed under a streetlight, that white-blond hair lit up like a beacon.

"Jesus Christ," I muttered. I had to give her credit. She had to live at least five miles from here, yet damn if she wasn't determined to walk home.

I started up my bike and rode until I could pull up in front of her. I cut the engine and slipped off my helmet.

"You planning to walk all the way home?"

"Yes."

"Do you want a ride?"

She stopped walking to consider my offer. "I guess."

I handed her the helmet. "Here, put this on."

"What are you going to wear?"

"I'm from Pennsylvania. No helmet laws. I'll be fine."

"Yeah, but this is New Jersey." The helmet was too big for her, but it was better than nothing.

"I'll go slow, I promise. If I get pulled over, it's only a twenty-five-dollar fine. I'll take my chances."

She climbed on and put her arms around my waist. I had to remind myself to focus.

"Am I holding you too tight?" she asked.

I smiled over my shoulder. "Just tight enough."

She loosened her grip, but as soon as I took off, she squeezed harder. Despite my promise to take it slow, if she held me tighter when I went faster, I might just have to do that.

At the first stop sign, I asked if she wanted to go for a ride or straight home.

"I'd love a ride, but not if you don't have a helmet."

"No problem." I leaned into the turn and headed up Cedar Hill Road. I had a spare helmet back at my apartment.

"You want to come in or wait here?" I asked after pulling into my driveway.

She made a face. "I need to use the bathroom, if that's okay."

"C'mon."

I was waiting in the living room when she came out. It gave me a crazy little thrill seeing her in my apartment.

"This is nice," she said, surveying the place. "A little sparse, but nice. You're very neat. Either that or you don't have enough stuff to make a mess."

"Both, actually. When I moved, I left everything with my ex."

"Oh. The rabbit."

"Scuse me?"

She grimaced and shook her head. "Nothing. Sorry."

"Better I found out before the wedding than after."

She didn't ask, but I could see she wanted to. So despite preferring to stick needles in my eyes rather than talk about what Jennifer had done to me, I voluntarily told her.

"I caught her cheating."

"You're kidding." She seemed honestly surprised. It was still painful, but her expression was comical. "I mean, I can't imagine someone cheating on you. You're just so . . . nice. And you're really attractive too. I mean really attractive."

"Well, thanks, but that didn't seem to matter—to her or my best friend."

"Ouch."

I shrugged. "It is what it is."

I could feel her discomfort as she walked around the room, looking at pictures of my nephew, my CDs. It was like she was trying to avoid me and tell me something at the same time.

Eventually, she decided to talk.

"You probably don't have too much respect for me, then."

"I don't follow."

"Me and Preston. He's got another girlfriend, you know. At least I think he does. Who knows anymore?"

I nodded. "You're too good for him."

She laughed. "Yeah, right."

"I'm serious. I don't really know you, but from what I do know, he doesn't deserve you. You deserve someone who sees in here." I tapped my chest maybe a little too hard, but I was feeling it. "You're a beautiful woman on the outside. Stunning. But you're also beautiful on the inside."

She bit her lower lip, and I went weak in the knees. I needed to change the subject. Here I had her to myself, and the last thing I wanted was to talk about was her jackass boyfriend.

I handed her the helmet. "Where do you want to go?"

She looked a bit bewildered. "I have no idea. Surprise me."

"Okay. How far?"

She laughed—musical notes again. "I don't know."

"How about this: what time do you have to be home?"

"I don't."

I grinned. "Ever?" At that moment, I was okay with that.

"Well, Izzy, my daughter, is away for the week with her father's parents, and I took tomorrow off to get caught up on some things I've been putting off. So technically, I don't need to be back until Sunday at three to fill in for Lynette. Otherwise, I wouldn't have to be back until Sunday night for Izzy." She gave me a triumphant smile.

"Well, my schedule isn't quite as open as yours, but if you're game, I have an idea."

"What?"

"You're psychic, you tell me."

"Funny." She made a face. "Is this like the last time?"

I shrugged. "Was kissing me really so bad?"

When she smiled, that carnival game went off inside me again. "No. It wasn't bad at all."

I eyed her sleeveless blue-and-white polka-dotted sundress, admiring how it curled snugly around her waist before flaring into a full skirt. I pulled a leather jacket from my closet and handed it to her.

"Where are we going? Canada?"

"It might get cool later, and you're not exactly dressed for riding. You'll thank me later. Unless you want to go back to your place and change." I hesitated to suggest it. I was afraid that once we got to her place, she might change her mind, but I also didn't want her to be uncomfortable on the ride.

She gave me a determined shake of her head.

"This is fine. I'm afraid Preston might go there once he realizes I'm not waiting obediently beside his car, and I don't feel like dealing with him anymore tonight."

"Okay, then. You're all mine." I buckled my helmet into place and then helped her with hers. "For a little while, at least."

After she settled onto the back of the bike, I could feel her hands rooting around underneath me. And damn if my dick didn't sit up and take notice.

I swiveled toward her.

"I suggest you hold onto my waist, not my ass."

"I'm tucking my dress under you so it doesn't blow up around me and I give everyone a free show."

I lifted up so she could finish.

"Good idea. We don't want to cause any accidents on the parkway."

"The parkway?" she cried as I revved the engine. "Where are we going?"

"Hang on!" I called over my shoulder and gunned it out of my driveway.

She wrapped her arms around my waist and pressed her body against my back. I was ready to ride all night.

CHAPTER NINETEEN

Chase

We rode for about an hour before I pulled off at a rest stop on the Garden State Parkway.

"How're you doing? You comfortable?"

She nodded and grinned. "What about you? Are you tired? You weren't expecting a midnight ride. I don't want you to fall asleep or anything."

With her tits pressed up against me and her arms tight around my waist, there was no chance of that happening. In fact, just remembering how she felt behind me might keep me awake for a days.

"I'm good, but I'm going to get some coffee. You want anything?"

She climbed off the bike. "Coffee would be good. I don't want to miss anything."

While I went up to Starbucks and placed our orders—regular coffee for me and some fancy mocha something-or-other for her—Rain waited at a table nearby, texting on her phone. I wondered if she'd be asking me to turn around soon.

I placed her coffee on the table. "Everything okay?"

She set her phone down and reached for her coffee. "I was just sending my mother a message so she wouldn't worry in case I'm not home when she opens."

I sat down across from her. "What time do you open?"

"She gets in around six, but we don't open until seven."

I liked that she wasn't sure what time we'd be getting back—and she was okay with that.

"I also got a message from Preston around midnight." She held the phone out for me to see what he'd written: Where the fuck are you?

What a jackass.

"You going to tell him?"

Her face clouded. I wasn't sure if she was angry or about to start crying.

"You want to talk about it?"

"Not really. I just want to ride." She smiled, but there was sadness behind her eyes.

We finished our coffee, and as we walked through the parking lot, I had to keep myself from reaching for her hand. It felt so natural.

"You ready to tell me where we're going?" she asked as she climbed onto the Harley behind me.

"Nope. You told me to surprise you."

"I know, but I don't usually like surprises."

"You'll like this one."

With Rain secure behind me and her arms around my waist once more, I got back on the parkway. It was the middle of the night, but even if I hadn't just had a large cup of coffee, I think I would've been just as alert.

I was pushing my luck where she was concerned. Even worse, I could be setting myself up to get hurt again. We were barely even friends, and I was in no way ready for another relationship. If I could wish this to be something more, I would, but she was in love with someone else, and stubbornly so.

What the hell was I doing?

"You okay?" Rain called over my shoulder.

"Great. How about you?"

"Good. Am I holding too tight?"

Not in a million years. "You're fine."

Before we exited the parkway, I pulled over to fill up and we each had another cup of coffee.

She studied my face and I found myself falling deeper into the clear blue of her eyes, still beautiful, even under the harsh lights outside the Wawa.

"Are you taking me to Cape May?"

I smiled and blew on my coffee.

Her face lit up and if it were possible, it made her even more beautiful. "Really?"

"I guess you are psychic. Do you like Cape May?"

"I've never been, but I've seen pictures. All those beautiful Victorian houses and the beach."

She was grinning. So was I.

I had cruised at or under the speed limit the entire trip, and even with the two rest stops, it wasn't yet three o'clock when we arrived. I wanted her to see the sunrise, and we still had over two hours to go. I rode along the main street to Ocean Avenue and then out to the lighthouse.

"This is so cool," she gushed over my shoulder. "I haven't seen a lighthouse this close since I was a little kid."

I parked near the walkway to the beach and led her toward the pounding waves. I held out my arm so she wouldn't trip; instead, she slipped her hand into mine and kept chattering away, animated by our spirit of adventure. Or maybe it was the two cups of coffee.

"Are you warm enough?" I asked.

"I'm fine."

When we neared the water, she pulled off her cowboy boots, threw them in the sand, and started running. There was enough of a moon that I could see her, but it worried me to have her so far out into the water at night. I pulled off my work boots and socks, tossed them alongside her boots, then rolled up my jeans and followed.

The water was splashing up her calves when I caught up to her.

"You're going to get soaked," I said. "That's going to be pretty uncomfortable heading back if you're all wet."

Waves rushed around our legs past our knees, and she grabbed my arm to steady herself against the drag of the tide. Moonlight cast her face in a blue-gray light, and with her hair floating around her face, she appeared delicate and ethereal.

"Are we heading back soon?" she asked.

"It's up to you. We can stay as long as you like."

"How about forever?"

Raising her arms, she twirled and then sprinted along the beach, darting in and out of the water. In the short time I'd known her, Rain had almost always worn a smile—at least until that asshole treated her like shit earlier—and been friendly and flirtatious. But now, it was as if she were also unburdened.

Considering how upset she'd been after the incident at Blondie's, I was pretty proud of myself, even if the fix was temporary. I started after her, not wanting her to disappear into the dark.

When I caught up to her, she was staring out to sea.

"Wouldn't it be cool if we could see all the way to France?"

I was about to say it would depend on which way she was facing and it was more likely we wouldn't see Europe at all, but there was no reason to correct her.

A ship passed, way off in the distance. I put my hands on her shoulders and turned her toward it.

"Look straight ahead. Do you see that blinking light?"

"Uh-uh."

I bent my knees until our eyes were almost at the same level. Her hair smelled like coconut, and I wanted to bury my face in it, wrap it around my fist, lose myself—

Down, boy.

My cock had been semihard since I'd picked her up outside Blondie's and was now straining uncomfortably against my jeans. I mentally adjusted myself. At least it was dark.

I shifted her so that the ship was directly in front of us. "Straight ahead. Follow the line of my arm."

"Oh! I see it now."

"That's the Eiffel Tower."

She was silent at first. Then, with her brow comically furrowed, she jabbed me in the ribs with her elbow. "Oh, it is not. But maybe they're sailing to France. Wouldn't that be something? To just get on a boat and go anywhere you wanted?"

She leaned against me, the top of her head skimming my chin. "It would be almost as nice as this."

Every part of me shouted no, but I did it anyway: I wrapped my arms around her.

"Thank you, Chase." She spoke softly, reverently. "This has been wonderful."

"It's not over yet. The best part's coming up in a little while." I checked my watch; we still had some time. "You want to walk, or you want to just sit here?"

She took in the wide expanse of open beach. "How about we go back there toward the dunes so we're protected from the breeze?"

"Are you cold?"

"A little. I'm kinda tired. That always makes me feel cold."

I took her hand and led her toward the dunes and a stand of beach roses. I dropped down onto the sand.

"If you want, sit here in front of me. You'll be warmer that way."

I expected her to refuse, but she plopped down between my legs. After a few moments, she leaned back against my chest.

"Are you comfortable?" I asked.

"I am, but I can't imagine you are."

"I'm fine. I'm more than fine."

I fought the urge to put my arms around her again. I had to keep reminding myself I was playing with fire, but in that moment, I didn't care if I burned to the ground. In fact, I welcomed it.

Other than the constant pounding of the surf and the whisper of the tall grass in the dunes, it was quiet. Neither of us spoke for a good long time.

"Do you want to know what I was upset about before?" she asked.

"Only if you want to tell me."

"Don't think less of me. Promise you won't think less of me. I couldn't bear it."

Fool that I was, I circled my arms around her. "I promise."

"I'd never met anyone like Preston before, and he seemed to be crazy about me from the very beginning. We'd been seeing each other for a few months before I found out there was someone else. By then, I was already in love with him."

She shifted closer and tucked her legs under her dress.

"And it's not as bad as it sounds. The reason he was still seeing her was that her mother was sick, and then she died. It would've been a shitty time for him to break up with her, right?"

If she expected me to give Preston a free pass, that wouldn't be happening. I didn't answer.

"It's been months now since he broke it off, and he's done nothing to make me think he's still seeing her, but I'm not really a part of his life. I went to his club once . . . That was a total disaster."

She swiveled toward me. "Did you know rich people eat all kinds of disgusting things?"

"Never having been rich, I can't say that I do.'

The way she shivered it could've been from the cold or the memory of eating at Preston's club. I held her a little tighter, so I didn't care what caused it.

"I dated a couple other guys when I'd thought it was over—nice guys—but my heart just wasn't in it. None of them were Preston."

I was a nice guy. I waited for her to end by telling me how she just wasn't into me.

"So what happened between you two tonight?"

"We'd gone to dinner, and like usual, we went to some hole in the wall an hour north. Diane insists he does that because he doesn't want to run into anyone he knows because he's still seeing Suzanne. Tonight I called him on it. He got really angry, and he swore it wasn't true. I want to believe him, but it's hard some days. It's hard when you've been dating someone for over a year and sometimes a week or two goes by before you see them again. He travels a lot for work, so I get it, but there are days when I just feel like a fool. Tonight, for some reason, I just couldn't seem to let it go. So we ended up fighting. I should've made him take me home, but he insisted on going to Blondie's. Obviously, that was a mistake."

I loosened my hold around her, but she didn't seem to notice. She just kept on talking.

"I've never seen him drunk before. Or so nasty. You saw how he was acting."

"I did." I'd wanted to bash his face in. No man who cared about his woman would treat her like that, especially in front of a crowd, and then let others demean her as well.

"So if he comes to you tomorrow and somehow proves that he's not involved with anyone else, do you believe the two of you will live happily ever after?"

She shrugged. If she recognized the bitterness in my voice, she didn't mention it.

"I used to believe that." She reached up and placed her hand on my arm and let her head fall back against my chest. "But honestly, I'm not so sure anymore."

We sat like that, resting against one another, for a long time, until the horizon turned from black to gray and the first strands of pink stretched across the horizon.

"You awake?"

"Mm-hmm."

Over the next fifteen minutes, from the comfort of the dunes and each other's arms, we watched one of Mother Nature's most spectacular light shows. The sky was a kaleidoscope of purples, blues, pinks, oranges, and yellows, fluid and constantly changing, until the sun burst out of the water. Any day I was blessed to watch the sunrise was a good day. To see it rise out of the ocean with this beautiful woman in my arms was a gift I hadn't known I deserved.

As the sun continued to climb and the light show faded to streaks of gold and blue, Rain sighed against my chest.

"Thank you," she said. "I think that was the most beautiful thing I've ever seen."

"You're welcome." I stood and pulled her up. "It's my favorite, but it was even more special watching it with you."

She turned her face toward mine. In the early light of day, her eyes were a lovely pale blue.

"Don't take this the wrong way," she said.

Before I could respond, she put her hand on my neck and pulled my mouth down to hers. I gave her a second, to see if it was an overly friendly thank you, but when she didn't stop, I gripped her waist, pulled her closer, and deepened the kiss. Her lips parted, and when my tongue brushed hers, and she gave a little moan, I kissed her even harder. She had to feel what she was doing to me.

After several minutes, I finally, painfully broke away.

"How can I not take that the wrong way?" I whispered, pressing my forehead against hers.

"I don't know."

I looked into her eyes, trying to see if I could understand what she was thinking, but all I saw was confusion. For now, I'd count that as a win.

"Are you hungry?" I asked. "There's a breakfast place nearby. They make a decent chocolate chip pancake. Nothing like mine, of course, but not bad."

"You cook?"

"I do," I said with a grin. "I'm quite a catch."

Her smile was electric, and I felt it everywhere. "I bet you are."

"So, pancakes?"

She nodded. "I'm starving, but don't we have to head back?"

"I deserve a day off too. I'll just call my brother. There's no place else I'd rather be—and no one else I'd rather be here with."

CHAPTER TWENTY

Chase

After breakfast we rode over to a little five-and-dime. Rain bought two large beach towels, two toothbrushes, a tube of toothpaste, and a bottle of water.

"Gee, thanks," I said when she handed me a toothbrush. "That bad?"

Laughing, she pushed her hand against my chest. "No. I just know I feel kind of yucky until I brush my teeth, and I figured you wouldn't want me to be all minty fresh while you're all nasty."

"I appreciate the sentiment," I said, holding up the brush. "Although by now, I need more than a toothbrush."

She shrugged. "You're fine. People will just assume we're homeless."

We took turns brushing our teeth at the edge of the parking lot, sharing a bottle of water to rinse our mouths, and then headed back to the beach. It was early and there were only a few people out on the sand. An older woman with a large floppy hat sat near the dunes, reading, while two small children played on a blanket beside her. There were a few joggers, including one with a black lab that kept darting in and out of the water, chasing the waves.

We hiked down close to the water, where Rain spread out the towels, then sat and pulled off her boots.

"So you don't think people are going to think it's a bit odd, even if I take my shirt off, that I'm lying on the beach in jeans and work boots?"

"You could always take off your boots."

I did exactly that, then took off my shirt, balled it up behind my head, and lay down. I was exhausted, and while I was enjoying the time we were spending together, I was worried about making the three-hour ride back to Millstone on no sleep.

"You taking a nap?"

I shaded my eyes and squinted up at her. "I think so. You mind?"

"Of course not. I'm going to take a walk."

"Want me to come with you?"

"Uh-uh. You rest. I want to enjoy this while I can."

Between the warmth of the sun and the pounding of the surf, I drifted off quickly. I don't know how long she was gone, but I woke when she rested her head against my arm. I cracked an eye open. She had moved her towel at an angle to mine and was using me as a pillow.

I couldn't figure her out. She was open, trusting, and physical. She touched, hugged, and even kissed without any reservations. She reminded me of a kitten, happy with whatever warm lap she found to curl up on. If that was the case, though, it didn't make me any more special than the next lap. I could've been anybody, and she would've been just as content.

I closed my eyes. Without thinking, I stroked her hair as if she were a cat curled up in my lap. At some point, I fell back to sleep.

The next time I woke, my skin felt tight. Sure enough, although I was already tan, a couple hours in the same position with no sun block had left the skin on my stomach a dark, reddish bronze. The tops of my feet were a much more uncomfortable red.

"Rain." I shook her gently. "Wake up."

She mumbled and rolled over.

"Did you get burned?"

She sat up slowly, and when I pulled off my sunglasses, she laughed. "You look like a raccoon."

I reached over and gently removed hers. "So do you." Her arm was a deep red and hot to the touch. I checked my watch. It was after one. "I think we better get out of the sun for a while.

"Or we could just roll over," she said with a coy smile. "We just shouldn't fall asleep again."

So that's what we did—only this time we lay side by side on our stomachs and talked.

The more we talked, the harder I fell for her. She wasn't just incredibly hot, and she wasn't just someone who needed protection from a lame-ass boyfriend. She was funny and smart—not so much book smart, but intuitive. I guess that was the part she claimed was being psychic.

I hated talking about myself, especially what I'd recently been through, but I found myself opening up about Jennifer and Gary and how foolish I'd been to ignore all the little signs: the unexplained gifts. The text messages at odd hours. Coming home to find Gary at the house so frequently it started to seem strange—but he was my best friend.

And then that last time, when I came home unexpectedly and found the two of them in our bed.

Until now, I hadn't told anyone that part; it was too painful and humiliating.

I almost told Rain about my dad and how he had walked out on us after cheating on my mom, but I didn't want to make her feel worse about her own relationship, since that's how it seemed she saw herself—the other woman.

I hadn't noticed at first—I guess because it seemed so natural—but the whole time I was talking, Rain kept her hand on my arm as if she could sense how difficult it was to share what I was telling her.

Wanting to move the conversation away from my sad, pathetic love life, I rolled onto my side and pointed to her back.

"You think you're done on that side yet?"

"Yeah. We should get out of the sun, or we're not going to be able to ride home."

I could think of worse things.

She stood and brushed the sand from her legs. "How about one more walk on the beach?"

I felt like I'd been deep fried. "How about this? We go have some lunch and maybe walk around town—in the shade—and then before we leave, we can come back. The sun will be lower in the sky." I pulled my sunglasses down just far enough for her to see me waggle my eyebrows. "Who knows? We may even have the beach to ourselves by then."

***

We found a restaurant near the water with plenty of shade and a nice breeze and ordered standard Jersey fare of fried shrimp and fries in a basket, with sides of coleslaw and iced tea. I think we were both in desperate need of caffeine.

"I'm having such a nice time," she said after the waitress took our order.

My heart did a little flip. "So am I."

We spent another hour talking over lunch. Then I left my Harley up at the Physick Estate, and we took the trolley around Cape May. It was almost five by the time we headed back to the beach for the walk I'd promised her.

We walked side by side, one hand holding her boots and the other in the crook of my arm. I was content for the first time in a long while. I had to keep warning myself that I was being foolish. I was becoming as conflicted as Rain claimed to be.

"You ready to hit the road?" I asked as we neared the spot where I'd parked.

"I guess," she said sadly.

She slipped her arm around my waist as we slogged our way through the sand back to the parking lot. I wanted nothing more than to pick her up, carry her up to one of the motels along Beach Avenue, and make love to her for as long as I could, even if it meant another night without sleep. I couldn't think of a woman who had enticed and enchanted me more.

It was no longer about sex. After spending the last twenty hours with her, I wanted more. I wanted to know everything about her. I wanted to listen to her laugh, hear her crazy stories, and learn about all of her predictions.

I wanted her. It was as simple and as difficult as that.

CHAPTER TWENTY-ONE

Rain

Chase pulled in behind the luncheonette, and I was glad to see the only car in the lot was mine. Not that I expected to see Preston sitting there waiting for me, but judging by the tone of his texts—from obnoxious to apologetic to worried, then frantic, and when I finally responded after he threatened to report me missing if he didn't hear from me immediately, back to obnoxious—I didn't know what to expect. My favorite text had been this one: How dare you make me worry half the night and all day.

How dare I, indeed.

I invited Chase inside, although part of me was afraid of what might happen if he accepted. Could he be thinking the same thing?

"I gotta go. I think if I stop for too long, I might keel over." He looked tired, but he still had an incredibly sexy smile. He definitely should smile more.

"Me too," I admitted, although at that moment, keeling over with him sounded pretty good.

He fastened the extra helmet to his bike. It was dark in front of my apartment, and we were standing outside the aim of the motion detector. I wanted to kiss him, and not just a simple thanks-I-had-a-terrific-time kind of kiss either.

It made no sense. I'd been hurting, thinking that Preston might still be seeing Suzanne, yet here I was doing almost the same thing. I'd just spent an amazing twenty-four hours with a very sweet, very good-looking guy whose kisses made me forget my own name. And I was pretty sure I wanted more.

Was I that fickle, or was I living up to the perception everyone had of me?

Chase stretched, and his T-shirt rode up over those amazing abs of his. He stifled a yawn. "I have to work in the morning, and we have a race tomorrow night. You coming?"

"I wasn't planning on it."

"If you change your mind, I'll be there."

Not knowing how to end this—whatever it was—started to feel a little awkward. I dug around in my purse until I found my keys, giving me something to look at other than that intense stare of his.

"Thank you again. I had the best time."

"I'm glad." He gave me another smile and raised his helmet. "I'll wait for you to get upstairs and inside."

If I stood this close to him one second longer, I was going to grab him by his T-shirt and drag him upstairs. Maybe not even a second. I backed away, then turned and raced up the steps before I could change my mind. When I'd unlocked the door and flicked on the outside light, he revved his engine and pulled away with a wave.

I stood in the doorway until I could no longer feel the vibrations of his Harley under my feet or hear the roar of his engine in the distance. Then I listened to the silence.

What an amazing day it had been.

It wasn't until I turned on the inside light and locked the door behind me that I noticed the huge bouquet of red roses on the kitchen table. I sank against the door as if the thorns on those roses had let all of the air out of me.

I love you. Forgive me.

As usual, there was no signature. Although red roses weren't my favorite—I preferred deep pink, but he'd never asked—they were beautiful and surely expensive, as they'd come from the best florist in the area. But it didn't matter. I still wanted to open the door and dump them over the deck and smash the vase in the parking lot.

Maybe I would go to the track tomorrow night. And maybe afterward, I'd kiss Chase exactly the way I was already regretting not kissing him tonight.

***

I woke around ten the next morning, and that was only because some asshole was pounding on my door. I opened it to find the asshole holding another bouquet of red roses. It wouldn't have surprised me at all to learn he owned his own greenhouse—or at least the damn florist.

"What the hell happened to your face?" he demanded.

"Really? That's what you have to say to me?" I tried to close the door, but he pushed it open and stepped inside.

"Do you know how sick with worry I've been? Where did you go? How did you get home?"

I glared at him. "If you were so sick with worry, why weren't you sitting outside my door when I got home last night?"

It looked as if a vein was about to burst on the side of his head.

"Last night? You didn't get home until last night?"

I blinked at him, struggling for the right words.

"Seriously, what happened to your face? You look like you fell asleep in the sun."

"Maybe I did." It was obvious I had. Why didn't I just admit it?

He set the flowers on the table next to yesterday's roses. "You going to tell me what happened?"

"Before or after you humiliated me at Blondie's?"

"After." His voice grew a little softer. "And I apologized."

"When? In a text message? After you demanded to know 'where the fuck' I was?"

"C'mon, baby." He slipped his arms around my waist. "I was drunk and upset. You know I don't like fighting with you." He kissed my neck. The scruff on his face scratched my skin.

"You're hurting me." I pushed against him. "I have a bad sunburn."

"I can see that." He continued to hold me and kissed lightly along my neck. In spite of the burn, goose bumps sprang up along my arms. "Why don't you let me rub aloe all over you?"

That sounded like a great idea, but I wasn't about to say so.

He kissed my shoulder and along my clavicle, then worked his way back up to my chin.

"I love you, Rain. I don't want to lose you. Please tell me you forgive me."

I pulled away. "It doesn't matter if I forgive you or not, because the way things are going, you're going to lose me for good."

"Baby, don't say that. You're killing me. I've told you, it's complicated."

I gave him a hard shove. "Stop it! I don't want to hear it anymore. In fact, I don't want to do this anymore. I'm done. I deserve more than this. I deserve to be with someone who loves me and who's not ashamed of me."

For as much as it hurt, physically and emotionally, I pulled away, walked to the door, and held it open. The fact that he actually looked stunned proved how out of touch he was with what he'd been putting me through.

But it didn't last. Within seconds, he was smiling as if he'd caught me bluffing.

When my tears spilled over, the cocky look on his face faded.

"Rain, don't do this. I'm not giving you up. It's not over."

I wiped my face with the heels of my hands, cringing from the sting. "Seriously. It was over before it began. I should've never let this go on. You're still hung up on someone else, and it isn't fair to her or to me. Go be with Suzanne. I'll get over it. I want to get over it, but I can't if you won't leave me alone."

"Fine, then I won't leave you alone." He plunked onto the couch with his arms folded and stared straight ahead.

I slammed the door with a loud bang and stomped into the kitchen to put on a pot of coffee. I'd slept twelve hours, and I felt as if I could sleep twelve more. When the coffee was ready, I poured myself a cup and ignoring him, went back into my room and lay down.

Just as I expected, Preston followed. He lay down beside me, his chest pressed against my back, his arm around my waist.

"I can't live without you."

"Yes, you can."

"Please don't be like this." He clutched me against his chest so hard it was difficult to breathe. I was about to tell him he was hurting me again when I realized he was crying. I pushed against him, but he held me fast.

"I don't want you to see me like this."

My sensitive skin throbbed, but I squirmed around in his arms until I was facing him. I'd never seen a man cry before. "Preston. Please, don't."

He buried his face in my shoulder. I held him against me, and when he finally looked at me, my heart broke. His eyes were red and swollen, and he looked so anguished that I felt guilty for pushing so hard, for threatening to end it.

And I felt guilty for the feelings I'd begun to have for Chase. While it had never made sense before when Preston claimed that things between him, Suzanne, and me were so complicated, I understood it all now.

I kissed his tearstained cheeks. I kissed his lips. And I gave in. Again. And he was more loving and tender than he'd been in a long time.

Afterward, Preston slept while I lay beside him, staring at the ceiling.

He'd made lots of promises to me over the past hour, but my heart still hurt. And not just because of Preston.

CHAPTER TWENTY-TWO

Chase

As tired as I was, I had a hard time sleeping Friday night. When the alarm clock went off, I wanted to stay in bed and just keep thinking about Rain, which is what I'd been doing most of the night. The only thing that kept me going through the morning was thinking that maybe I'd see her that night at the track. And then afterward, who knows? I was pretty sure she felt something as well.

Unfortunately, it wasn't Rain who showed up that night. It was Preston.

"Where's my girl?" Wally called out when he saw Preston coming into the pit area where we were getting the car ready.

"She's not feeling well. I left her home to sleep. I'll check on her later."

I wanted to kick something—preferably Preston. I finished making a gear change while he walked around shaking hands, acting like he'd funded the entire operation because his fucking name was painted on the side of the car. I hated this creep. I didn't care how many tires he'd paid for.

"So how's it going, buddy?" he asked, coming up to me and holding out his hand. At least the asshole wasn't looking to fist bump. I took his hand and shook it, knowing full well mine was covered with grease. Disgust registered on his face as he looked around for something to wipe it on.

"Sorry, man." I shrugged and pushed my sunglasses up on top of my head, now that the sun had dropped behind the grandstands. "That's the danger of being in the pits." I wiped my hand on my jeans and almost dared him to do the same, which he didn't.

An odd look came over his face. "Get a little sun?"

I nodded.

"Looks like you fell asleep at the beach."

"Maybe."

I had nothing to hide, but I wasn't willing to share anything with him either. Given the way he was staring at me, I'm guessing he'd figured out that Rain and I had matching sunburns.

"You really should use sun block," he said before turning away and looking for something to clean his hands.

I went straight home after the race. I was disappointed Rain hadn't come and disappointed that she and Preston had made up. And I was more than disappointed with myself. I had rushed headlong toward her, knowing she was in love with another guy.

I pulled a bottle of whiskey from the cabinet over the sink, then filled the glass halfway. I stretched out on the couch to watch the end of the Phillies game, but when the closer blew another save, I nearly put my foot through the set.

Disgusted, I turned off the TV, picked up my cell phone, and pulled up the picture I had taken of Rain on the beach just after we'd watched the sun rise. Her hair was blowing in the breeze, some of it across her face. Her smile was wide, and her eyes matched the morning sky behind her. I had every intention of deleting that photo, and if I had a brain, I would have.

But I didn't.

Instead, I stared at the image for so long, I heard the pounding of the surf and the cry of the seagulls. I tipped my glass, finishing off the whiskey, then I powered down my phone and tossed it on the glass-topped coffee table.

Too bad there wasn't some way for me to power down the memories.

CHAPTER TWENTY-THREE

Chase

I stayed away from Blondie's for two weeks. Rain knew where to find me if she was interested. Considering she didn't show up at the track or at Diane and Wally's once while I was there, I assumed she was avoiding me too.

I was a little sick about the whole thing and more than a little lovesick in general.

That Saturday, we got rained out. The crew was heading to Blondie's, and since Rain didn't work every Saturday, I figured I'd take a chance.

I heard her laugh before I saw her, but I couldn't leave now. If I walked out, it would be too obvious. I'd already taken enough ribbing from the guys, who'd figured out the matching raccoon masks.

She turned toward the door as we walked in, and in that instant, I was certain she knew I was there before she saw me.

I led the way to the far corner near the pool room, not knowing if she was working that end of the bar or not, since Lynette was also on. At least here, I could escape to shoot pool easily enough if I felt the need.

Turned out Rain was working the other half of the bar, but she came over to say hello.

"How are you?"

In her eyes, curiosity mixed with regret, only I couldn't tell if the regret was over what had happened between us or what hadn't happened since.

"Good. You?" I sipped my beer and tried to look nonchalant while waiting for her answer. It wasn't easy.

"I'm okay." She was being honest. She didn't smile or flirt, and she wasn't looking for my sympathy, which she'd be hard pressed to get.

Oh, who was I kidding? For as much as I cared about her, I didn't want to see her hurt, even if it meant that jerk was the one who was making her happy. But to be honest, she didn't look all that happy.

"Hey, darling." Wally said. "Where've you been hiding?"

She flashed him a wide grin, and the mask slipped back into place. Her eyes even regained their sparkle. She had shown me her true self, and in spite of everything, I tumbled a little harder.

I excused myself to the back room, where Fish and Dennis were racking up balls, and slapped a few quarters on the table, intending to play the winner.

My mind wasn't on the game or even in the room. The only entertainment there was Fish, staggering around the table.

While the two of them were settling up, I ducked out to grab another beer. Rain was on her side of the bar, waiting on a group of women, several of whom were noticeably drunk and giving her a hard time.

Wally was watching the scene unfold.

"This isn't good," he said quietly. "I think that's Preston's old girlfriend."

A short girl with long, dark hair had climbed onto the rail and was leaning across the bar, while Rain stood stiffly in front of her. I carried the Heineken Lynette had just handed me further down the bar and sat where I could hear what was going on.

"Yes, girls," the woman said, slurring her words slightly and taking in the bar with a sweep of her arm, "this is what slumming looks like."

"What would you like?" Rain asked, her voice tight.

"Hmm. First, I'd like a cosmo. And second, I'd like you to stay the hell away from my boyfriend."

I glanced at Wally. With a quick nod, he headed for Lynette.

Rain leaned closer, although she spoke loudly enough.

"The thing is, he keeps coming after me. Where do you think he was last night, you cold-ass bitch?"

Lynette and Irena were moving toward Rain, but it was too late. The girl reached out and grabbed a handful of Rain's hair. Rain pulled back her arm, her hand clenched in a fist. It was go time.

I scaled the bar and reached her just before she could connect. I carried her off kicking and swearing, almost taking out an entire shelf of bottles on the way. I didn't stop until I had her inside the pool room.

I turned in time to see two of the girl's friends barreling toward us. The girl-friend, or ex-girlfriend, whatever the fuck she was, was howling on the other side of the bar, claiming Rain had hit her.

"Wynocha! Out!" Irena yelled.

Judging by the sounds coming from out there, more people had jumped into the fray. Rain was pushing against me, trying to escape, while the two girls on the outside were calling her a variety of unsavory names.

I tossed Dennis my keys.

"Bring my truck around back to the kitchen door."

Rain was still trying to get back into the bar. I was afraid that if she did, all of her anger and frustration with Preston would come pouring out and she'd end up in jail.

I was relieved when Wally's enormous shadow filled the doorway.

"Keep them away," I called over my shoulder as I picked Rain up and moved her to the back of the room.

"Hey!" I yelled, setting her down. "Knock it off."

She looked so stunned that I'd shouted at her, she stopped fighting me.

"That bitch is claiming you hit her," I said, "and even though she's lying, if she presses charges, she's just going to cause a huge mess for you. And I'm pretty sure that's exactly what she's angling for."

"I never laid a hand on her! You pulled me away before I could deck her." She stood on her toes and shouted over my shoulder. "You fucking bitch!"

"I know that, but it'll be your word against hers. I'm betting her posse out there is going to claim you hit her—or at the very least, say that they didn't see, which still leaves it at your word against hers."

"She started it! She came in knowing I was here." Her face crumpled, and she started to cry. "She pulled my hair."

"I know," I said in my most soothing voice. I put my arms around her.

"Then why can't you say that I didn't hit her?" she sobbed into my chest.

"I will, but that doesn't mean they'll believe me."

The sound of a siren grew louder and Rain's sobs with it.

"I can't go to jail. I can't afford a lawyer. I don't even have bail money."

"You're not going to jail," I assured her, although depending on what the women told the police, she could get nailed with a battery charge.

Dennis returned and handed me my keys. "Can you believe someone called the cops?"

"Who is it?" Rain asked, dabbing at her eyes with the edge of her shirt.

"Staties," he said. "Local cops must be busy."

"Oh, swell," she muttered. "Just put the cuffs on now."

"The state police have it in for you?" I asked, doubting that seriously.

She frowned. "Just some of them."

Dennis patted her on the shoulder. "I'm sure it'll be fine."

He pulled a chair over, and I had her sit. I squatted in front of her.

"You need anything?"

"Yeah, a shot of tequila and a public defender."

I laughed in spite of the potential seriousness of the situation, glad to see a bit of her usual sparkle had returned.

"I promise if they throw you in jail, I'll bail you out, get you a lawyer—whatever you need, okay?"

She made a face. "I can't ask you to do that."

"You didn't. Remember? I'm one of the good guys."

"I keep forgetting." She smiled, although briefly.

Dennis stuck his head around the corner, then called over his shoulder. "I'm not sure I recognize either of them, so you should be okay."

"What the hell did you do that you have to worry about the state troopers?" I asked.

Dennis chuckled, and she shot him a dirty look. "It's not funny."

"Sorry." He ducked back into the bar.

When she realized I expected an answer, she explained that she'd briefly dated one of the troopers, and because of Preston, it hadn't ended well.

"I didn't mean to lead him on. I liked him, really. He was very sweet."

"I told you, nice guys finish last." Would she be talking about me some day, saying what a nice, sweet guy I had been?

Two uniformed troopers entered the pool room. One was older, maybe mid-forties, but the other looked to be in his mid-twenties and was a dead ringer for Matt Damon.

Rain groaned, then stuck her arms out to be handcuffed. I should've recognized another nice guy when I saw one. Maybe we should form a club.

I stepped aside as the troopers approached. The older one looked puzzled at Rain's submissive behavior, but the younger one frowned.

"Knock it off, Rain," he said quietly. "I just need to ask you a few questions."

He listened intently as she explained what happened, including balling up her fist to hit Suzanne and how I had grabbed her and carried her out before she could do so.

"She claims you landed a punch on the side of her head."

"She's a liar," Rain said.

I kept my mouth shut, but when he looked at me, I shook my head. "Rain didn't touch her. In fact, the other girl reached over the bar and pulled Rain's hair. That's when I went over the counter and grabbed Rain, because I figured that was exactly what the other girl was looking for, to start trouble. If her friends are corroborating her story, then they're lying as well."

"Actually, they're saying they didn't see anything, but they did hear Miss Langmore yell when Rain allegedly struck her."

"I'd like to strike her," Rain grumbled.

The trooper warned her not to make threats or he would charge her on that alone.

She huffed sharply. "What about name-calling? Can you arrest her for calling me names?"

I leaned over and whispered. "She didn't call you a name. You called her a cold-ass bitch. Her friends called you names."

"Yeah, well." She sniffed. "If the shoe fits."

The older officer, who had gone back out to the bar, returned.

"No one says they saw Rain hit her, although a few say they did see the Langmore girl grab her first and pull her hair, and they did see Rain attempt to hit her. But everyone confirmed that this guy pulled her away before anything happened."

"So can I press charges for her attacking me first?"

"Do you really want to?" Matt Damon asked.

She shook her head.

"I'll talk with her and see if I can get her to let it go, but she'll have the option to press charges or go after you for any other perceived injuries you may have caused her."

Rain made a throaty sound. "Such as to her ego?"

"Not to her ego," He stifled the slightest smile. "But she could still claim that you hit her. To be honest, I doubt a girl like that wants to go to trial for being involved in a bar fight. I think she's trying to send you a message, Rain."

I felt bad at how uncomfortable Rain looked, although I silently agreed with him in one respect. Someone like Suzanne wouldn't even admit that she had been in a place like this, let alone gotten into a fight.

On the other hand, although I don't know if he'd meant to, the trooper had implied that Rain wasn't "a girl like that." By the hurt look on her face, I assumed she had realized the same thing.

"I suggest you head home for the night and cool off," he said. "Give me your phone number and address, for the record, in case I need to follow up, but I'd be surprised if she really wants to pursue this, all things considered."

Rain gave him the information he asked for, then followed it with a sad smile. "Thanks for not running me in, Brian, and for believing me."

He didn't look at her as he tucked his notepad into his shirt pocket. "I'm just doing my job."

After the officers left and I was sure the women were gone as well, I led Rain to the kitchen to collect her purse and jacket. When she stepped outside, she headed for her car.

"We can get that later. I'll take you home."

I expected her to argue, but she didn't. She obediently stood next to my truck and waited for me to open the door. She remained quiet on the ride back to her apartment.

"Do you want to come in?" she asked when I pulled up in front of her door.

"Do you want me to come in?"

She hesitated for only a second. "Yeah. I think I do."

CHAPTER TWENTY-FOUR

Chase

Rain's apartment was small, with sloped ceilings on either side except in the kitchen and bathroom, so since I'm nearly six-three, I had to stay toward the center of the living room. The place was clean and bright, although it was obvious a child lived there, as there were toys and dolls on shelves around the small dining area and in the living room. There was a single bedroom to the right as we came in, with two beds, a double for her and a single for her daughter, I presumed.

It certainly didn't look like the apartment of a woman of the reputation Rain had garnered.

"How do you stand up in here?" I asked, joking. She had to be at least five-seven.

She shrugged. "I hit my head a lot, especially when I'm cleaning. My mom owns the building, so it doesn't cost me much, although I still pay rent; otherwise, she couldn't afford the mortgage. I could live with her for nothing, but I want to make my own way. Although, I feel bad knowing she could get more for this place than I give her."

She pointed at the couch. "Have a seat. Just be careful when you stand up."

Since the steep slope was above the left side of the couch, I opted for the right. "Where's your daughter?"

"With my mom. She usually stays over on nights I work. I used to pick her up, especially when she was younger, but it's not so easy to carry her anymore. If she wakes up, she doesn't want to go back to sleep, and if she has school in the morning, it's hard. My mom brings her to the restaurant in the morning, and we have breakfast together before she goes to school."

"Pictures?"

She looked surprised. "You want to see pictures of my kid?"

"Yeah. Absolutely."

She jumped up and just missed striking her head on the ceiling. She pulled several albums from a set of low shelves and dumped them on the secondhand coffee table in front of me.

"What do you want to drink?"

"Whatever you're having."

She disappeared into the kitchen and came back a few minutes later with a bottle of tequila, shot glasses, a shaker of salt, and a plate of cut limes.

"Rough day?" I teased.

She rolled her eyes and laughed as she poured two shots. "You could say that."

We did our shots, then she settled in beside me and opened the first album.

"You're going to be sorry you asked." She wore the unguarded smile I liked so much.

"I doubt it."

In the first pictures she showed me, I hardly recognized her. Her hair was darker and she looked like a kid herself, holding her daughter in the hospital bed, tired but smiling.

"My mom took that right after Izzy was born."

"You look so young—I mean, barely even legal."

"I wasn't. I was almost seventeen when Izzy was born."

"Where's her father?"

"Who knows? We met when he was a senior, and I was a sophomore. Captain of the football team, all that stuff. I was a cheerleader, of course." She gave me a wicked smile. "If you're good, I'll show you my pompoms."

There was the flirt again.

"Anyway, I went a little wild after my dad was killed. My mom didn't have it in her to straighten me out, and even if she'd tried, I would have fought her. She was grieving and withdrawn, and with no one to keep me in line, I was out of control, which was probably what Jeff liked about me. Diane's mother finally sat me down and threatened to kick my ass into the next decade, but by then I was already pregnant. Jeff and I broke up as soon as he found out. He went away to college. He was around after he graduated, but he took a job out of state a few months ago and hasn't seen Izzy since. His parents used to see her more often, but since they moved away, other than that week they took her back in August, she doesn't see them much either anymore."

She poured another two shots. "I don't usually drink at home, but I think I deserve it today."

I hoisted my glass, and clicked the rim against hers. "I didn't say anything."

"I just don't want you to think I'm an alcoholic or something."

"I don't. Besides, who cares what I think?"

Her eyes caught mine, round and serious. "I care."

I couldn't ever remember having that feeling like butterflies in my chest—that was some girl thing—but damn if I didn't get them when she looked at me like that. This girl was so far under my skin, it almost scared me. Almost.

We looked through more of her photo albums. I could see the gradual transformation from Rain the wild child teenager to Rain the single mother to Rain the white-hot blond bombshell and potential Playboy centerfold.

I flipped to another picture of her daughter. Izzy's hair was naturally the color Rain dyed hers, and she had the same ice-blue eyes. The only difference was her naturally curly hair and her missing front teeth, at least in the most recent photo.

"Your daughter is beautiful," I said. "She looks just like you."

Rain looked pleased. "Everyone says that. I don't really see much of Jeff in her, which is fine by me."

"Your mother's no slouch either," I pointed out.

Dorinda wasn't quite as tall as Rain. She didn't look much past her early forties and had a similar build and coloring.

"She'll be happy to hear you think so. She thinks you're pretty cute too, by the way."

I couldn't hold back my grin. "You've talked to your mother about me?"

"Don't get too excited. My mother wants to fix me up with every man who walks in who's over twenty-one, under eighty, and not wearing a wedding ring." She grinned. "You, my friend, are at the top of her list."

Terrific, I was in the friend zone.

She poured another shot, but I stopped her before she poured one for me.

"I have to drive, remember?"

The way she hesitated, the way she bit her lip, I wondered if she was going to ask me to stay. Or was it wishful thinking? And if she did, would I?

Given what she was going through and the fact that she was still clearly in love with that clown, I couldn't. I didn't want to desert her, but I needed to protect myself—and I was already feeling pretty damn exposed.

She downed two more shots.

I considered taking the bottle away, as she was already drunk.

"I know this is none of my business, and you certainly don't have to answer, but I'm wondering what you're planning to do."

She looked at me, somewhat askew. "About what?"

"About your situation with Preston." I hated even saying the son of a bitch's name.

"I don't know," she said, and then buried her face against my chest and began to cry.

I hated it. I hated that I'd pushed her. I hated that she loved someone else and that he was clearly too stupid to make her the priority she deserved to be.

I also hated that if he hurt her in the worst way possible, by dumping her, it might be the only chance I'd have to make her mine. I wanted to be there for her, regardless, but what kind of a friend wants to see you hurt?

A selfish one. That's what kind.

She pushed herself off of me and sniffed. "I think I'm drunk."

Even with a tearstained face and black streaks under her eyes, she was beautiful.

I tucked her back under my arm and kissed the top of her head. Like a friend would do. "I think you're right."

I held her for a long time, even after she fell asleep against me. It was almost three, and I was fried. Gently, I lifted her off of me and carried her into her bedroom, where I placed her on the bed. I pulled the blanket over her, and even though it made me feel like some kind of creeper, I kissed her cheek. It was warm, and that intoxicating mix of vanilla and coconut wrapped itself around me.

I debated whether to head home or sleep on the couch, and since I didn't know if she'd need help with her car in the morning, I opted for the couch. I helped myself to one more shot of tequila, hoping it might help me sleep.

It was hard enough to sleep at home, thinking about her on the other side of town. With nothing but a wall between us, it might be damn near impossible.

CHAPTER TWENTY-FIVE

Rain

I didn't see Chase again after he took me to get my car. In a way, I was glad. It was confusing being around him. I definitely had feelings for him, feelings I didn't understand.

And then there was that vibration running through me every time we touched. I still had no idea what the hell it meant, but it no longer scared me, and I was no longer worried for his health.

Maybe what I was feeling was just because he was so damn nice. In the short time I'd known him, he'd proven to be someone I could depend on. And I did care about him. I just wasn't sure if I felt about him the way I suspected he felt about me—and if not, then what? I couldn't bear to hurt another nice guy. It was hard enough seeing Brian after what had happened with him, and the risk that he could have been a real SOB and arrested me for assault was scary. A lot of guys would have done exactly that just to get even.

Then there was Preston.

I'd given him my heart, and while I loved him, and I believe he loved me, it had never felt right. It was a hard truth to accept, and I wasn't sure I fully accepted it. Acknowledge was a better word. I was acknowledging the possibility that Preston was treating my heart like another one of his possessions. Like one of his sports cars. It was his to do with what he wanted, when he wanted, and then park it in his climate-controlled garage until he felt like firing it up and taking it out for spin.

But I wasn't a thing to be owned and played with.

After our last fight, Preston had sworn it was over with Suzanne. And I, of course, had believed him. But if he was telling the truth, what was the other night about? It had to be difficult for a girl like Suzanne to come into Blondie's and confront me, even with her entourage. And the fact that she'd obviously had a few too many cosmos told me she needed the liquid courage to do so. But would she have done it—drunk or not—if she and Preston weren't together? Possibly. Maybe it was a way to scare me off, make me think they were still together so I would break it off with him and she could sweep back in and claim him.

It was a pretty elaborate and risky thing to do on her part, but if there was one thing I'd become certain of in the past eighteen months, I didn't know shit about rich people.

And that included Preston.

I hadn't seen him since before the incident with Suzanne. I called him the next day and left him a voicemail telling him what she'd done and told him not to contact me unless she was completely out of his life. I didn't want to hear about social circles or clubs or family ties.

That was a week ago, and I'd heard nothing back. I don't know if that meant he was with her or mad at me for not believing him. Or too busy with work to answer.

Maybe all of the above.

As stressed out as I was, it was no surprise that I ended up with a wicked upper respiratory infection. After I begged and pleaded with her, my Aunt Donna, who worked for a doctor, was able to get me a prescription for antibiotics and cough medicine, saving me a visit to the urgent care center.

I was so sick I missed two days of work. I went back Thursday but came home after prepping for the lunch rush and spent the rest of the day in bed, only getting up when my mother brought Izzy home. Not long after I'd put her to bed, I crashed on the sofa.

I opened my eyes feeling fuzzy and confused, especially about the steady tapping on my door. The apartment was dark except for the ghostly blue light from the television. The clock on the cable box said it was almost eleven.

I grabbed the hammer I kept nearby and crept toward the door.

"Who is it?" I whispered, not wanting to wake Izzy.

"Me."

"I don't know who 'me' is," I said, although of course I did.

"You know damn well it's me, Rain. Open up."

I unlocked the door, still holding the hammer. I didn't step aside to let him in. "What?"

"C'mon. Let me in."

"Look, I don't feel well. Unless you have something new to tell me, then there's no reason for you to come inside."

"I have to talk to you. I have something to give you."

"Preston, please. Don't do this to me."

"Baby—"

I started closing the door.

"I won't leave until you let me in and talk to me."

"Fine." I tried to close the door the rest of the way. "You can sit there all night if you want."

He pushed his way inside.

"Preston!" I was practically hissing, which triggered a fit of coughing. He waited patiently until I stopped. "I want you to go," I croaked.

"Marry me."

My heart slammed against my rib cage, then plummeted down into my stomach. "It's really over? No more Suzanne?"

"Tell me you'll marry me."

"Get out."

"No." He pulled me into his arms. Mine hung limp at my sides. "I love you, Rain. If I can't see you anymore, it'll kill me."

It was déjà vu all over again. It might be a cliché, but it was true.

"You know," I said, beginning to cry even though it angered me to do so. It may have been more related to being tired and feeling sick than it was to matters of the heart. "I think there's something seriously wrong with you. If you love me so much you can't live without me, why the fuck can't you break it off with her?"

"Because I'm weak," he whispered into my neck. "Because I can't risk angering my father, or I could lose everything. When he retires, everything becomes mine. We're talking millions, Rain. I can't take a chance. But once he steps aside, and everything is signed over to me, it won't matter who I disappoint. It's complicated. I've told you that. My parents? They're all about their clubs and the way things look, and they expect me to marry Suzanne."

He kept kissing me, tugging at my nightgown, determined to have me. He begged me to change my mind, forget my ultimatum. But his words, even in my foggy, weakened state, solidified my decision—and broke my heart. I would be no one's "disappointment." I deserved more.

I pushed against his chest. "I can't, Preston. Please. I won't do this to myself anymore. It's over."

He snatched me up and carried me to the couch.

"No," I whispered, thinking of Izzy in the next room. "Please go."

I was in tears, but he kissed them away until I gave in. He made love to me quickly and quietly, and if it was to be the last time for us, it was hardly a flicker compared to the fire that had once consumed me.

It was more than fitting.

While he dressed, I lay naked, wrapped in a quilt, sneezing and coughing, my head throbbing. Disgusted with myself for caving.

He sat on the coffee table across from me and pulled a small blue velvet box out of his pocket.

"I'll stay away. Give you space. For now. But I want you to wear these every day until you change your mind."

When I didn't take the box, he opened it. Inside was a pair of round diamond earrings. They were huge—so big that no one I knew would ever believe they were real. And proof that his "proposal" had been nothing more than a way for him to buy time. Had he been serious, there would have been a ring in that box. And I still would have rejected it.

"I don't want them."

"Don't be ridiculous," he said, pushing them toward me and bumping his hand into my breast.

I slapped his hand away.

"I said I don't want them!"

"Do you have any idea what those are worth?"

I sat up so quickly the room began to swim. "I know exactly what they're worth: more than a year of my life, my self-esteem, the hurt feelings of some very special people, and the loss of someone who might have made me very happy."

I grabbed my nightgown off the floor and yanked it over my head.

"I'll still make you happy, baby, I promise."

"You asshole! I didn't mean you!"

I walked to the door and held it open. He set the box on the coffee table. As he passed, he leaned down to kiss me. I pulled away.

"Suit yourself," he said, no longer sounding as desperate as he had when he arrived.

I snatched the box off the table and waited by the door as he made his way back to his precious Stingray.

"Preston," I called as he opened the car door.

When he looked up, I aimed the box at his head and threw it as hard as I could. It glanced off the roof and bounced into the parking lot. Horrified, he ran his hand over the spot where the box had struck the car. I would have loved to have left a dent in that damned Corvette, but I didn't have that kind of luck.

The only thing cracked and dented, was my heart. And my self-esteem.

Dents could be fixed. I just hoped mine weren't too deep.

CHAPTER TWENTY-SIX

Rain

Diane showed up at my door a few days later.

"You okay?"

"If you mean the head and chest cold from hell, then yes, I'm feeling better. If you mean the man who stole eighteen months of my life only to break my heart, then yes, also fine. It was time. If he can't make a commitment to me, I'm done."

I filled the basket in the coffeemaker. I hadn't been sleeping well, other than a few naps here and there, and while I already had enough caffeine in me to last a week, I had things to do.

Diane grabbed two mugs from the cupboard and settled in at the kitchen table.

"I've got to go grocery shopping today, so I don't have anything to snack on other than animal crackers."

She shook her head. "I'm good. I didn't come to eat."

I grabbed the creamer from the fridge and joined her at the kitchen table while we waited for the coffee to brew. "What's up? You hiding from Wally?"

She tucked a strand of flame-red hair behind her ear. "You don't know, do you?"

I hadn't noticed it when she came in, but I did now. She looked sad and a little nervous.

"I don't think so. What are you talking about?"

She linked her pinky with mine, something we hadn't done since around the time my father had died. Whatever it was, it had to be bad.

She inhaled deeply and then spoke rapidly, like she was pulling off a Band-Aid.

"Preston and Suzanne are getting married. He gave her a ring and everything." She searched my face. "I'm sorry, Rain."

I stared at our joined fingers. Numb. That's what I felt. I'd pushed him away, and he'd gone right back to Suzanne. Or maybe that had been his intention when he showed up the other night. He wanted to solidify my spot on the shelf while he went on with his life.

I should feel devastated. I should be crying. Ranting. Cursing him. But I wasn't. Other than a pinch in my chest, I was numb.

"Are you okay?"

"Yeah, I think so. I just feel . . . kinda weird, ya know? And maybe a little empty."

"He's a jerk. I've always thought so, and this is just proof. Wally said that girl is a bitch. If that's who he wants, they deserve each other."

She was probably right. But that didn't mean it didn't hurt—but shouldn't it hurt more? Maybe the antibiotic was affecting me mentally.

Diane rose and grabbed the coffee carafe, then filled our mugs. When she returned to the table, she covered my hand with hers and squeezed. "Do you want to go shopping? We could go look at shoes. That always makes you happy."

"Thanks, but I just want to be alone. I think I need to lie down."

"You want me to take Izzy?"

"That's okay. My mom is picking her up later. She and my Aunt Donna are taking her to the Bloomsburg Fair."

"Well, let's get her ready, and I'll take her home with me. She can play with my nephews, and then I'll bring her to your mom's after she closes the shop. This way you can rest. Okay?"

I finished getting Izzy ready to go, made her promise to be good, and told her I'd see her in the morning.

Although my plan had been to spend the day catching up, I was fresh out of energy. With Izzy gone, I would have an entire twenty-four hours to wallow. I had a pile of dirty clothes and hardly any food in the house, but I had plenty of wine, my favorite tearjerker movies, and a stack of magazines. I wanted to cry Preston out of my system, once and for all.

After a long, hot bath, I slipped into my favorite pair of yoga pants and a T-shirt, grabbed a bottle of wine and a blanket, and curled up on the sofa.

When I was finally able to cry—which only started during P.S. I Love You, when Gerard Butler kept sending Hilary Swank all those letters after his death—I was hard pressed to put my finger on exactly why. Was I crying because Preston had proposed to Suzanne? If he were to show up at my door today, tell me he'd made a huge mistake, would I take him back?

For as much as I believed I'd loved him, the answer would be no. I'd been hurt and strung along, but while I'd once loved him, I was no longer in love with him.

The realization stunned me.

And if that was the case, why was I crying?

My heart and my head leaped to Chase. I'd surely blown it with him. If Preston hadn't been in the picture, things between us could have been very different. The times I'd spent with him had been some of the best I'd ever had. Chase made me feel special in a way I hadn't felt since my dad died.

Thinking of my father made me cry harder. What a fucked-up life I'd been living.

Between the crying and the wine, my head was pounding. I took some aspirin and climbed into bed.

When I woke, the pounding in my head was gone, only to be replaced by a muffled pounding in my ears.

Shit. The possibility of Preston standing outside my door frightened me. I couldn't do this again. I didn't want him. I just wanted him to go away.

I pulled the blankets over my head, but the knocking grew louder.

A male voice called through the door. A voice that did not belong to Preston. "Rain?"

I tugged the comforter off the bed, wrapped it around my shoulders, and went to the door.

"Who is it?"

"Chase."

I unbolted the door and pulled it open to find Chase standing on my deck holding a bottle of tequila, a bag of limes, and a pizza.

"I thought you might want some company. Is that okay?"

It was more than okay, but before I could answer, the tears were back.

He set everything down on the deck, wrapped his arms around me, and led me to the sofa. I cried even harder.

When I'd finally settled down to soft, quiet gulps, Chase made me drink a glass of water and eat half a slice of now-cold pizza. My headache had faded, leaving me groggy and a bit disconnected, like I was floating.

"Can I do anything for you?" he asked. "Get you anything?"

I nodded. "Yeah, two shot glasses in the cabinet over the sink. There's salt and a cutting board on the counter and knives in the drawer near the stove."

When Chase returned and joined me on the sofa, I sliced a lime into wedges while he filled the glasses.

Before we took the first shot, I clicked his glass.

"What are we toasting?"

"I'm not sure. How about endings and beginnings?"

He nodded and raised his glass, then threw it back.

We did another shot after that one, but instead of feeling numb and disoriented, I was heating up. When he poured a third, I climbed onto his lap, straddling him. I slid the elastic from his hair and ran my fingers through the silky strands, pushing them to the side, exposing his neck. His head tipped back, and when he swallowed, I kissed the base of his throat, and licked my way up to his chin. He already tasted salty, but I sprinkled more on him, licked it off, drank my shot, and bit the lime.

While I did, he steadied me with his hand around my waist. I knew by the way he looked at me, the way his nostrils flared, and the way his breathing hitched that I had him—which was good, because I wanted him.

"Your turn," I purred, sliding off his lap and rolling onto my back on the coffee table, a wedge of lime between my teeth. I raised my shirt and waited.

He knelt between my legs and ran his tongue from my navel up to my breasts, then sprinkled my belly with salt. When he poured the tequila into my belly button, I squealed from the cold.

He leaned forward and drew his tongue over me slowly, following the path of the salt, lapping up the tequila. He bit the lime in my mouth, then lifted me up, pulled the rind from my mouth, and kissed me like I'd only been kissed twice before.

Both times by him.

My body buzzed like a neon sign, like a plug being inserted into a socket. The sparks I'd felt the very first time we touched had ignited into something that already felt like it was burning out of control, and I was consumed. Nothing had ever felt like this before.

Nothing.

Chase's response was more than I could've hoped for. I was so overwhelmed and emotional, and probably a little drunk, that I almost started to cry again. When we stopped for air, I rolled onto the floor with him, pulled his T-shirt over his head, and pushed him down.

"It's your turn." I worshiped the ridges of his rock-hard belly with my hands and my tongue.

We did more body shots, kissing long and slow in between, until it grew so dark in my apartment it was difficult to see.

I tried to stand without breaking our kiss and tugged him to his feet.

"I want you," I whispered, nipping his lower lip.

"Are you sure?" he asked, kissing my neck as he did. "I think you might be drunk."

"I'm positive. And I'm not that drunk." I pulled back and cradled his face in my hands, feeling the scruff along his jaw, and looked into his eyes—eyes with a fire so hot, I could feel the burn. "Just please don't hurt me. I don't think I can stand any more hurt."

He lifted me into his arms.

"Never," he said, before kissing me again. "I swear, Rain, I will never hurt you."

CHAPTER TWENTY-SEVEN

Chase

I carried Rain into her room and gently set her on the bed. It was so much like the last time I'd done this, only then she'd been asleep. Now, despite more shots of tequila than I could remember, she was wide awake. I was more than wide awake. I was wired for sound.

Of all the women I'd ever been with, I couldn't remember ever wanting one as badly as I wanted her. I reached behind my shoulders, tugged my T-shirt over my head, and tossed it in the corner. My jeans hit the floor next.

Rain lay on her back, propped up on her elbows, watching me. When I tossed my briefs onto the rest of my things, her small pink tongue swept her bottom lip, and my dick almost smacked me in the chin.

I knelt on the edge of the bed as she sat up and removed the skimpy T-shirt she'd been wearing, and I almost cried. I'd wanted her for so long, it seemed like forever. This felt more right than just about anything I'd ever done. Or anyone I'd ever done.

She shimmied out of her yoga pants and sent them sailing across the room.

She was a vision. Tiny waist, slender arms and legs, beautiful face, blond hair falling over perfect breasts. Even her feet were gorgeous—which was where I started, planting kisses on her instep, biting her toes.

I wasn't rushing this. I'd waited too long to have her. If I gave in to my want, it might be over in minutes. And that would be a damn shame.

When I'd kissed and licked my way up to the apex of her thighs, she squirmed beneath me. It seemed a ridiculous time to pray, but it's what I wanted to do. Among other things. Because surely, I was as close to heaven as I'd ever been. I licked and teased my way closer, gripping her toned thighs, pushing them further apart. She pulled her knees up, dragging a foot across my back and digging in with her toes.

I couldn't wait any longer. I had to taste her. I wrapped my arms around her thighs and pressed my hands gently against her belly, holding her in place. When my tongue found her center, her body stiffened and arched upward, and the low growl she emitted nearly made me come, even though my dick was nowhere near her.

I wanted to give her everything before I even thought of taking something for myself, no matter how badly I'd been craving her. Craving this very moment. I wanted to make her forget anyone before me, because without even trying, she'd made me almost forget that there had ever been any other women in my life, including the one who had almost destroyed me.

Rain writhed and moaned. Her hands gripped my hair and her nails dug into my scalp. I thought for sure I was going to lose it, but I dug in and held her until she exploded, moaning loudly, pulsing against my tongue, her body convulsing and nearly levitating out from under me.

As her orgasm faded, I ran my tongue over her gently, relishing the taste of her, the wetness, and still holding back even though I wanted to be inside her more than I'd ever wanted anything. When I felt her body begin to relax, I climbed my way up to those magnificent breasts. I captured a nipple in my mouth, teasing it with my tongue, while my hand tested the weight of her other breast, finding it as perfect as I'd expected.

She tugged on my hair, and I lifted my head, running my tongue between her breasts and up to the curve of her neck, where I nibbled gently.

"You need to be in me," she said, her voice throaty and intoxicating on its own.

"I agree." And without another moment's hesitation, I buried myself deep inside her, as deep as I could go.

Her arms wrapped around me, and her hand stayed in my hair, touching, pulling, rubbing my scalp. It was so fucking sensual, I didn't think I'd last a minute.

"Fuck me," she moaned.

So I did. I fucked as hard as I could, because I had to. Because for months, it had been all I could think about. Because I needed her more than I needed my next breath.

CHAPTER TWENTY-EIGHT

Rain

I woke in the morning to an empty bed, a pounding head, and whispered giggles coming from my kitchen. I propped one eye open to find a glass of orange juice and three aspirin on my nightstand. I took them gladly, then lay back down and closed my eyes again.

From the giggling, I assumed my mother had brought Izzy home. I was disappointed not to wake up with Chase beside me, but I was used to it. Like Preston, he must have disappeared sometime during the night. I climbed out of bed, moving slowly in deference to my massive hangover. I found my robe on the floor, cinched it tightly, and headed for the kitchen, ready to face my mother's third degree.

What I found nearly tore my heart in two. Or maybe it stitched some of the broken pieces together.

Izzy stood on a chair at the counter with one of my aprons doubled over and wrapped around her, while Chase helped her measure a scoop of flour into a bowl. On the kitchen table was a tray with a coffee cup and one of my bud vases holding one lone stem that must've been plucked from the potted mum on the deck.

I leaned against the doorjamb. "Morning," I croaked, still more asleep than awake.

"Mommy!" Izzy cried. "Go back to sleep! We're making you a surprise."

"Sorry, sorry." I was about to ask Chase if he minded, but the smile he gave me answered that question. In fact, it melted my heart.

"Yeah, Mommy, go back to sleep," he said.

I was desperate for coffee but I obeyed, right after I ducked into the bathroom to brush my teeth and pull my nightgown on.

Izzy was whispering noisily outside my door, so I closed my eyes and pretended to be asleep.

She climbed into bed beside me and yelled "Surprise!" in my face. I tried not to grimace.

"Hey!" Chase whispered, almost as loud. "Mommy has a headache. No yelling. We don't want her to be grumpy, right?"

I cracked one eye open. "I'm never grumpy, am I, Iz?"

She looked solemnly at Chase and shook her head.

"See?"

"Good to know." He winked at me.

I pulled myself into a sitting position. "So what do we have here?"

"It's a tradition," Izzy explained as Chase set the tray on my lap.

I looked up at Chase and waited for clarification.

"I told her making chocolate chip pancakes on Sundays is a tradition for me."

"I like tradition," Izzy announced, snuggling in beside me.

Chase left the room and returned with a plate of pancakes for her and one for him, then settled down at the foot of the bed.

"These are great." I hadn't been hungry earlier, but I was suddenly ravenous. "The coffee is good too." I took another sip, hoping he'd brewed a large pot. "You remembered how I take it?"

"Light and sweet—just like you." His smile had me melting like the chocolate chips in my pancakes.

When Izzy finished, I gave her permission to go watch cartoons. She left the room but leaned back inside the doorway a moment later. "Don't forget to ask her," she whispered loudly.

"I won't," he whispered back.

"Ask me what?"

"I told her I'd like to take you both fishing today but said it was up to you."

"Fishing? She wants to go fishing?"

"Apparently. She asked me what my other traditions were, and I said sometimes on Sunday I like to go fishing. She asked if she could go too, so . . ."

"Isn't fishing supposed to be a time for quiet reflection? Do you know how quiet a six-year-old can be? We'll scare all the fish."

He wrapped his hand around mine and rubbed his thumb back and forth over my skin. "I don't care. I'd love to spend the day with both of you. If she wants to go fishing, she can scare all the fish she wants. You up for it?"

"Maybe. I'm a wee bit hungover, but I'm feeling a little better. Must be this first-class room service."

When I finished eating, I snuggled back under the covers. Chase nestled in beside me.

I curled into his side, feeling like I belonged there, and rested my hand on his hip. "You know, when I woke up and you weren't in bed, I figured you'd left during the night."

"I wouldn't do that," he said, kissing my forehead.

"What did my mother say when she dropped Izzy off?"

"She asked if you were okay."

"And?"

"I said I thought you would be. Then she gave me a wicked smile."

Way to play it cool, Mom. "That sounds about right. I told you she liked you."

"Good, and so does Izzy, I think. I'm hoping you might too."

I focused on his blue-green eyes and stroked his cheek. "You're definitely three for three."

***

After a shower and a lot more coffee I was ready to go fishing. We stopped at Chase's apartment so he could shower, change, and pick up his equipment. Then he insisted on stopping at Walmart for a pole for Izzy and a fishing license for me.

"I don't need a license. I'll just watch."

"Do you plan to see me again after today?"

I was dumbfounded. "I hope so."

"Then you need a license."

He took us to a quiet spot along the north branch of the Raritan River, where he spent the better part of the afternoon unhooking my fishing line from low-hanging trees and taking tiny fish off Izzy's Hello Kitty fishing pole. Unlike me, Izzy was experiencing an abundance of beginner's luck.

In spite of barely getting his own line wet, Chase seemed to be having a good time. He laughed and smiled and held Izzy in his lap when she got tired and refused to lie down on the blanket. He held my hand when he could and kissed me just about every chance he got.

We stopped at the diner for dinner, and Izzy immediately claimed the bench seat next to Chase. "Are we having pancakes next Sunday?"

He glanced at me and smiled. "That's up to your mommy. If she says it's okay, then it's okay with me."

"Please." She looked up at me with her big blue eyes and blinked several times. Like mother, like daughter.

Twenty-four hours ago I'd been lying in bed, drinking, and crying. Today, I had a license to fish. I couldn't help but agree things were looking up. "We'll see."

"Please, Mommy. If you and Chase have another sleepover, then he can make pancakes."

I rolled my lips together to keep from laughing and looked up at the ceiling.

Chase, however, couldn't help himself.

"Please? We can have another sleepover."

When I lowered my eyes, he was grinning.

"We'll see, Iz," I repeated. "You just be good, okay?"

He lowered his voice. "Why does she need to be good? You're the one who should be good."

"So should you," I answered, teasing.

Izzy was still begging for Sunday pancakes when I tucked her in later. Then she insisted on Chase reading her a story. Listening to the peals of laughter coming from the bedroom, I wondered if she would ever be able to fall asleep, but it seemed an afternoon of fishing had worn her out. She was snoring softly by the time he came out of the bedroom and joined me on the couch.

I was tired as well, but I couldn't help smiling.

He returned my smile. "What?"

"Where did you come from, Chase Holgate?"

He pointed toward the bedroom. "In there. I was just reading Izzy a story."

"That's not what I mean and you know it."

He shrugged.

My love life had been one for the books so far. But Chase? He was exactly what I'd always wanted; what I'd dreamed about. Steady. Kind. A beautiful soul. And let's not forget sexy as hell.

"I'm not a lucky person. And you seem too good to be true."

"I told you I was one of the good guys, and I meant it. I'm also crazy about you. I have been since I met you. At first, it was for the obvious reasons." He waggled his eyebrows; in case I didn't follow. "But as I got to know you, it was because of the person you are."

"You hardly know me."

He slipped his arm around my shoulder, and I curled up against him. "I know that you're a good daughter and a good friend and a great mother. You're friendly and easygoing. You don't take anything or anyone for granted, and you're spontaneous. Add that to being so incredibly hot—and that you're pretty damn good in bed—and you're the real deal, baby."

Although I believe he meant the last part, he said it as if he were teasing me. His words slipped under my skin and warmed me in a way that was new and exciting. I wanted him to write them down so I could read them over and over again.

"What about me?" he asked. "Think you know me?"

I thought about what to say maybe a bit too long, because he began to look a little uncomfortable. I finally nodded.

"I'm pretty sure I do. In addition to being so incredibly handsome and just about the sexiest man I've ever met, you're strong and quiet. You're dependable but not predictable. I think you're trustworthy and honest, kind, loving, gentle, and I think you may also be very sensitive." He was smiling, and I kissed him several times before I finished. "I think you just might be the prize in the bottom of my Cracker Jack."

"Cracker Jack?"

"You know how when you buy a box of Cracker Jack, it's because you think you want the sweet, sticky popcorn and nuts, but what you really want is the prize? In order to get to it though, you have to eat all that popcorn, and before you know it, you're sick to your stomach and miserable because you had to go through all that to get to your prize. But once you have that whistle, or tiny plastic horse, or little shoe, it's yours, and if you want, you can keep it forever."

He pulled me into his lap and kissed me until my lips were swollen and my cheeks burned from the scrape of his whiskers. I fumbled with his belt, but he grabbed my hand.

"Your daughter's asleep in the next room," he whispered.

"She's out like a light."

"I don't want to take a chance."

I stood and pulled him up behind me, then led him into the bathroom and locked the door behind us. He hoisted me up onto the counter.

"Rain," he mumbled into my neck. "I know I'm a day late with this, but I don't have any protection on me, and I know damn well I didn't use any last night. We're playing with fire here."

"Would you stop if I told you to?" I asked, knowing the answer.

"If I need to, I will."

The way he sighed made me laugh. "It's okay. I'm on the pill."

"Oh, thank god."

We tried doing it with me sitting on the countertop and Chase standing, but that didn't work. He was too tall. Then we tried with him sitting on the lid of the toilet and me straddling him, but once we got busy, the toilet rattled so much he was afraid it would come apart. So we moved to the edge of the tub. He faced out, stretching his long legs into my tiny bathroom, while I straddled him again, facing the tub. It not only worked, I had another amazing orgasm. In less than twenty-four hours, I'd had several of the most intense orgasms of my life.

We stayed on the edge of the bathtub afterward, speaking in low voices.

"I should probably go," he said into my hair, making no attempt to move.

I planted tiny kisses along the side of his neck. A soft, low noise came from deep in his throat.

"I don't want to leave."

I kept kissing him and worked my way to his ear. "I don't want you to go either," I whispered.

"You can come to my place."

I leaned back and frowned. "You're worried about my daughter walking in on us, but you're okay with leaving her home alone."

"Of course not. We'd bring her with us. I have two bedrooms."

"I can't do that. What kind of mother takes her kid from her warm bed and drags her out in the night so she can go have sex?"

"A horny one." He sunk his teeth into my shoulder.

It took a while, but we were finally able to tear ourselves away from each other. He left only after I promised that Izzy and I would stay at his apartment the next night.

Later, I lay in bed and tried to process the past couple days.

It seemed sudden and crazy, but I had feelings for Chase. Strong ones. I'd tried to ignore them, but they were real. Obviously. And during that time, while I was getting to know him, I think I'd been emotionally letting Preston go, even if I hadn't been aware of it.

At that moment, I would have given just about anything to have Chase lying next to me.

I had almost drifted off when my phone vibrated on the nightstand.

I miss you.

My smile faded when I realized the text wasn't from Chase.

CHAPTER TWENTY-NINE

Rain

We spent Monday at Chase's apartment, and then Tuesday after I worked at Blondie's, he followed me back to my apartment, since my mother had Izzy. On Wednesday and Thursday, we went back to his place.

On Friday, Diane stopped by work to find out what the hell was wrong with me.

She followed me around the back of the restaurant as I pulled together the ingredients for a vegetarian chili.

"There's nothing wrong with me." I wiped my forehead with my forearm. It was unseasonably warm for late September.

"A week ago you were ready to jump off the Landing Lane Bridge. Now you're spending every night with Chase."

And I thought I was the dramatic one. I frowned and shook my head. "I wasn't 'ready to jump off a bridge.' And I thought you liked Chase."

"I do. My ovaries explode every time I look at him, and I think you two would be great together. But shouldn't you give yourself a little time to breathe?"

"She's right, Rain," my mother said, darting into the kitchen for another bag of hoagie rolls.

I frowned at her as well and gave her a thumbs-up. "Thanks for the support, Mom."

"Just saying. You need to figure out what you want."

The chopped onions, celery, and peppers sizzled in the hot oil when I dumped them into a large Dutch oven. I gave them a quick stir and then waved my spoon at them.

"Did it ever occur to either one of you that maybe I've been developing an interest in Chase over the past few months?"

"No," they said in unison.

"Well, that just proves you don't know anything, because I was. I saw him a couple times, and I realized there was something special about him."

I lowered the heat under the veggies so I could focus on the conversation.

"In fact, I felt something the first time he touched my hand." I turned to my mother. "Remember how Daddy said he knew that man was going to die when he shook his hand?"

"Oh, dear god!" My mother made the sign of the cross and clutched her chest. "Rain! Don't say things like that. You think Chase is going to die?"

"No!" I shook my head vehemently. "Jeez, Ma! But I felt something like low-voltage electricity running through his hands into mine. That's never happened before. And it's gotten stronger since then. And warmer." It was hard to explain how it felt, and judging by the way they were looking at me, it wouldn't matter what I said.

Diane rolled her eyes. She believed in my psychic abilities when it suited her purposes, like whether it would rain on her wedding day—it did, but the sun came out by the time she came out of church, which I predicted—or whether she would pass Algebra I even though she didn't study—she didn't, which I also predicted. But when she didn't like what I had to say, she didn't want to hear it.

After years of listening to my father's predictions, and that he hadn't seemed to know about his own death, my mother wasn't interested either.

"Would you just trust me to know what's right for me?" I asked.

My mother looked at me thoughtfully.

"You know, I hate to encourage this psychic crap because you know how I've always felt about it, but what you just said reminded me of something."

"That you should trust me to know what I want?"

She waved her hand, aggravated. "No, not that. What you said about electricity. Remember? Your father used to say something like that about me. I can't remember exactly what it was, but he said the first time we touched, he knew. He'd felt it, some vibration or electricity or something, and he said he knew we'd be together the rest of his life."

Her eyes filled. "See what you made me do?" She dabbed at her eyes angrily and gave me a look that was meant to come across as annoyed.

I could see right through her. I set down my spoon and put my arms around her. My father may not have been here to explain to me what the feeling I had when I touched Chase meant, but my mother, without realizing it, had just delivered the message for him. Loud and clear.

"Daddy always said he knew from the very first moment. And he was right, Mom. I hope I might be just as lucky."

"Okay." She gave me a quick pat on the tush and stepped away. "That's enough. I can't be waiting on all these people with mascara running down my cheeks." She picked up the bag of rolls. "Just be careful, Rain. Promise me. I don't want to see you hurt again."

I nodded, feeling a little too emotional to say anything else.

But while my mother might have understood, at least a little, Diane wasn't convinced.

She grabbed my hand before I could turn up the vegetables again. "Listen, Rain. I don't want you to get hurt again either. Wally says Chase just went through a really bad breakup before moving here, and he might be doing the same thing you are. You might just be his rebound, you know?"

"I know all about it. And he knows what I've been through, so we both have our eyes wide open."

At least, I knew my own eyes were open. When he knocked on my door last Saturday, I'd been certain I hadn't wanted it to be Preston, and that had shocked the hell out of me. When it turned out to be Chase, I'd been so relieved I couldn't stop crying.

But did that mean I wanted Chase, or was I just happy it wasn't Preston?

And what if Chase really was on the rebound? I was twenty-three and had only been in two relationships, and both had nearly destroyed me in different ways. Jeff had taken my youth, and Preston, my self-esteem.

The smart thing would be to let a relationship develop naturally. See what happened. Take it slow.

I turned up the heat on my vegetables, gave them a stir, and let them sizzle.

CHAPTER THIRTY

Rain

"Move in with me."

So much for taking it slow.

I snapped the light on beside me and stared at him. "Are you crazy? Don't you think it's too soon? It's only been a couple weeks."

We were lying in Chase's bed. Izzy was asleep in the room down the hall.

"Not for me, it isn't." He rolled onto his side, facing me, and propped his head up on his hand. "Move in with me. There's plenty of room. Keep the apartment. If you aren't happy, you can go back. What's crazy is all the back-and-forth. I want your kiss to be the last thing I feel at night and your smile to be the first thing I see in the morning."

I shook my head. It was crazy. I knew that, and he should have known that. What was even crazier was that I wanted to. Logic be damned. But with my track record, I wouldn't chance it.

"What if this is a rebound relationship? I don't think it is, but what if I'm just trying to get over Preston and you're still getting over the rabbit?" I was so stunned I couldn't remember her name.

He wrapped his arms around me and pulled gently until I was again lying beside him. "Then we'll take it slow."

"How is moving in with you taking it slow?"

"Do you want to see anyone else?" he asked.

"No."

"Neither do I. How about this? Let's play house for a week and see how it goes."

I slipped my hand under the covers, grabbed his semihard dick, and giggled. "Is this what you call playing house?"

It took a second for him to regain his focus. "That's part of it—but all the rest of it too. Who takes Izzy to school and picks her up from day care? Who does the grocery shopping? Who cleans the bathroom, cooks dinner, walks the dog?"

I sprang up again. "You have a dog?"

"No, but I've been meaning to get one."

"One thing at a time," I warned. "So is the answer to all those questions me? I run Izzy back and forth, do the shopping, clean the house, cook dinner?" A dog wasn't even on my radar, so I let that one go.

"Absolutely not. That's what I mean by playing house. If the first week works out, we can do it for another week, and then we'll reevaluate and see about week three." He brushed a strand of hair from my face. "C'mon, Rain. Give us a chance. We have something special starting here."

He flipped me on my back and pushed inside of me.

"You're making it hard to say no."

"Then don't."

"Chase, it's too soon." I wrapped my legs around his waist in case he tried to pull away. He didn't. He just lowered his forehead onto my shoulder. "But it doesn't mean I don't want to see where this goes. I do. I agree. There's something special between us. I felt it the first time we touched—even though I didn't understand it at the time. But if we're wrong and it doesn't work out, I can't uproot my daughter like that. As it is, she's already crazy about you."

"I'm crazy about her—about both of you."

I threaded my fingers in his hair and lifted his face so we were eye-to-eye.

"I don't want to mess this up." I kissed him, deeply, hoping he would believe me. "I know I don't want anyone else, but I can't move in with you. I can stay here overnight, and you can stay with me when Izzy isn't home. We can spend weekends together. Then in a couple months, let's see how we feel. You might find that I drive you crazy."

He traced his nose along my jaw until he reached my lips. "Oh, you drive me crazy all right, Rain Storm. In the best way possible."

"Ditto."

CHAPTER THIRTY-ONE

Chase

Maybe it was crazy to want Rain and Izzy to move in with me.

It had only been eight months since Jennifer tore my heart out of my chest, shredded it into tiny pieces, and then stomped all over it. To discover it was still here with me, beating, doing somersaults over another woman, surprised the hell out of me. I hadn't believed it possible I could ever fall in love again or allow anyone to get this close to me, but Rain was all I could think about. It didn't matter how fast it had happened.

She was intoxicating, and I wanted her more than I'd ever wanted anything or anyone. No woman had ever had this kind of an effect on me, not even my ex-fiancée. To be able to have her, to make love to her, was indescribable. I was no novice in the bedroom; I'd had my share of girlfriends and even girls I'd hook up with for a good time.

But with Rain, a touch of her hand, a flick of her tongue, and I would happily have signed over the title to my truck as well as my bike. She should teach classes, write books, you name it—she knew what to do to make me nearly lose my mind, and she did it well. I could understand why Preston didn't want to let her go. The difference, as far as I was concerned, was that I also saw the person Rain was. I saw what was hidden behind those baby blue eyes. I saw the woman.

But while I saw who she really was, everyone else just saw great tits and legs that went on for miles. I'd seen how guys looked at her and talked to her, especially at Blondie's. While it had bothered me in the past, now that we were together, it was making me a little nuts. I was never one for jealousy before, but now, every time I caught some guy look like he was trying to picture Rain naked, I wanted to rip his face off. Making it more difficult was that Rain left little to the imagination, especially when she was tending bar. Even when it was too cold for shorts and tank tops, she was more exposed than covered. I didn't know if she realized it. I think she'd been dressing that way for so long it was just who she was. I didn't want to start trying to change her, but either I was going to have to spend every night she worked sitting on a bar stool for eight hours, or I would just have to suck it up and trust that she could handle herself.

In spite of this newfound insecurity, things between us were great. It had been four weeks, and I couldn't have been happier. For as much as was falling in love with Rain, I was also falling in love with Izzy. I hadn't thought I was ready to be a father, but it sure as hell seemed that way. That little girl had me wrapped around her finger, maybe even more so than her mother. I was at their mercy.

I came home from work on the Friday before Halloween to find Rain and Izzy in my living room. Izzy was wearing black tights, black shorts, and a black sweatshirt, on the front of which Rain had painted a white oval. A glittery headband with pointy black ears perched above her excited little face, her nose and cheeks painted to look like a cat. Rain was pinning a tail on her when I walked in.

"Uh-oh," I said when Izzy gave me one of her big grins. "Better tell the mice to go hide—the cat's out of the bag."

She held up her paws and was about to make a run at me, but Rain held her back.

"Wait, Iz. You're going to tear your tail off." She finished what she was doing, then gave Izzy a pat on the bottom. "Go."

Instead of the hug I was used to, Izzy got on her knees, rubbed against my leg, and meowed.

"What do you think, Mommy?" I asked. "You think this kitty is ticklish?" I didn't even have to move, and Izzy collapsed into a giggling mass at my feet.

"How was school today?" I asked.

"Good," she rolled onto her back. "I got to pick a prize from the treasure box."

"Nice work!" I held out my hand, and she high-fived me.

"So if you're going to be a cat, should I be a dog, and Mommy can be a mouse?"

"Uh-uh. Mommy's going to be a bunny."

I looked at Rain. "A bunny?"

She flashed me a salacious grin, and I felt a little nauseated. Rain was working the Halloween party tomorrow night at Blondie's, and she'd told me she'd be wearing a costume.

"You want to model that costume for me?" I asked, praying it came with lots of white fur and a basket of colored eggs.

She winked. "Maybe later."

***

Just as I feared, Rain wasn't dressing as the Easter bunny. Nope. She had a genuine Playboy bunny costume complete with tall, semi-erect ears and a big, fluffy tail.

"Well? What do you think?" She strutted around the bedroom in four-inch heels and fishnet stockings. "How about you get one of those smoking jackets? Like Hugh Hefner?"

I shook my head. "I don't think so."

"C'mon, what are you going to wear?"

"A hard-on, just like every other guy who sees you in that."

She frowned. "Don't be ridiculous. It's just a costume. I'm hardly showing any more than I normally do."

I must've grimaced, because her eyes flashed.

"Do you have a problem with the way I dress?"

I shook my head. I did, it seemed, but I sure as hell wasn't about to say so.

On Saturday, I dropped Rain off at Blondie's, fed Izzy, and then took her to Rain's mother's to spend the night, promising I'd wait for her to get home before making our Sunday pancakes.

When I got to Blondie's, the place was standing room only. Rain gave me a wide grin and dragged a bar stool out from behind the counter.

"Reserved seating," she yelled over the jukebox as I took my seat. She looked me up and down. "I thought you weren't wearing a costume."

"Who says this is a costume?" I was wearing a dark suit, white shirt, and dark tie. I'd slicked my hair back into a ponytail and sported a pair of dark aviator shades. An old Bluetooth ear piece was tucked against my right ear.

"Seriously," she made a face as she tried to figure out who I was supposed to be, "who are you?"

I lowered the glasses so she could see my eyes. "I'm your bodyguard."

The guy sitting beside me burst into laughter. Rain smiled and shook her head. "You're ridiculous, you know that?"

At least she was laughing.

"Heineken?"

I shook my head. "Tequila shooter for me and one for the bartender."

"Are you trying to get me drunk, Mr. Holgate?" She batted those sinfully long eyelashes at me.

"Not yet, but I'm hoping to get lucky later."

She leaned across the bar and reached for my face with both hands, then kissed me.

"Oh, baby. You can count on it."

CHAPTER THIRTY-TWO

Rain

On Monday night we took Izzy trick-or-treating. We did the neighborhood thing, stopped by my mom's, and ended up at Diane and Wally's. Chase took Izzy out to see the race car while Diane made me a cup of tea.

"So you really are domesticated now, aren't you?" she said with a laugh as she poured the boiling water over my tea bag.

I yawned. "I don't know about that. I would definitely say we are in a honeymoon phase." I smiled, then yawned again.

"He must be keeping you up nights. It's barely seven thirty."

"A little, I guess. I think all the back-and-forth has got me kind of worn out. It's nice, though."

"Just nice?"

"More than nice. It's great. It's so good I'm almost scared." I spooned sugar into my tea and stirred.

Waiting for it to cool, I twirled the string from the teabag around the mug handle.

"I found another note."

"Are you kidding me?" she asked. "What the hell's his problem?"

I wrapped my hands around the mug to warm them.

"Who knows?" Preston had left a note on my car on Thursday. He hadn't come inside Blondie's, but twice now I'd found notes tucked under my windshield wiper when I left work. And there had also been that one text message.

"Do you think he knows about Chase?"

"Maybe. For fuck's sake! He's engaged. Besides, I told him it was over, and I meant it. And honestly, the more I think about it, the more I believe it was over for me long before then, but I was too stubborn to admit that I had wasted all that time. Is that crazy or what?"

Her face puckered. "Why are you even asking me if I think you and Preston were crazy? You already know the answer to that. So what did Chase say?"

"Are you kidding? I can't tell him. He'd blow a gasket. If he thought Preston was hanging around, he'd be furious."

"I can't blame him."

"Yeah, but I think he needs to trust me to handle it. Right?"

Diane poured a splash of milk into her tea and stirred it slowly, staring into her cup as she did. I waited while she raised the cup and took a sip.

She set the cup down and cleared her throat. A lecture was coming my way.

"Don't take this the wrong way. You know I love you, but you're a big flirt, Rain. Shit, I've caught my own husband patting you on the ass, and if he does it again, I might break his hand. But most of the guys we know are like that. I've seen the way some of them leer at you, and I'm sure Chase sees it too. Guys are possessive, and you're his now. He doesn't want someone looking at you like that."

Even my best friend had no faith in me. "Diane!"

"I'm serious. Think about it. How would you like it if women were making obscene remarks as he walked by or flirting with him down at the gas station while he worked on their engines?"

I set my cup down slowly, pulled in a deep breath, and pinned her with a look. "I trust him. I wouldn't think anything of it. In fact, I'd think it was a testimony to my excellent taste."

"Bullshit. And besides, even if that were true, guys don't think like that. They think with their dicks, and they beat their chests, and they know that every other guy is thinking the same thing they are. That's why they get all macho and want to start pounding on each other."

The engine of the race car started up outside, and I pictured Chase in the driver's seat with Izzy in his lap. Diane stood and closed the door to block out the noise.

"Did you tell him about the photo shoots with Antoine?"

"Not yet."

"Are you kidding me? Preston may have been okay with that shit, but I have a feeling Chase isn't going to be on board. At all."

"To be honest, I was thinking of giving it up anyway. I'm spreading myself way too thin lately. The extra money was nice, but I'm worn out. I've been sick twice already this year, and I feel like I'm coming down with something again."

"Good girl. I can't see him being okay with it."

"When did you get so smart about men?"

"Since I regularly have a crew of them in my garage. And because my husband is a blabbermouth and tells me what they say."

I remembered about how miserable Chase had looked Saturday night when he'd dropped me off at work in my bunny outfit, and how he'd eye me up before I'd leave for work at the bar, never saying anything about the way I was dressed, but always looking like he wanted to. "You think maybe I should tone it down a bit? You know, at Blondie's?"

"Wouldn't hurt. So should I plan on another person for Thanksgiving?"

"Actually," I said a bit sheepishly, "Chase says his sister-in-law usually cooks dinner, and his mother will be coming in from Allentown, and he wants me to meet her."

"Oh, fuck. You have to have dinner with Lorraine the Pain?"

I laughed. "Shh! What if Chase heard you call her that? I told him I knew Lorraine from school. I never told him she detested me."

"Well, that sucks. Maybe you can come for dessert, then."

I nodded and stifled another yawn. "Speaking of dessert, you have any cookies or anything? I'm starving."

"No cookies, but I have a bowl of Halloween candy." She went to fetch the bowl from near the front door and set it down on the table between us. I helped myself to a peanut butter cup. "Just promise me that now that you're in a relationship and you're all happy and shit, you're going to get fat."

I popped the candy in my mouth. "I'll see what I can do to help a girl out."

She snatched up a fun-sized Milky Way. "That's all I ask."

CHAPTER THIRTY-THREE

It had been a hectic week, and by Sunday evening, I was exhausted. I'd cleaned my apartment, done several loads of laundry, driven over to Chase's and made dinner, and gotten Izzy off to bed. Chase offered to do the dishes and insisted I take a long, hot bubble bath. He even set out candles, poured me a glass of wine, and brought me my iPod so I could listen to music.

A girl could get used to being treated like this.

I'd been soaking for a good long while when he knocked on the door and poked his head in and to ask if I needed anything.

I slid up into a sitting position. "No, just you. Want to join me?"

"I thought you were relaxing."

"If I get any more relaxed, I may slide down the drain."

"Well, I wouldn't want that to happen." He stepped out of the room for a moment and returned with another glass and the bottle of wine.

I made room for him, but it was a tight squeeze.

"We need a bigger bathtub," he pointed out as I settled in between his legs.

I leaned back against him, one knee drawn up and the other leg hooked over the side of the tub. "Not much you can do about that, is there? But wouldn't that be great? Imagine all the wicked things we could do in a nice big bathtub."

"Well, now that you mention it, I was meaning to talk to you about that."

"Getting a bigger bathtub? That would be kind of crazy, since you rent."

"I know, which is why I'm thinking of buying a place."

My heart might have skidded to a stop. "You're moving?"

"If you come with me."

"Where?"

"Here—well, somewhere around here. Things are great between us, and I still want you to live with me." He pointed to the collection of hair products around the tub, the panties drying on the shower rod, and all my makeup piled on the counter, not to mention the basket of Izzy's tub toys sitting in the corner. "You've got half your stuff here and the other half on the other side of town. I want you under my roof. I want you to know I'm taking care of you and Izzy. I want to make your life easier. I want you to feel safe and protected. I want to trip on Izzy's toys when I come home from w—"

I gave him a gentle shove. "You say that now, but step on one Barbie shoe barefoot and you'll be singing a different tune."

"I'm serious, Rain." He leaned as far forward as he could, given the tight quarters, and wrapped me in his arms. "I love you. I've been afraid to say it because I don't want to freak you out, but I've loved you for—"

I twisted toward him and pressed my fingers against his lips, feeling the magnitude of what he was telling me.

"Stop. Listen to me. First, I don't need someone to take care of me and Izzy. I've been taking care of the two of us, more or less, since she was born. That's important to me." He started to speak again, but I pressed harder. "Second, we've only been together for six weeks. And third, I'm pretty sure I love you too."

I took my fingers away, but kept them close to his mouth in case I needed them again. "But it's still too soon to live together. I don't want to fuck this up. I like the way things are. We're together every night as it is. Why jeopardize things between us?"

"Exactly—we're together every night. How would we be jeopardizing any-thing?"

I loved him. I didn't care who thought it was crazy or too soon, and I could see someday making a commitment to him, much bigger than just living together. But being independent was a big deal for me, and I wasn't sure I was ready to give that up. My heart was still pretty bruised, and I didn't think I could survive if he changed his mind about us later. So for now, even if it meant disappointing him, I had to protect what was mine.

Disappointed, he flung himself back against the wall. Water splashed out over the sides and onto the floor. "Fine. But I'm still going to look for a house. And you're coming with me. If nothing else, we'll have a bigger fucking bathtub."

I pressed my lips together to try and hide my smile.

"I could totally get behind a bigger bathtub."

CHAPTER THIRTY-FOUR

Chase

About a week before Thanksgiving, I met with a real estate agent, and since I wanted Rain and Izzy to live with me in whatever house I bought, I dragged them along whenever I went to see a listing.

Rain refused to comment, insisting this was all on me and her opinion didn't matter, but I could tell just by watching her what she was thinking.

If her eyes widened, her lips quirked slightly, or she ran her hand over something slowly—like granite countertops—that meant she liked it. If her eyes narrowed, her nostrils flared, or her lips twisted—as they did for no bathtub in the en suite—it was a no.

And she thought we didn't know each other well enough to move in together.

When I told my brother I was house shopping and that I hoped Rain would eventually agree to move in with me, he gave me a strange look.

"I don't know, man. I mean, she's hot, don't get me wrong, but you don't want to get mixed up with someone like that. I mean . . . c'mon, Chase. I hope you're keeping it wrapped up, because from what I've heard, she's slept with half the damn township."

"What the fuck did you say?" If my brother was as smart as I believed him to be, he'd better watch how he rephrased that.

"All I'm saying is watch your step. There's nothing wrong with having a good time, and after what you've been through, you deserve it, but—"

My ratchet hit the floor of the bay with a loud clatter as I stalked toward him.

"Whoa!" he cried, holding his hands up. "What the hell's gotten into you?"

"You watch your fucking mouth." I aimed a finger in his direction.

"Are you serious? You're coming after me over some little piece of—"

"Don't!" One more word and I didn't care if he was my brother.

"What the fuck is your problem?"

"I mean it, Dylan. Don't talk about her like that. You'll respect her, or I have nothing to say to you."

He stared at me, his mouth working, but he had enough sense to keep it shut. He stormed into his office. After a few minutes, he returned and held out what at first looked like a spiral bound book. It turned out to be a calendar.

"Here," he said, waving it at me. "Check out Miss February."

My belly twisted itself into a knot, even though I had no idea what he was talking about. Given the smug look on his face, I didn't want to find out.

"Go ahead. Take it."

I turned the calendar over in my hands. Beautiful Bartenders of New Jersey 2012.

"February," he repeated. "Comes right after January. However, I'm betting a lot of guys come right after checking out Miss February."

I didn't even know why yet, but I wanted to punch him. I flipped up the cover and turned the first page: January . . . February.

If I'd been much older than twenty-seven, chances were good I might've had a heart attack, although the chances of my having an aneurysm were still pretty high.

Rain's arms were crossed above her head. She was dressed in a tight, long-sleeved red turtleneck, cropped high enough to expose the bottom half of her perfect breasts. The matching bikini bottoms were cut in a low V. Her lips and nails were blood red, and her nipples pointy enough through the stretchy fabric to cut glass. The stem of two dark red cherries was gripped between her teeth.

"We cannot tell a lie," the caption read. "Miss February has us tongue-tied."

Fuck.

"Does your wife know you have this?" I asked, trying to deflect some of what I was feeling.

The son of a bitch had the nerve to snort. I tore out the page and tossed the calendar on the floor.

"What do you think that's going to do?" he laughed. "It's last year's calendar, Chase, and they printed thousands of them. More than half the guys in New Jersey probably still have their copies."

"You know what? I think you're jealous. You couldn't get a girl like Rain, so you have to piss all over me because I can."

"That's what you think? You ever notice how many notches she has on her bedpost? You're the latest in a very long line, little brother." He took a few steps back. "And that's not all she's done. Your little plaything poses for magazines as well. She must be one hell of a mother. Maybe you should get her kid a copy of the latest issue so she can take it to school for show and tell. I bet no one would even be surprised."

The blood was pounding in my head. "I think you better shut the fuck up."

He walked toward his office, shaking his head. Before he entered, he turned back.

"Suit yourself, Chase. You say you know what you're doing. I hope so. But don't say I didn't warn you. And if you were planning on bringing her for Thanksgiving, don't. Lorraine won't have her in our house, and I'm standing by my wife." The door to his office slammed shut.

"We weren't coming anyway!" I called after him.

I finished changing the tie rod on the Caravan I'd been working on, then grabbed my stuff and left, even though it was only a little past three.

Rain had gone Christmas shopping with Diane. If I hadn't offered to pick Izzy up at her mother's and bring her to my place, I'd park my ass at the bar on the corner and drink until I didn't want to bash my brother's face in. But I wouldn't drink and drive with Izzy, not even one beer. Besides, if anyone could get my mind off Dylan's bullshit, it was Izzy.

I also wanted a clear head when I talked with Rain later. She looked incredible in that calendar, but the thought of some hairy fuck jerking off to her picture made my skin crawl. And if there were other photos of her out there, more calendars or, god forbid, magazines . . .

The turkey club I had for lunch threatened to reappear.

I checked my phone before starting my truck and found a text.

Rain: Could you stop at my apt for Harvey? Forgot to pack him.

Another reason she should live with me—all this back-and-forth was nonsense. I fired off a text telling her I'd take care of it.

The luncheonette was closed when I got there, and the parking lot was empty. The weather suited my mood, cold and miserable. Between the low pressure and my fucking brother, my head was pounding. At least I knew where Rain kept the aspirin.

I let myself in with my key. On the small kitchen table was a large bouquet of red roses. There had to be at least two dozen. I debated for less than ten seconds. It was wrong, but I opened the card anyway.

One for every month I've loved you. Missing you. P

I crushed the card in the palm of my hand and pulled out my phone.

"Dorinda? I'm in Rain's apartment. Did you put these flowers in here?"

"Yeah. She'd left by the time they came, so I just put them upstairs. Why'd you send her flowers?"

"They're not from me."

Several beats of silence followed.

"Oh. Crap."

I wanted to throw the vase against the wall. "Listen, I'm going to be a little late picking Izzy up."

"Don't do anything foolish, Chase. Rain doesn't even know. Just throw them out."

"Oh, I'm going to throw them out all right." I hung up before she could say anything else.

I grabbed the flowers and threw the arrangement on the floor of my truck, splashing water onto the carpet and the door, which pissed me off even more. The notes, and now this? This loser was lucky I wasn't heading for his house instead of his office.

I was still pissed that Rain hadn't told me Preston had been leaving notes on her car, having to find that out from Wally, but I understood why she wasn't telling me. She had nothing to do with it, and I couldn't hold what Preston was doing against her.

But I could sure as hell could hold it against him. Like maybe against his throat.

Jamison Architectural Associates was a two-story glass-and-metal building. Fancy topiaries, pruned into balls and cones lined the walkway from the parking lot to the front door. I grabbed the vase and the roses, half of which were now broken, and stormed in through the front doors.

The receptionist eyed me hesitantly. "Can I help you?"

"I want to see Preston."

"If you have a delivery, I can take it." Given the condition of the flowers, she must have thought I was the worst delivery man ever.

"This is personal. I need to speak with him myself."

"Which Mr. Jamison?" she asked. "Junior or the third?"

"There's three of them? Fucking unbelievable. The third, I guess."

She glared at me and then punched a few numbers into her switchboard.

"Mr. Jamison, there's a delivery man here to see you . . . No, sir. He said he needs to see you personally."

She hung up and gave me a smug once-over. "He'll be right down."

Good. There would be a witness to what I was about to say.

The jackass kept me waiting a good ten minutes while I paced the lobby, carrying the beat-up roses, which didn't improve my mood at all. A door opened on the second floor, and Preston appeared behind a glassed-in wall and then descended a flight of open stairs into the lobby.

"Hey, Chance. Am I right?" He held out his hand, greeting me genially, although casting a wary glance at the battered arrangement I held in my arm.

"Save it, Preston." I shoved the vase into his hands, spilling what remained of the water over his slacks and shoes and sending petals spiraling onto the travertine tile. "The next time you send something to Rain or make a personal delivery to her car, I won't return it to your office. I'll bring it directly to your fiancée. Understood?"

"How is this any concern of yours?" he asked, his voice low enough so that the receptionist couldn't hear him, although given the bent of her body, she was listening intently.

"It's my fucking concern because she's my fucking girlfriend, and I want you to stay the hell away from her."

He reached out to grab my arm, I assume to pull me farther from the front desk, but I raised my hands and stepped back. "I really wouldn't do that if I were you."

"You? Rain's boyfriend? You've got to be kidding. Since when?"

He laughed, and if there hadn't been a witness sitting right there, I would have knocked some teeth down his throat.

"Longer than you might think."

"Oh, really? So when she slept with me last time we were together, she was cheating on you?"

My fist caught his upper lip, cutting my hand in the process. He staggered but was able to right himself before he went down. Several drops of dark red blood dripped from his mouth onto his bright white shirt.

He was smart enough not to fight back, probably for two reasons: one, I was angrier than he was and could inflict a hell of a lot more damage, and two, he didn't want anyone asking questions. The ruckus had already attracted several bystanders, and the receptionist threatened to call the police.

"I don't think that's necessary, Valarie," Preston said. "I think this gentleman is leaving. But if he shows up again," he announced as I made my way to the door, "you will call the police."

I issued him a warning as well.

"You stay away from Rain—or next time, it won't be you I'm coming to see."

CHAPTER THIRTY-FIVE

Chase

I'd been in bed for a while when Rain came home. The door to the guest room clicked open. She'd stopped to check on Izzy. A few minutes later, I heard water running in the bathroom. Afterwards, she slipped in beside me, put her arm around my waist, and snuggled in, pressing her naked flesh against me. I put my arm over hers, but I didn't turn around.

"You awake?" she whispered.

"Sort of."

She giggled, and in spite of how worked up I'd been, I smiled. I loved that laugh.

"How was your day?" she asked, assuming that being "sort of awake" meant I felt like talking.

"Not good."

"I'm sorry. You want to talk about it?"

"Not really."

She was quiet for few beats, then asked if she'd done anything wrong.

"No," I said, but because I was a fool, I added, "not really."

"'Not really' isn't the same as no. What did I do?"

"It's fine, Rain. Let's just forget it."

She sat up and turned on the light. I groaned. I should have just kept my mouth shut.

I rolled over and squinted up at her and those perfect tits.

"Jesus, cover up. I can't argue with you while you're sitting there naked."

"Now we're arguing? We went from zero to sixty in less than ten seconds. You want to tell me what the hell I did?"

"I said you didn't do anything wrong."

"You said 'not really.' That means something."

"Lower your voice or you'll wake Izzy."

"You're pissed. You're wearing pajamas."

"I was cold."

"You never wear pajamas."

"Yes, I do."

"Liar."

"Now you're pissing me off." I rolled away from her and pulled the covers up.

"What the hell happened to your hand?" She grabbed my wrist.

"Nothing."

"You were in a fight."

"Go to sleep, Rain. We'll talk about it in the morning."

"The hell we will. We'll talk about it now."

I huffed loudly and rolled over again. "I had a fight with my brother—"

"You hit your brother?"

I glared up at her, trying to avoid her breasts. "Would you let me finish?"

By the set of her jaw, I knew I was pissing her off. I was pretty fucking pissed myself.

"Afterward, I left work early and I went to your place to pick up Harvey." Who I'd forgotten anyway. "And I found a bunch of roses sitting on the kitchen table with a card that read, 'One for every month I've loved you. Missing you.' And signed with a big, fat 'P.' I called your mother and she thought they were from me, so she put them in your apartment."

"I didn't see any flowers." Her jaw was so tight I was surprised she could speak. "What did you do with them?"

"I undelivered them."

"What?"

"I undelivered them. And I told him the next time he sends you something or leaves a fucking note on your car, I would undeliver them to his fiancée."

Her eyes widened.

"Why didn't you tell me about the notes?"

"Because I didn't want you to get upset. I threw them away. How did you find out? The only person I told was—" She shook her head and frowned. "Wally, right?"

"Yep."

"Why didn't you say anything?"

"Because I trust you, and I figured you didn't tell me for the exact same reason you said. Although you know, for as much as you cared about him, part of me still has to wonder—"

She leaned over and kissed me. Every time I tried to speak, she did it again until I seemed appropriately silent.

"Let's get a few things straight," she said. "I'm nuts about you. Okay?"

I nodded.

"Also, you shouldn't open my mail or my deliveries, but in this case, I understand and I forgive you. But it's not okay to go over there. Please tell me you didn't hit him."

She wasn't the only one who could set her mouth in a tight, thin line.

"Chase!"

"Why? Do you care what happens to him?"

"No. But I care what happens to you. Didn't you think he might have you arrested or sue you for damages or something?"

"Yeah, which is why I didn't throw the fucking vase through the windshield of his Corvette."

"Oh, baby." She climbed on top of me and pulled my undershirt up over my head. "I love that you're defending my honor and going around beating people up for me, I do, but you don't have to. You're all that matters. Preston can send me all the flowers and jewelry he wants, and it won't change a thing. I don't want him back. I've been happier in these past couple months than I've been in my entire life." She kissed my neck and started working her way down my chest. "I mean that."

"Jewelry? He sent you jewelry?"

She shook her head. "Not really."

"What do you mean, 'not really'?"

She sighed and sat up again. "A few days before he and Suzanne got engaged, he showed up at my place late at night. First he asked me to marry him, which was a desperate, bullshit move on his part, and then he begged me not to shut him out. He gave me all the same lame excuses he's been giving me since I found out about Suzanne. I told him not to bother me anymore, but he got upset and he made me feel guilty—"

"He made you feel guilty?" I snorted. "That's rich." I couldn't believe I was hearing this.

"Yes, I felt bad, but I told him it was over. I was pretty sure I wanted it to be over, even if he had ended it with her." She drew her finger down my chest and smiled. "You see, I'd met this very handsome mechanic—"

"You felt so bad you slept with him, right? In spite of telling me now that you already had feelings for me at the time."

The second the words left my mouth, I knew I'd made a huge mistake.

She climbed off me and stood before I could grab her, then stormed out of the room.

I snatched her robe off the floor and followed her into the living room.

"You're standing in front of the window naked."

She wrenched the robe out of my hand. "I don't give a fuck."

"I'm sorry." I put my arms around her. She struggled, but I was a lot stronger. When she calmed down, I relaxed my grip. Which is when she elbowed me in the stomach.

"I'm with you. Isn't that enough?" she demanded. "I don't owe you any explanation for anything I did or who I did it with before we were together. Did he tell you I slept with him? Is that why you hit him?"

"Yeah."

"I'd like to hit you both."

She turned away and stared out the window. I waited a few minutes, hoping she'd cool off, then carefully put my arms around her. She didn't fight me this time.

"I love you," I whispered, watching her reflection in the glass. "I'm sorry I'm acting so crazy. I don't know what's come over me." I rocked her gently. "I've never been jealous or possessive before, and I do trust you. It's everyone else I have a problem with."

"I'm not interested in anyone else."

"I know." I kissed the top of her head. "I'll try my best to start behaving like I belong in this century, okay?"

I could tell from her reflection that she was smiling.

We'd cleared one hurdle, but it probably wasn't a good time to ask her about the calendar.

CHAPTER THIRTY-SIX

Chase

I told Rain my brother and sister-in-law were going to her family's for Thanksgiving and taking my mother with them, so if she wanted, we could go to Diane and Wally's for dinner. I hated lying to her, but I couldn't tell her the truth either. I hadn't spoken to Dylan since our fight unless I had to. He didn't appear in any hurry to speak to me either.

When I called to invite my mother for dinner on Friday so she could meet Rain, things didn't go any smoother.

"Chase, your brother is worried about your relationship with that woman."

"He's jealous."

"Don't be ridiculous."

"I'm not. You need to meet her for yourself—and before you come over here with any preconceived notions, which I assume are coming from Lorraine for some reason, since Dylan doesn't even know Rain. I'm asking you to judge her for yourself. I'm in love, Mom, and I don't need to justify my feelings to you or Dylan or to anyone else."

"You're being awfully defensive, sweetheart."

"I'm sorry, but I didn't expect my brother to uninvite me for the holiday because his wife doesn't like my girlfriend."

"From what I understand, he didn't uninvite you. He just didn't invite this young woman."

"Same thing. And as far as Rain is concerned, you all are going to dinner at Lorraine's parents' house. I'm not going to hurt her feelings and tell her she wasn't invited. And I'll tell you another thing: until Dylan apologizes, he's on my shit list."

"He's your brother!"

"Exactly." I was being rude, but I didn't care, even if it was my mother. "He should know better. I'll see you Friday night. Enjoy your Thanksgiving."

My mood hadn't lightened much by Thursday, which only served to remind me of the way my family was responding to Rain and to me, by extension. I'd promised to try to handle this jealousy thing better. It was a completely new and unexpected emotion for me.

When I picked Rain up at her apartment Thursday afternoon, I was relieved to see she was wearing a simple, light-colored lace dress with a high neckline. It was still tight and short, but it was one of the most conservative things I'd ever seen her wear. She looked beautiful—and yes, sexy—and I told her so as she slipped into her coat.

She grabbed two apple pies off the kitchen counter as we headed for the door.

"I thought you were making a pumpkin pie." Pumpkin was my favorite.

"I was, but when I opened the can, it made me gag. It must have been bad, so I tossed it and made another apple. My mom's making a pumpkin pie and bringing it with her, so you'll have your pumpkin pie. Oh, and I invited her for dinner tomorrow night, so she can meet your mom too."

She gave me a big smile and I smiled back.

"That will be nice."

Actually? It might be anything but nice.

I loved Dorinda. Rain took after her in a lot of ways, so how could I not love her mother? She was sweet to me even before Rain and I were a couple. And she was in my corner, and for that I was grateful. But like Rain, she was a bit flashy. She was only in her mid-forties but dressed like she was in her twenties. She easily pulled it off, but I cringed at what my mother would think. My mother was the grandmotherly type—and a bit judgmental, which worried me.

"Will Chase's mommy be my new grandma?" Izzy asked from the back seat.

"Izzy!" Rain spun around. "What did I tell you about asking those kinds of questions?"

I glanced in the rearview mirror. The kid must take after her mother in the psychic department.

Izzy's little face crumpled. "Sorry."

I couldn't help laughing. "What kinds of questions has she been asking?"

I glanced over at Rain. She didn't blush easily, but her cheeks were pinker than usual.

Before she could answer, Izzy did.

"I only asked if you were gonna be my daddy."

"Izzy!"

"And what did Mommy say?" I persisted.

"She told me to mind my pool cues."

"P's and Q's," Rain corrected her.

"I don't like peas," Izzy said.

Rain sighed. "Never mind. Just don't ask questions like that. It's not polite."

I reached across the console, took Rain's hand, and gave it a squeeze. "I don't have any problem with questions like that."

She shot me a look, but I caught the light in her eyes. "You mind your pool cues too."

I smiled all the way to Diane and Wally's, but it faded almost as soon as Rain took off her coat. I was waiting to hand her the pies when Wally whistled.

Rain's somewhat conservative dress wasn't conservative at all. A heart-shaped cutout exposed most of her back, enough to see that she wasn't wearing a bra. She was all smiles with the attention, and as she turned to carry the pies into the kitchen, Wally swatted her bottom with an open palm.

I took off my jacket and jammed it against his chest. I leaned in close enough so that only he could hear me.

"You do that again, and you and I are going to have a serious problem."

He looked about to laugh, but when he realized I wasn't joking, he checked himself.

"C'mon, man. I don't mean nothing by it. I've always done that."

"Well, it's going to stop. And if you know of anyone else who thinks it's okay to put their hands on her, then you better let them know I won't tolerate it. She'll be treated with respect just like everybody else's wife or girl, or I'm going to start busting heads."

Wally rubbed the spot on his chest where my fingers had connected. "What the hell's gotten into you?"

Maybe I was overreacting, but my blood was boiling. No one had the right to do that to her, although she should've been the one to say something about it. It had been going on so long, I don't think she even knew it was wrong anymore. That was just the way they treated her. My chest tightened as I thought of the calendar. For some reason, she treated her body like it was a public commodity—like sharing it was part of who she was. Well, it was going to stop. I had no idea how I'd get that across to her, but I would.

"Just . . . don't. Okay?"

He raised his hands in surrender and directed me to a cooler on the deck with the beers. "Take two," he suggested.

When I came back in through the kitchen, Rain was trying to extricate herself from an older man, probably Diane's great-uncle, who seemed intent on dancing with her, even though there was no music. I assumed she could read my mind, because when she saw me watching, the look on her face said: Let it go. I'm handling it.

I shook my head, found a seat on the couch, and watched Green Bay get trounced by the Lions for the next two hours.

***

Izzy fell asleep in the truck on the way home. I carried her into the house, slipped off her coat and her shoes, then tucked her under the covers. Before I left the room, I dropped a kiss on the top of her head and ran my fingers over her soft, golden curls. We'd planned to read another chapter from The Lion, the Witch and the Wardrobe tonight, and I'd been looking forward to cuddling with her. Our nightly ritual had become one of my favorite parts of the day.

"She's out like a light," I said, returning to the living room.

Rain stood by the door, her coat still on.

"I think she wore herself out with Diane's nephews," I said, slipping off my jacket. She still hadn't moved. "What's wrong?" I asked.

The look she gave me bore through me like a laser beam.

"What are these?" I caught a flash of red on glossy paper. My jaw stilled into a tight line.

One perfect eyebrow arched upward. "Well?"

She held up at least a dozen months' worth of February, torn from calendars throughout Millstone.

I felt like I'd swallowed the Sahara. My tongue cemented to the roof of my mouth. I blinked. Twice.

"Chase."

I might even have stopped breathing. Or maybe I was just buying time because I didn't have a defensible answer.

Still gripping the evidence, she folded her arms and angrily tapped the toe of her cheetah-print stiletto in my direction.

I jutted out my chin and tried to look indignant. "What were you doing in my glove compartment?"

Suspicion flashed across her face. "That's your answer? How long have you had these? And why?"

Shit. She probably thought I was a fucking stalker.

"Not long." I stared at the wall above her head, afraid if I made eye contact, she might incinerate me.

"Just one, I might be flattered—but there are fourteen here, Chase. Fourteen. That's creepy. And a little stalky."

My eyes slid down to meet hers. I frowned. "I'm not a stalker."

"You're something," she sighed, slipping out of her coat. When she turned to hang it in the closet, I got another panorama of her bare back.

I didn't dare say what I was actually thinking: That the way she dressed sometimes made me act like a crazy person; a maniac running around town and demanding the month of February from anyone stupid enough to admit they still possessed a year-old calendar.

"That's it?"

I shrugged.

She tossed the calendar pages on the coffee table and headed for the bedroom. I forced my feet to follow.

"Because I don't like the idea of other guys looking at you like that. I can't help it. I'm a guy. I know how we think. I look at that picture, and my damn jeans get tight, but that's okay. You're supposed to make my jeans tight. I just don't want you making anyone else's jeans tight."

She pulled a face. At first she looked like she would lash out at me, but she spoke to me as if I were a child. Why not? I was acting like one.

"Relax, okay? Very few men have ventured where you've gone." She gave me a sassy little smile and shrugged. "Besides, it was a fundraiser for pediatric cancer. And I wasn't even naked. I was wearing a turtleneck, for god's sake."

A turtleneck? Seriously? I struggled to format an answer to this that wouldn't piss her off, some way to point out that while her get-up did in fact have a neck and sleeves, it had no middle or bottom.

"And I might as well tell you, I've done some other modeling for the photographer who shot the calendar. Just some artsy black and white stuff. I'm not even sure what he does with them." She shrugged again, as if that were that, then slipped her arms from her dress and let it fall to the floor. Just as I'd suspected. No bra. I peeled my eyes off her breasts.

"And if this bothers you that much, then you should be glad I turned down that other offer."

"What other offer?"

"The magazine," she said, slipping into her robe and cinching it tight. "After I did the calendar, I got a call from a magazine offering me twenty-five hundred dollars to pose naked. I didn't take it—so relax, okay?" She gave me a dismissive shake of her head. "Good thing. Not that I have any problem with posing naked, but after this, I could just picture you driving all over the country and pounding on doors, demanding that men hand over their copies of Delicious." She frowned.

"And just so you know, there would've been an additional twenty-five hundred if they'd used me on the cover."

Brains. Mine. All over the bedroom wall.

"What?" She looked annoyed.

"Nothing." I shook my head, the same head that was trying to wrap itself around what she was telling me.

"It's no big deal, Chase. Jeez." She whipped open the robe and threw it on the floor, knowing damn well what she was doing to me now. "It's just a body. Everyone has one. Some people can sing, some can paint, some are good at math, some can tune an engine until it hums. My talent is this. I don't even have to work at it."

She strutted past me and into the bathroom. Again, it was as if my feet had grown roots.

"You'll probably have a problem with this too," she called out over the sound of running water, "but I was a life drawing model at the college last spring." I could tell from her garbled voice that she was brushing her teeth. "I'm sure if you go up to Rutgers, you might be able to bribe someone to give you a list of all the students in that class. If most of them live in the dorms, you won't even have to travel too far to strong-arm them into giving you their work."

When she noticed me leaning against the doorjamb, she wiped her mouth and grinned.

"Funny," I growled.

"You're the one who's funny, caveman—"

I didn't let her finish. I grabbed her around the waist and tossed her over my shoulder. "I can't help it. This," I said, slapping her bare ass, "is mine. I don't want anyone else seeing it or touching it—or any of your other assets."

I tossed her on the bed, and was relieved to see the annoyed look in her eyes had been replaced with something I could work with.

She gripped my T-shirt in her hand and pulled me down on top of her.

"You're a caveman, all right. But you're my caveman."

***

"How about roast beef and mashed potatoes tomorrow night?" Rain asked after some pretty amazing makeup sex. Not that we'd had a fight. It had been more of a loud discussion. But I still needed to make it up to her, because in my head, it could have gone much worse.

I opened my eyes. "Who doesn't like roast beef?"

"I know you like it. Does your mother?"

"I guess. Don't fuss."

"I'm meeting your mother for the first time. I want her to like me. I want her to know I can cook, and I'm taking good care of you."

"I told her you're taking great care of me. She'll love you." I planted a kiss on her forehead and rolled away. It was hard to face her when I was worried that my mother might not love her, at least not right off the bat, thanks to my brother and his busybody wife.

Which was why I stupidly asked what she would be wearing tomorrow night.

"Why?"

"Just wondering. My mom's kind of old-fashioned, you know?"

"No, I don't know. Is there something wrong with the way I dress?"

Yes. "No. It's just that it wouldn't hurt for you to cover up once in a while. You're a beautiful girl, Rain. You'd look good in anything."

"Except what I usually wear? What was wrong with the dress I had on today?"

I flipped back toward her. "It had no back. Weren't you cold?"

With the look I was getting, the temperature had dropped in the bedroom.

"I was fine. It was a nice dress."

"It was. It would have been great for cocktails at a club in Manhattan, but it was a little much for Thanksgiving dinner with friends."

"Oh, now it's too much. I thought it wasn't enough."

I rolled on top of her, pinning her in place, and stared down at her until I could see a crack in her stern facade.

"Fine," she said, trying to hide a smile. "I won't wear that dress when your mother comes tomorrow. But I do have a red turtleneck I could probably wear."

CHAPTER THIRTY-SEVEN

Rain

Chase had to work Friday and since I had the day off, I didn't set the alarm and ended up sleeping until well past nine. When I woke, Izzy was watching cartoons in the living room with a bowl of cereal and a half-gallon of milk, half of which seemed to have pooled on Chase's glass-topped coffee table.

"Izzy, you're making a mess," I said, rushing into the kitchen for the paper towels. "Did you climb onto the counter to get the cereal down?"

She shook her head, not even bothering to look at me, entranced by the cartoons.

"Uh-uh. Daddy left it on the table for me with a note that said not to wake you."

Oh my god. Not this again. "Izzy! It's Chase. Don't call him Daddy."

Twin pools of icy blue stared up at me. "He said it's okay."

My daughter wanted a daddy, and I couldn't think of a better one, but that still didn't make it right. The last thing I wanted to do was scare him away, even though he was the one pushing for us to live together. It was all too good—except for that whole jealousy thing—that I kept waiting for the other shoe to drop.

After cleaning up Izzy's mess and getting her dressed, I made a quick pass around the apartment, scrubbed the kitchen and the bathroom, and then Izzy and I went to the grocery store.

Roast beef was a specialty of mine. I was also making Chase's favorite mashed potatoes, glazed Brussels sprouts, an autumn chopped salad with dried cranberries, and for dessert, chocolate cake from scratch. My mother was bringing the wine.

Back at Chase's apartment, I put the cake together first, and while it was baking, I prepped the rest of the dishes. I fried bacon and toasted the nuts for the salad, chopped the cranberries, and washed the lettuce. At four o'clock, I seasoned the roast and left it to rest on the counter, then set the table.

Izzy was playing in the guest room, which was looking more and more like a little girl's room than a spare bedroom in a bachelor pad, and I still needed to shower. But first, I needed to figure out what I was going to wear. After allowing myself a few moments of panic, I settled on black leggings and a belted sweatshirt tunic. It was the most conservative thing I had with me, although now that Chase had made me feel self-conscious about how I dressed, I worried that it still wouldn't be stodgy enough for his mother.

I laid the items out on the bed and myself alongside them. I needed to rest my eyes. Just for a few minutes or I wouldn't make it through dinner.

It was dark when Chase shook me awake. "Babe. Rain. Wake up!"

I squinted up at him, trying to make out his face.

"What time is it?"

"It's almost five thirty."

"Why are you waking me so early?"

"In the evening. My mom will be here in a half hour, and you haven't even put the roast in yet."

I sprung up. "What? How? Are you sure?"

"Yeah, come on. I put the oven on, but I don't know what temperature."

"Shit. I just lay down for a second. I'm sorry." I flew into the kitchen and cranked the oven up to three seventy-five—higher than I'd usually cook a roast, but I didn't have time to do it slow. I put the roast in, slammed the oven door shut, and flew back down the hall. Chase had stripped out of his work clothes.

"I need a shower," I announced.

"So do I."

"We can take one together."

"Yeah, because that will make us get in and out faster." His frown showed how ridiculous he thought that was.

"I'm serious." I yanked my T-shirt over my head and tossed it in the corner. "I need to get in the shower too. You'll just have to keep your hands to yourself."

What a joke. He didn't even try to keep his hands to himself, and by the time we got out of the shower, I was hoping his mother would stay for about five minutes and leave, so we could pick up where we'd left off. I'd been so tired lately I was falling asleep almost as soon as my head hit the pillow.

Being in a normal relationship was wearing me out.

When I opened the door to dart down the hall to the bedroom, Izzy was speaking with someone in the living room.

"Chase is going to be my new daddy."

"Oh god," I whispered as I stepped back into the bathroom and pushed the door closed quietly.

"What are you doing?"

"I think your mother's early. Either that or Izzy just told the UPS lady that you're her new daddy."

"Will you stop freaking out about that?"

"It's been two months, Chase. You and I haven't even discussed it." I was practically hissing. "Do you think my daughter and your mother should be the first to hash it out?"

"Don't worry about it." He poked his head out the door and when the coast was clear, he motioned for me to make a dash for the bedroom. As I did, he went out to greet his mother wearing a towel. I knew she'd seen him that way before, but it probably didn't reflect very well on me.

"Everything's fine," he said, joining me a few minutes later as I yanked a comb through my wet, tangled hair. I hadn't had nearly enough time for conditioner. "Oh, and your mother just arrived."

"Are you kidding? She's late for everything and today she decides to be on time?" I slipped into my clothes, but I still had to dry my hair and put my makeup on.

"That's not all. She brought Bert."

Bert was my mother's latest boyfriend. Although he was funny, he could be loud and a little obnoxious. He was also a little grabby, especially with my mother. Not that she seemed to mind.

"Could you set another place at the table and see what they all want to drink? The roast has another hour yet, and I didn't plan any appetizers. You think your mother would mind if we started with chocolate cake and worked our way backward?"

"Stop worrying. Everything will be fine. She's gonna love you." He gave me the fastest kiss ever and left me to finish getting ready.

While Chase entertained everyone and hopefully put a lid on Izzy, I dried my hair and pulled it into a loose bun. I was about to skip the eyeliner, but I just couldn't do it. I did, however, forego my usual wings in attempt to be more conservative.

It wouldn't have mattered if I'd taken twice as long to dress. The moment I met her, I sensed that Mrs. Holgate didn't like me. What I also knew was that her entire opinion of me had been formulated long before we met, thanks to Lorraine. When I'd told Chase I knew Lorraine from school, I'd failed to mention that her best friend had been dating Izzy's father, who dumped her for me.

If Lorraine still hated me for that, then so be it. She wasn't the first person to be wrong about me.

"Mrs. Holgate." I held out a clammy hand and tried to smile. "It's so nice to meet you. Please forgive me for being so late. The day just got away from me. Welcome."

She gave my hand a limp bob. "I've been here before."

"Of course you have. I guess you should welcome me, then." My laugh erupted like a donkey's bray. Chase looked startled, and my mother wore a pained expression. "What can I get you to drink? Anyone? Maybe I better have a drink."

"Why don't you have a seat?" Chase said. "I'll get you a drink."

I nodded and crossed over to my mother to give her a kiss. She pulled me into a bear hug.

"Calm down," she whispered between gritted teeth. "You're acting like a fool."

"Thanks, Mom," I whispered back. "Oh, and thanks for making me look like the conservative one."

"No problem." She winked as I pulled away. Mom wore skintight black jeans and a black V-neck sweater that showed a considerable amount of cleavage. She also had on a pair of leopard-print stiletto ankle boots, and when she moved, her chunky gold jewelry tinkled like a tiny symphony.

In contrast, Chase's mother wore flats, dark slacks, and a gray sweater set that might have been cashmere. The requisite single strand of pearls was draped around her neck. The only thing that surprised me was that she wasn't clutching them.

"Hi, Bert." I'd only meant to acknowledge him, but he caught me off guard, treating me to a face full of thick chest hair courtesy of his overly enthusiastic hug.

When he finally freed me, I saw that Chase had set out a bowl of nuts, a bowl of olives, and some cheese. At least his mother wouldn't starve to death while waiting for dinner. I squeezed onto the sofa beside my mother.

Chase handed me a glass of wine. I took a mouthful, then popped up like a timer on a roast chicken. "I have to finish the potatoes and check the roast."

I had cooked the potatoes earlier. I heated some cream and butter and then mashed them, grated some cheese, and popped them in the oven to bake while the roast finished cooking. I checked the temperature. Hopefully, Mrs. Holgate liked her meat rare, because that was how I was serving it. Twenty more minutes and then a few minutes to rest. If I could keep everyone happy that long, we could start the salad.

Conversation during dinner was polite. Chase kept trying to draw his mother out, but she wouldn't cooperate. Used to a more animated dinner table, even when it was just the two of us, Izzy was surprisingly quiet, which was probably a good thing, given her new focus. My guess was that she was as uncomfortable as I was.

When dinner was over and I stood to clear the table, Bert and my mother stood as well.

"Sorry, darling, we're meeting friends for drinks and we're already late."

"You're leaving?" I gave her a pleading look, but she ignored it.

"Sorry. Save me a piece of cake." She smiled down at Mrs. Holgate. "Rain makes the best chocolate cake. When I put it on the menu, we sell out within a half hour."

"I thought you were a bartender," Mrs. Holgate said, ignoring the comment about my cake.

"Just a few days a week to make ends meet. I cook at my mother's restaurant. That's my real job."

She lifted her eyebrows. "Hmm."

"Rain is a wonderful cook, obviously," my mother said. "I wish I could pay her what she's worth."

Mrs. Holgate's face contorted into something that resembled a smile, but she didn't comment on dinner one way or another.

After my mother and Bert left, I finished clearing the table and put on a pot of coffee. I had given Izzy a piece of cake earlier, and now I told her to say goodnight. She was polite with Mrs. Holgate, but when she came to Chase, she wrapped her little arms around his neck and begged him to put her to bed.

"Not tonight, sweetie," I said. "Chase hasn't seen his mommy in a while, so I'll put you to bed and read you a quick story. He can put you to bed tomorrow night."

My daughter was not happy.

"I promise." He leaned in and whispered loudly, "and it won't be a quick story either. The Lion, the Witch and the Wardrobe. Tomorrow night. Three chapters. Just you and me."

"It's a date." She squeezed him tightly.

That time, Mrs. Holgate's smile seemed almost sincere.

Despite wanting a longer story, Izzy fell asleep quickly. I had almost pulled the door closed when I heard angry whispers coming from the dining room.

"You have nothing in common with this girl," Mrs. Holgate said. "And what happens to that poor child when you finally realize that? You'll disrupt her home, her life. I can't believe you're being so foolish. This isn't like you to rush into something like this. I would think you would take your time and find the right woman. Maybe try to make things right with Jennifer. I understand looking to have a good time. Have your fun. That's all girls like that are good for. God knows your father—"

"That's enough, Mom. I don't know if it's Dylan or Lorraine telling you this, but I expected you to make up your own mind and not listen to either of them."

"I'm basing my opinion on what I see with my own eyes. For god's sake, Chase, that outfit looks like it was painted on her."

I took a few deep breaths, then pulled the door closed with a snap. The voices fell away.

"More coffee?" Chase asked his mother, louder than necessary.

It hurt for him to pretend that what I'd just heard hadn't happened. The child in me wanted to climb into bed and crawl under the covers. The teenager wanted to march into the other room and tell her to fuck off. The adult me plastered a smile on her face and returned to the dining room.

"No, darling," Mrs. Holgate said, standing as I entered. "I should be going. I promised your brother I wouldn't stay out late. I don't want them worrying about me driving those dark roads by myself."

I wanted to be the gracious hostess and encourage her to stay, even offer to drive her home and drop her car off in the morning so she could stay later. I'd looked forward to hearing about Chase from the person who knew him best. I wanted to do all those things, but I could hardly open my mouth. I could barely manage a smile as she thanked me for dinner.

"Your mother's right. You're a very good cook, Rain."

Chase slipped his arm around my waist so ferociously I almost stumbled. I tried to swallow the lump in my throat, then croaked out something resembling a thank you.

"Will you be staying in the area long, Mrs. Holgate?" I asked, toying with the masochistic idea of trying to win her over with another dinner.

"Um . . . No. Actually, I'm heading home tomorrow."

Chase had told me she would be staying until Tuesday. Deer hunting season started Monday, and Chase and Dylan had been planning to head into the woods early that morning. Lorraine had to work, so his mother was going to watch the boys. Chase no longer had plans to go hunting. Maybe Dylan wasn't going either.

"That's too bad." I smiled up at Chase. "I was hoping to hear some stories about Chase when he was younger." When I looked back at her, I saw no warmth in her eyes. "Perhaps next time."

I knew that as far as Mrs. Holgate was concerned, there would be no next time. She slipped her arms into the coat Chase held out for her. I wanted to thank her for coming but caught myself. I didn't want to be reminded again that it was not my place to thank her for coming to her son's home.

Instead, I held out my hand.

"It was nice meeting you, Mrs. Holgate." I left it at that.

She looked down at my hand before accepting it into her own, mumbled something I didn't catch, and without meeting my eyes, she turned to go.

While Chase walked his mother to the car, I began stashing leftovers. That would be all I could manage tonight. I wanted a glass of wine and a hot bath, but I knew he'd want to climb in with me.

For the first time since we'd been together, I didn't think I could manage his affection. I felt raw and inferior, and I didn't want him to know I'd heard them talking. I didn't want him to be embarrassed—or worse, to learn that she had convinced him that she was right.

It was like meeting Preston's parents all over again, but this time, it hurt a lot more.

I was wedging the last plastic container into the refrigerator when he came back inside. He slipped his arms around my waist and kissed the spot behind my ear. My knees wanted to bend, and the rest of me wanted to lean into him and have him prove that whatever his mother had said didn't matter.

But I remained stiff. I'd had plenty of practice at trying to protect my battered heart. Granted, I usually failed, but at least I knew what steps to take.

To his credit, he didn't speak. He didn't lie and tell me it went well or that his mother really liked me. He turned me around to face him.

I hoped he couldn't read anything in my eyes.

"Do you mind if I get this in the morning? I'm not feeling too good. I'm just going to head off to bed."

He rested his hand against my forehead. Then replaced his hand with his lips. "I'll clean up. You go rest. Can I make you tea or something?"

I shook my head. "I'm just tired. I'm sure I'll feel better in the morning."

He tilted my mouth up to his. "Thank you for this evening. Everything was amazing."

I swallowed, then smiled. My head bobbing up and down.

"I love you," he called as I pulled away.

"Love you too," I called over my shoulder, afraid to face him. Afraid for him to see the sting of shame branded on my face.

CHAPTER THIRTY-EIGHT

Rain

"No, no, no!"

I stared at the little white wand in my hand. One pink plus sign. I grabbed the package directions again. Just in case the plus sign meant you were positively not pregnant. Nope. Positively pregnant. And stupid. Definitely stupid. What was the sign for that?

I padded around the bathroom, muttering to myself. It had been a week since Chase's mother's disastrous visit. Chase was working. He always worked Saturdays, which made his brother even more of a jerk in my opinion. Not that I knew the guy. I had a feeling Lorraine had already worked her magic on both Dylan and their mother, which would more than explain the family's hostility.

"Focus, Rain." How could I be pregnant? I was on the damn pill—had been since Izzy was born. I loved my daughter, but I wasn't about to do that again. It had to be a defective test.

I snatched Izzy up, buckled her into the car, and made it to the pharmacy just before it closed.

An hour and two more defective tests later, I was still pregnant.

I sat on the edge of the tub and tried to quell the roiling of my stomach. I'd always imagined that the next time I had to reveal I was pregnant, I'd be sitting across the table from the man I loved—my husband, preferably—over a candlelit dinner in a fancy restaurant. I'd take his hand, look lovingly into his eyes, and give him the good news. He'd gather my hands in his, get up from his chair, and pull me into his arms. He'd kiss me and tell me how happy he was. And we'd dance. In my dreams, we'd always dance, because we were that happy.

I let go a deep breath. It came out as a sob.

There would be no restaurant. No handholding. Definitely no dancing. And who knows? Once Chase found out, I might not even have the man I loved. It's not like it hadn't happened to me before.

I read the wand again. Maybe the whole batch was defective.

As much as I hated having to put out the money for a doctor's visit, especially when I wasn't sick, I didn't have a choice.

First thing Monday morning, I'd call my gynecologist.

***

"How?" I wailed at Dr. Hart Monday afternoon. "I'm on the pill."

Shaking her head, she scanned my chart. "The pill is over ninety-nine percent effective when used properly. Are you sure you didn't miss a dose? Even one could be enough."

"Positive." I felt nauseated—nerves or the baby growing inside me, it didn't matter which. I wanted to barf.

"Have you been sick?"

I shook my head. "No. Just a cold a couple months ago."

Her eyebrows shot up. "Did you take anything?"

Seems like we were getting a bit off topic. I was having a life crisis, and she wanted to talk about how to treat a cold.

"I drank lots of fluids and tried to rest, but I was going through a really difficult time. I think stress just brought on the cold in the first place. I'm usually pretty healthy."

"Head cold, chest cold? Flu?"

Was she kidding?

"Chest cold. Cough."

"Drugs?"

"I don't do drugs. Never have."

She smiled. "Not those kind. When you were sick, were you on any kind of medication? Antibiotics, maybe?"

"Yeah. Amoxicillin or something."

"There you go." She closed the chart and set it on the counter. "Lie back so we can see what's going on."

"There I go what?" I cried, not lying back.

"There you go, as in antibiotics affect the efficacy of oral contraceptives. If you were downing lots of grapefruit or OJ as well, that could've helped give those little swimmers even more of a fighting chance."

"What?" They must have heard me in the next room. Maybe even the next town. "Why didn't anyone tell me that? Don't you think it should be on the box or something? I'm pretty sure Minute Maid doesn't warn you that your chances of getting knocked up increase with every glass."

Dr. Hart wasn't doing a very good job not laughing. I, on the other hand, wasn't amused.

"The chances of the orange juice itself being responsible for your pregnancy are pretty slim. I'd point my finger at the antibiotics, and I'm going to bet there's a warning somewhere in that teeny-tiny print you probably didn't bother to read. I'm just surprised the doctor who prescribed your antibiotics didn't recommend you use another method of birth control during your course of treatment."

Too bad Aunt Donna wasn't a doctor, nor had she told me any such thing. And since I'd likely gotten pregnant while on that course of antibiotics, that also meant there was a chance that Chase wasn't the father.

The room started to tilt, and saliva pooled in the back of my throat. Seconds later, my breakfast, including that sneaky glass of orange juice, found its way to the bottom of Dr. Hart's trash can.

CHAPTER THIRTY-NINE

Rain

I didn't know what to expect when I told Chase, so I asked my mother to keep Izzy overnight. Although I probably looked like a zombie when she asked if I was okay, I insisted I was and that I was just tired and needed a little alone time with Chase.

Izzy was disappointed. I think if the opportunity had presented itself, she would have dropped me off at my mother's so she could have a little alone time with Chase instead.

I whipped up another roast beef, since it was Chase's favorite, and made sure the fridge was stocked with Heineken. I grabbed myself a bottle of wine, then put it back. Even though I needed it, I wouldn't be drinking any. Dr. Hart had discussed my options with me, and I knew no matter which side of this development Chase landed on, I would be having a baby.

When Chase's Harley roared up the street and into the garage, I tried to remain calm. It wasn't easy.

He came in through the front door and hung his leather jacket in the closet.

"Roast beef on a Monday? How come you're not working?" His slow, warm smile warmed me all the way to the base of my spine.

I tried to smile back.

"Irena didn't need me, and I had a little extra time, so I thought I'd make something special."

I stuck my head into the fridge for a Heineken. They were right in front of my face, but he didn't need to know that. Feeling only slightly more composed, I grabbed a bottle, slipped the neck into the bottle opener he'd screwed into the side of the counter, and popped off the top. When I handed it to him, he pulled me in for a long, slow kiss.

"Where's Izzy?" he asked after letting go.

"Spending the night with my mom."

I drained the potatoes and began pounding them with the potato masher as if my life depended on it. Chase watched me, an odd expression on his face, then asked if he had time for a shower.

"Yep, about twenty minutes. You want salad?"

"Not if you don't. I'm good with anything," he called as he disappeared down the hall.

"We'll see about that," I muttered.

***

"So," Chase said, slicing into the meat I'd piled onto his plate. "What's going on?"

"What do you mean?"

"Just the two of us and my favorite dinner on a Monday. I figure something's going on."

I frowned. "Why does there have to be anything going on?"

He speared a piece of roast beef. "I don't know. Just seems strange is all. And I miss playing twenty questions at dinner, although I do enjoy having you all to myself."

He put the meat in his mouth and chewed. I should've gone for a tougher cut. It would've kept him busy longer.

He looked up to find me watching.

"What?"

I should probably wait until after dinner. No point having him choke on his roast beef. He was a pretty big guy for me to attempt the Heimlich.

I jumped up from the table. "Want more gravy?"

"It's right here." He held up the gravy boat.

"That's not hot enough. Let me heat it up for you."

"It's fine."

He grabbed my wrist and pulled me back down. Then he set his fork down and pushed his plate away.

"What's going on?"

"Nothing."

"Rain."

"Nothing. Jeez."

He leaned back and folded his arms. I stared at the indentation that separated the long, lean muscles in his forearms, the road map of veins running the length of his arms, the strong hands, the nails that were never quite clean no matter how hard he scrubbed them with Gojo. He waited patiently while my eyes traveled up his Mötley Crüe T-shirt to his face. His lips were pursed. The eyes that always sparkled for me were serious.

"What's going on?"

I took a deep breath and opened my mouth. What came out was a low moan that quickly morphed into a sob.

He pulled my chair from the table with me in it, knelt before me, and took my face into his hands. I kept my eyes closed. It hurt too much to look at him.

"Baby, what's wrong?"

I cried harder.

"Is it your mom? Izzy?"

I shook my head and sobbed louder. He helped me stand and led me into the living room, with me crying the entire way. When we reached the couch, he pulled me into his lap, which only made me cry harder.

"Rain, please." He brushed strands of wet hair off my face. "Tell me what's going on?"

The room was dark. He reached for the lamp, but I grabbed his arm. It would be much easier to say if I couldn't see his reaction, especially if he hated me.

I wiped my eyes with the edge of my sleeve.

"Right around the time we got together—actually a few days before—I was sick. I had some kind of upper respiratory thing, and my aunt got me some antibiotics."

I glanced up to see if he was following me. I could see enough of his face to tell he was clueless, although he looked worried, like I was about to tell him I had something fatal. I pushed ahead.

"Anyway, I was on antibiotics for ten days to help with the infection."

While I spoke, his thumb traced circles on the top of my hand. I stopped speaking for so long that he finally asked if I had gotten sick again. I shook my head.

"Not really."

"Not really?" He rested his forehead against mine. "Please just tell me. You're scaring me."

"Don't hate me."

His hand gripped mine. "Never. I could never hate you."

"Never say never."

He stiffened. "Is this about Preston?"

"No! Um . . . not so much. God. I don't know."

The tears were back. They consumed me as Chase dropped my hand, lifted me off his lap, and stood, looking down at me.

"You're going back to him?"

The accusation was so shocking, I stopped crying. "No! Absolutely not. How could you even ask me that? I love you."

"Then what is it? Whatever's going on here has you bawling your eyes out and me scared shitless. Just say it already, for fuck's sake."

I rolled my lips together and nodded. I blinked several times and squeezed my eyes shut.

"I'm pregnant." For as much as I was afraid of his reaction, I didn't want to miss it either. As the words left my mouth, I squinted up at him.

He ran his hand through his hair.

"Again. Tell me again."

"I'm pregnant?"

It was impossible to read him.

He dropped back onto the couch.

"I thought you were on the pill."

"I am, but when I was sick, I was on antibiotics. Did you know the pill doesn't work if you're on antibiotics?"

He shook his head.

"Me neither. Obviously. And then there's the whole orange juice conspiracy—"

"You're doing this, right?" His eyes met mine. I nodded, and he wove his fingers between mine.

"Okay. When"—he cleared his throat—"when is the baby due?"

"Probably the third week of June."

He nodded, staring down at our entwined hands.

"Chase," I began, "you know there's a possibility—"

He pressed his fingers against my lips. "Stop. Stop talking. If it's okay with you, then as far as I'm concerned, we're having a baby. You and me. We are having a baby."

Fresh tears filled my eyes, and my heart felt as if it would beat right through my ribs.

"Are you sure?"

He lifted my chin and brought his face close to mine.

"I'm sure." His lips brushed mine gently. "I've never been more sure of anything in my life."

CHAPTER FORTY

Rain

Telling my mother turned out to be easier than telling Izzy. We sat at her kitchen table, her drinking coffee and me drinking tea and craving a cup of now-forbidden caffeine.

"If I've learned anything, Rain, it's that life doesn't turn out the way we expect it to. There are things that are much worse than creating a new life." She gave me a sad smile. "Are you happy?"

I pressed my lips together and blinked. "Yeah. Scared, but happy."

"Then that's all that matters." She stood and pulled me in for a hug, kissed my forehead, then she told me to quit Blondie's.

I groaned. Chase was already on me about working two jobs, and now that he had a good excuse to get me out of the bar, I expected him to double down on his efforts.

My mother didn't ask. She just assumed the baby was Chase's. So did Diane. Everyone would assume that. Chase and I were the only ones who understood I could be carrying Preston's child. As far as I was concerned, his name wasn't to be mentioned, like that Michael Keaton movie Beetlejuice—I figured if we avoided saying his name, he'd never materialize. It worked for me.

Surprisingly, Izzy had a meltdown when we told her. We took her to see Santa at the Bridgewater Commons, and then afterward, we stopped for ice cream. She had been chattering away about what she'd asked Santa to bring her, hoping he'd be sure to get her the American Girl doll with the blond hair and blue eyes, and matching pajamas for her and the doll. When she slowed down long enough to stick a spoon into her clown sundae, I told her she was going to be a big sister.

She looked from me to Chase, blinking slowly as her eyes filled with tears. Then she swallowed and set down her spoon.

This was not the excited reaction I had expected. I nervously glanced at Chase.

"Iz, what's wrong?" I asked. "I thought you wanted to be a big sister someday."

The edges of her mouth drooped and quivered. She looked up at Chase, and the first fat tear spilled over and rolled down her cheek into the chocolate syrup at the edge of her mouth.

"What's the matter, sweetheart?" he asked.

"Does that mean you can't be my daddy now?"

Chase's lips parted, but he was at a loss as to what to say. His eyes swept from her to me, a look of near panic on his face.

I swiped at a tear of my own.

A lock of hair escaped from Chase's ponytail as he leaned forward. He pushed it behind his ear, then did the same to one of Izzy's long, gold curls. "Of course not. If it's okay with Mommy, I would love to be your daddy."

He gave me a pleading look. I bit my lip and nodded, praying that I wouldn't start bawling too.

Chase took a deep breath and smiled at me. Then he stood, and in front of Izzy, in the middle of a crowded Somerville Friendly's, he dropped to one knee.

"Isolde Storm, you are my favorite girl, and I've come to love you very, very much. Would you do me the honor of becoming my daughter?"

The nearby tables had gone silent except for an audible gasp from the table beside us. Or maybe it was me.

I don't know how it was even possible, but at that moment, as my daughter hurled herself into Chase's open arms, I fell even deeper in love with him. And it wouldn't have surprised me one bit if just about every woman in that restaurant had fallen in love with him, as well.

CHAPTER FORTY-ONE

Rain

It was the best Christmas I'd ever had, even counting the ones before my father died. Chase put his beautiful heart into everything he did, which was considerable since I was always tired. The doctor reminded me this would pass by the end of the first trimester. I was counting the days.

In the meantime, I had to finally admit working two jobs was getting to be too difficult. While living with Chase made parenting easier, splitting my free time between him and Izzy and still having family time for the three of us was damn near impossible. I'd miss it, but I gave my two weeks' notice at Blondie's. New Year's Eve would be my last day.

I don't think I could have given Chase a better Christmas present. He'd been hinting around that I should quit ever since I agreed to move in with him after we learned I was pregnant. He wanted to take care of his family, he said—me, Izzy, and eventually the new baby. And while I was used to carrying my own load, knowing there was someone who wanted to be there for me night and day, every day, was pretty fucking fantastic.

I also gave him a watch for Christmas, which he said he loved. But I'm pretty sure quitting Blondie's meant a lot more.

Chase gave me an antique silver heart on a chain with a tiny silver key—his heart and the key to it, he said. I loved it, and I hadn't taken it off since he fastened it around my neck Christmas morning.

As for Izzy, he was thoroughly spoiling her. It worried me at bit, at first, but when her own father's postdated check didn't arrive until Christmas Eve, I didn't mind as much. She was six. Was I supposed to wrap the stupid check and stick it under the tree? The least he could've done was send it early enough that I could buy presents and put them under the tree and say they were from him.

So while Christmas itself was the best and New Year's Eve would be my farewell to bartending, we had one other holiday event sandwiched in between: a visit to Chase's mother.

I couldn't say I was looking forward to it, but Chase insisted she'd invited us—all of us. It was obvious how she felt about me, and I had assumed she would have invited Chase to visit on his own.

I'd offered to invite her to our place for Christmas, but he'd told me she would be spending the holiday with her sister.

To be honest, I'd been relieved. She radiated such negative energy, and I didn't want to have to endure that on our first Christmas together. It didn't often get that kind of a reading on someone, which made me think it was especially strong where Mrs. Holgate was concerned.

"Are we there yet?" Izzy moaned from the back seat. Other than a handful of trips to visit Jeff's parents, Izzy's car rides averaged about fifteen minutes, if that. We never really had anywhere to go before.

"Almost, pumpkin." Chase smiled at her in the rearview mirror.

I swiveled in my seat to face her. "You're going to be on your best behavior, right, Iz?"

"Yes, I told you already," she said dramatically.

I bit my lip to keep from laughing. She was six going on sixty.

"Yeah, Mommy," Chase said. "I'm pretty sure I heard her tell you that the last twenty times you reminded her." He wrapped a warm hand around mine and squeezed. "It's going to be fine. What're you so worried about?"

Your mother thinks I'm not right for you, I dress like a streetwalker, and the only thing I'm good for is to have fun before you move on to a real relationship.

"Nothing," I lied. "I'm just not sure I made a very good first impression, and I want her to like me. To like us."

"Nonsense," he lied right back to me. "Last time was great."

The familiar buzz was there as he held my hand, but there was something else, something almost painful. It passed too quickly to register. He let go of my hand, put on the turn signal, and slowed to a stop in front of a roomy brick ranch.

"We're here, Izzy. This is where I grew up."

Her seat belt was off before he'd parked the car. She knew she wasn't supposed to do that, and normally I would've scolded her, but I didn't want to risk walking into Mrs. Holgate's house with a cranky six-year-old.

"Will your daddy be here?" Izzy asked.

"Izzy . . ."

Chase's hands tightened on the steering wheel, but when he answered, his voice remained gentle. "No. My father moved out a long time ago."

While Chase went around to grab the gifts for his mother, I climbed out of the truck and opened the back door to get Izzy. As I helped her down, I whispered against her ear.

"I know it's hard and you want to know all about Chase and his family, but maybe today isn't the day to ask those questions. Let's just have a nice visit and make sure to say all our pleases and thank-yous. Can you do that for me? Please?"

She nodded solemnly. I was asking too much from a child her age, which showed how desperate I was for Mrs. Holgate's approval.

He opened the door without knocking and waited for me to step inside first. Such a gentleman, damn him. I'd have much rather followed him—or better yet, waited in the truck until it was time to leave.

All I could see was beige carpeting, so I wiped my feet like a madwoman, fearful of tracking one speck of dirt on the rug, and then I made sure Izzy did the same.

"Chase!" Mrs. Holgate bustled down the hall toward her son, arms out, ready to grasp him in a hug. I wondered how weird it would be to hug her, but I didn't get the opportunity. She took the bag of gifts from Chase and held out her hand, waiting for his jacket. At least she smiled at me.

"Nice to see you again, Rain. Merry Christmas."

"Merry Christmas, Mrs. Holgate. Thank you for having us—Izzy and me," I added quickly, so she wouldn't point out that her son was family and welcome in his own home any time, or something along that line.

"It's nice to see you too, Isabel."

"Isolde, Mom, not Isabel," Chase said.

I flapped my hand. "Oh, it doesn't matter. Isabel. Isolde. Same difference."

Chase looked at me like I'd lost my mind. "No, it's not. Her name isn't Isabel."

I looked at his mother and shook my head. "Really, you can call her Isabel."

Of course my daughter jumped in. "But that's not my name."

Chase rested his hand on the small of my back, and I focused on the warm vibration, letting it flow from his hand, grounding me. I tried to smile. "Actually, we call her Izzy."

His mother looked at me like I was a bit off my nut.

"Yes, well."

She draped Chase's jacket over a chair in the foyer and motioned for us to do the same. "Let me just put these under the tree. I have some appetizers we can nosh on while we open gifts."

Pictures of Chase and a boy I assumed was Dylan, lined the walls of the foyer. I spotted what must've been Chase's senior picture. His hair was just a little shorter than it was now and slightly blonder, like he'd spent the summer outdoors. His features weren't quite as chiseled, but he had the same strong jawline and full bottom lip. I noted with some satisfaction that Chase was by far the better-looking brother. Not that there was anything wrong with Dylan, other than his taste in women.

Dylan and Lorraine's wedding picture hung on the opposite wall. There appeared to be an equal number of framed photographs of both Chase and Dylan, but while many of Dylan's included Lorraine, an equal number of Chase's included Jennifer. Prom photos from two different years hung side by side. There were a few vacation shots from the beach, probably Cape May, and I couldn't help but feel wildly jealous. Another photo—fuck me—looked to be their engagement photo.

I dragged my eyes back to Chase's senior picture.

"So that's you, huh?"

He followed my finger and groaned. "God, yeah. Don't laugh."

"Are you kidding? You were so cute." I leaned closer. "I would've totally gone all the way with you in high school."

He ran his hand along the back of my neck and gave it a gentle squeeze. "You would've made all my high school dreams come true, and then I would've kicked anyone else's ass if they even thought about getting near you."

"I would've liked that."

His mother's voice interrupted our musings on an imagined past. "Chase, are you coming? I think Isolde would like to open her gifts."

With his hand on the small of my back, Chase guided me to the living room sofa, where he sat down beside me. I'd begun feeling somewhat calmer, but the smell coming from the kitchen hit me in the pit of my stomach. Whatever was cooking had a disagreeably sweet, sickly aroma. I'd carried my bag into the living room with me, thank god, and dug around until I found a peppermint. I popped it into my mouth.

"You okay?" Chase asked, looking concerned.

I willed the saliva gathering at the back of my mouth to stand down. "Uh-huh. I think the ride unsettled my stomach a bit."

Mrs. Holgate picked up a cut-glass plate holding a shivering pink mold of some sort surrounded with crackers and held it in front of me. "Shrimp dip?"

I loved shrimp, but the thought of it embedded in cream cheese, mayonnaise, and tomato soup was more than I could handle at the moment. Not to mention the addition of the peppermint candy.

"You know, I think I'll just have a cracker for now." We'd been here less than ten minutes, and already I'd insulted her. "But it looks delicious."

I swiped two crackers off the tray and nibbled one slowly, praying it would calm the turbulence building in my gut.

"Isolde?" She held the plate in front of Izzy.

"Yuck!"

God help me.

"Iz, we don't say yuck."

Izzy looked up at Mrs. Holgate apologetically. "No thank you, please."

Chase's mother laughed. "Very good. Chase, at least I know you love shrimp dip." She set it down on the coffee table in front of him.

He picked up the gingerbread man dip spreader and scooped so much shrimp dip onto his cracker that I was surprised it didn't break. He must really love that stuff.

"I have some cheese, if you and your daughter would prefer," Mrs. Holgate said. "I could cut some up for you."

"That's not necessary. We're fine. We wouldn't want to ruin our dinner."

"I like cheese," Izzy insisted.

"I know, sweetie, but—"

Mrs. Holgate stood. "I'll get her a few pieces. It's no trouble." Looking down at Izzy, she asked, "Would you like to help me?"

Izzy scrambled to her feet. "Yes please, thank you."

As soon as they left the room, I slumped against Chase. "I'm sorry. I eat practically anything, but this pregnancy has my taste buds all fucked up. I thought I was finished with the nausea by now, but today of all days, it's back with a vengeance." I popped the second cracker into my mouth. "And what is that awful smell?"

"Smell? Like a bad smell?"

It seemed to be getting stronger. I nodded.

He shrugged. "The only thing I smell is roast leg of lamb. It's my mother's specialty, which just proves you're wrong and that she does like you."

My mouth filled with saliva, and I could have sworn Mrs. Holgate's couch was rocking like a small boat on a stormy sea.

"Bathroom?" was all I could manage to get out.

Chase helped me to my feet. "Through the foyer, down the hall, turn, and it's the last door on the right."

I sprinted from the room, narrowly missing Izzy carrying a small plate with sliced cheese and followed by Chase's mother. I prayed the bathroom wasn't as far away as it sounded.

The door slammed behind me and I dropped to my knees, careful not to puke all over the plush salmon-colored toilet lid cover, which reminded me way too much of the shrimp dip. The chocolate chip pancakes Chase had made for breakfast escaped in a rush. I sat on the floor, waiting for another wave to pass before I was ready to rinse my mouth and return. We'd planned to tell his mother about the pregnancy after dinner, but at this rate, it was going to happen sooner rather than later.

I was leaning against the sink when there was a light tap on the door.

"Babe?"

I opened the door to find Chase wearing a worried expression.

"You okay?"

"Not really. I hate lamb, even the smell of it, and that's when I'm not pregnant. And it appears this baby isn't a fan of lamb or the shrimp dip."

"Who can blame it? I hate that stuff." He bent over the sink and rinsed his mouth out.

"You're gobbling it down like you haven't eaten in weeks."

"My brother likes it. I didn't want to hurt her feelings, especially with you and Izzy not eating it, so I figured I'd take the bullet."

I started to laugh. "Do you at least like lamb?" Just talking about it made my empty stomach do a flip.

"I do." He brushed a damp strand of hair off my cheek. "I think it's best if we don't wait until after dinner. This way you'll have an excuse not to eat it, okay?"

Although the thought of telling Chase's mother that her darling son was having a baby with the girl meant just for fun didn't calm me in any way, having to eat lamb to try to make nice was far worse.

I slipped my hand into his. "Yeah, we don't have a choice. But you get to do all the talking."

CHAPTER FORTY-TWO

Chase

Walking back into my mother's living room, I almost lost my nerve. I had no idea how she would react when she found out Rain was pregnant, and if it went badly, I hadn't thought about how that would affect Rain. The last thing I wanted was to cause Rain any more hurt or stress. Her life had been filled with it, and I loved her too much to allow her to experience any more pain, especially from my family.

"Everything okay?" My mother was showing Izzy one of her holiday musical snow globes. The tinkle of "O, Little Town of Bethlehem" played while Izzy watched snow fall on a nativity scene.

"Yes, I'm fine, sorry," Rain said.

I scooped Izzy up in my arms and put the snow globe back on the shelf. "Come sit with me." She wrapped her arms around my neck.

"Are we going to open presents now?"

"In a few minutes."

"This child's been waiting long enough," my mother insisted. "If Rain is okay, we should forge ahead." She glanced at her watch. "The lamb has to rest for twenty more minutes, so we have enough time before dinner."

Rain squeezed my hand. "Let's open presents first."

I squeezed back.

It surprised and pleased me when my mother asked Izzy if she would like to pass out the gifts. Maybe she'd had a change of heart. At least she was trying, even though I'd practically had to twist her arm to invite us over for dinner. She'd wanted just me to join them at my brother's on Christmas Day, which was bullshit, and exactly what I'd told her. Since Dylan and Lorraine—or more likely, Lorraine—wouldn't relent when it came to Rain, if my mother wanted to see me for Christmas, she would see all of us.

Like most things she did, Izzy took the task of distributing gifts seriously. The first one she picked up was for Rain from my mother, and a surge of relief rushed through me. I hated to admit it, but I'd worried that my mother might have bought gifts for only me.

Smiling, Rain tore into the brightly colored paper to unveil a perfume gift set. There were six or seven different kinds in the box, and since I wasn't familiar with any of them, I assumed none of them were pricey selections. It was probably something she grabbed at Target, but at least it was a gift.

"Thank you," Rain gushed as if it were the thing she'd most wanted this Christmas.

I rubbed my palm atop her thigh. I loved the way she smelled, and I hated the idea of her changing her scent in any way.

"I didn't know what type of fragrance you wore, so I bought you a selection," my mother explained.

Izzy clapped her hands. "Open it, Mommy. I want to smell."

Oh, hell no. The last thing we needed was Rain to get a whiff of something that didn't agree with her, and she'd be off to the bathroom again.

"Hey, Iz. Isn't there something under there for you?"

Fortunately, six-year-olds were easily distracted, even those as precocious as Izzy. While she searched through the boxes under the tree, I tucked the perfume gift set on the floor beside me.

"Here's one! And it's heavy." Izzy tore into the paper, ripping it to shreds.

"Thank you," Rain whispered.

I wrapped my hand around hers. "I got you. Don't worry."

Izzy stared down at the cardboard box from Amazon that she'd just unwrapped, then looked up at my mother. "Thank you for the nice box."

My mother just looked surprised, while I tried not to laugh out loud. Rain was struggling as well.

"I bet there's something in that box." I crouched on the floor beside Izzy, and using my car keys, slit open the tape sealing the box shut. I let her open it the rest of the way.

"Books!" Izzy cried, trying to lift a boxed set of Anne of Green Gables out of the box.

My mother seemed genuinely happy at Izzy's response. "I loved these books as a girl. I hope you don't already have them."

"I don't," said Izzy. "Daddy, will you read these to me?"

Rain tensed beside me, while my mother recoiled as if a snake had slithered out from under the tree.

"Of course I will. I'd be honored."

Izzy stepped over the torn wrappings, approached my mother, and threw her arms around her neck.

"Thank you. I love them."

My mother gave her a quick hug, ending it with a little tap on the back. "You're very welcome. Chase, I have some gifts here for you, of course."

"Izzy, why don't you give Chase's mother her gift from us first?" Rain said.

I had wanted our gifts to my mother to be from both of us, but Rain had insisted she wanted to buy something from her and Izzy. She'd found an antique music box with Clara holding the Nutcracker. When you wound it up, it played the "Dance of the Sugarplum Fairy." It had been far too expensive, but she'd insisted on buying it herself. It was beautiful, and something my mother would love, but it made me sad to think Rain felt that she had to buy my mother's affection.

My mother unwrapped the gift and lifted it out of the box. "Oh, how nice. A music box. Thank you." She returned it to the box.

"It plays the 'Dance of the Sugarplum Fairy,'" Rain said.

"Yes, that would make sense, wouldn't it?" She folded the lid on the box and slid it under the tree.

Heat flooded my face. I'd never thought of my mother as petty. She'd instilled manners in us from the time we could talk. I wanted to ask her to step into the other room, just like she would have done if I'd been that rude. Since that wasn't an option, I tried to coax an appropriate response out of her. "It's an antique, Mom," I added.

"Yes, I could see that. It's very nice." She pulled several boxes out from under the tree and handed them to me. "Here, you should open these so I can get dinner on the table."

I did as I was told, but there was little joy in opening any more gifts. My mother had already overreacted to Izzy calling me Daddy, and we hadn't even broached the topic of Rain's pregnancy. I opened my gifts quickly with little commentary—not that there was all that much to say about shirts and jeans. I even found it hard to raise much enthusiasm for Brent Celek's Eagles jersey.

Rain tugged the jersey out of my hands. "What's this, Holgate? You never said you were an Eagles fan. This puts things in a whole new light."

She was kidding, of course. For the past three months, we'd watched football together practically every Sunday. Rain had even taken to making me a feast fit for a five-star tailgate, from chili to wings and everything in between, not to mention the rumble in my living room when the Giants and the Eagles faced off in October. She'd plopped down beside me at the start of the game in a too-tight Giants jersey and been a thorough distraction, complete with eye black under her eyes. She'd even dressed Izzy as a Giants cheerleader. When the Eagles pulled from behind in the first quarter, she'd stopped sharing her popcorn.

"If you don't like it, you can always take it back," Mom said. "I'll find the receipt."

What? "No. I love it. Rain's kidding, Mom. She knows I'm a die-hard Eagles fan."

Ignoring my comment, my mother stood. "Well, you know best. Come, dinner's ready." She rose and left the room.

Izzy followed, while Rain tugged on my arm.

"When are you going to tell her?"

"I guess I can tell her when we sit down. I don't want to ask her to hold dinner any longer."

Rain nodded. "I guess, but I can't eat that lamb. I can't even smell it."

More and more, I was sorry I hadn't just taken a ride out last weekend and told her when it was just the two of us. I don't know why I'd thought it would be easier this way. Or maybe I was taking the coward's way out, hoping she wouldn't say anything negative if Rain and Izzy were here to hear it. I no longer believed that, but I prayed I was wrong.

The table was set with my mother's best dishes, and platters of sliced lamb, parslied potatoes, and buttered green beans filled the table along with a crystal bowl of mint jelly. There was also a large tossed salad, which I'd never been happier to see in my life. That mix of iceberg, romaine, and loose-leaf would hopefully buy me enough time to spring the news without Rain having to turn down yet another offering from my mother without good reason.

My mother set a glass of milk down in front of Izzy, who was surveying the table with her nose scrunched. It seemed her mother wasn't the only one who didn't like lamb.

"What would you like to drink, Rain? I have red wine to go with the lamb, but if you prefer a white—"

"No wine for me, thank you. Water is fine. Or milk."

"Milk?"

"Mom, why don't you let me handle the drinks? You sit."

"Chase, I'm perfectly capable—"

"Of course you are, but why should you? Sit."

I poured a glass of milk for Rain, and two glasses of red wine, one for me and one for my mother, although honestly, I would have preferred a six-pack of Heineken.

After we said grace and the salad had been passed, I cleared my throat.

"So, Mom, we have news." I lifted Rain's hand and tucked it in mine. "We're having a baby. Rain's pregnant."

Despite my fear over how my mother would react, the smile on my face was sincere. I was happy. I loved Rain, and I wanted to spend my life with her. We were just getting off to a faster start than most people might have expected.

Mom's fork clattered onto her plate. "You're what?"

Her eyes darted back and forth between me and Rain. She even swiveled to her left and looked at Izzy, perhaps to see if she would be the one to cry, "Just kidding!" Instead, Izzy nodded, her blond curls bouncing.

"But you—I don't understand. You just . . ." Her mouth opened and closed like a fish's. "Chase! This is irresponsible. You hardly know one another."

Rain tugged at her hand, but I strengthened my grip. "It wasn't planned, no, but we're happy about it. Rain and Izzy have agreed to move in with me. We're a family, and in June, we'll be a bigger family." I zeroed in on my mother and hoped that my look would communicate my expectation that she would at least be civil and levelheaded. "You're going to be a grandmother."

"I'm already a grandmother. Your brother has a child and another on the way—or have you forgotten them already?"

I guess she didn't understand the look I'd given her, because that didn't sound exactly civil.

"Of course I haven't forgotten."

Rain pulled harder, and her hand slipped free.

"Look, Mrs. Holgate, this wasn't planned. Unfortunately, things like this happen. But even still—"

"I would guess you're an expert in that department."

I threw my napkin down. "That's enough."

There was a slight pressure on my arm, not a panicky grip this time. It was meant to soothe. Rain sensed I was about to lose it on my mother, and she was stepping in. For as nervous and afraid of my mother's reaction as she'd been, the tables had been turned. Right now, she was the calm, focused one.

"Yes, Mrs. Holgate, for better or for worse, I am an expert," Rain said. "And I consider myself blessed in both cases." She smiled at Izzy, who sat quietly, eyes wide open, not fully understanding what was happening. "And I do love your son, if that makes you feel any better."

For all she looked as if she'd been sucking on a lemon, my mother remained quiet. Thoughtful. Her back was ramrod straight, her jaw tight, and her chin raised. It was a familiar posture to me—Queen Geraldine, my brother and I used to call her. It was her body's immediate reaction to any mention of my father, as if he were so far beneath her that she wouldn't deign to acknowledge his existence.

It bothered me to see her react to Rain's heartfelt confession, but at least she'd ceased the attack. For now.

But then the facade cracked, and she smiled. "I'm so sorry. You just caught me off guard. I was feeling a little peaked before you came from not eating earlier." Her fingers flew to her chest, and she fingered the single strand of pearls that my grandmother had left her. "Please forgive me."

She swiveled toward Izzy. "And you, young lady! A new brother or sister. You must be very excited."

With her usual serious expression, Izzy nodded. "Yes, ma'am, but I don't like that." She pointed to the plate piled high with lamb.

"Oh. Of course. How about peanut butter and jelly? I have some grape jelly that I made myself." She smiled at Rain. "Did Chase tell you we have our own grape arbor? I know you're a wonderful cook, but have you done any canning? It's so satisfying. I'd love to teach you, if you're interested."

To say my head was spinning was an understatement. I'd never witnessed such an about-face, but I wasn't going to question it, especially when my appetite was returning and I was surrounded by the three people I loved the most.

"I would love that, Mrs. Holgate. I adore grape jelly—and if you wouldn't mind, could I also have a peanut butter and jelly sandwich? I'm not a huge fan of lamb, and thanks to this little one, there are too many things I can't eat right now."

My mother pushed her chair back from the table and stood. "It's no trouble at all. And please, call me Geraldine."

CHAPTER FORTY-THREE

Rain

Who knew homemade grape jelly tasted so much better than the stuff from the grocery store? If Mrs. Holgate—it was going to take me awhile to feel comfortable enough to call her Geraldine—wanted to teach me, then I would be her willing student.

I picked up the empty salad bowl and the half-empty plate of lamb, trying to breathe through my mouth, and carried them into the kitchen. Mrs. Holgate had excused herself for a moment—to the bathroom, I guess, although she seemed the type to never admit to something as base as that—and when she returned, she scolded me for clearing the table.

"Rain. Sit! I insist. How about a nice cup of tea?" She began filling the teapot with water. "Herbal or decaf?"

"Decaf is fine, thank you."

When Chase entered the kitchen with the rest of the dishes, I gave him a bright smile and a thumbs-up. He responded with a wink.

"Chase, why don't you take Izzy and show her your room?" his mother said.

"You mean the shrine?"

She batted his arm lovingly. "My boys tease me because I've left their rooms the same as when they were here. All of Chase's trophies and awards are in there, including his jersey and his state champion football medal." Her eyes were a bit damp as she continued. "You're a mother, dear. You'll see."

Chase ran a paper towel under the faucet and used it to gently clean Izzy's face and hands. "C'mon, Iz. Let's go see my shrine before my mother starts singing the Parkland alma mater."

Izzy slipped her hand in his. "What's a shrine?"

"It's a tribute to my misspent youth."

Shaking her head, Mrs. Holgate chuckled softly. "Misspent youth. Hardly."

She carried two mugs of tea to the kitchen table, placed one before me, and sat. "Chase had a wonderful childhood, despite his father's trying to tear our family apart."

The way her eyes suddenly bore into me, it was like I'd had something to do with his father's abandonment. Chase had never said much about his father, and I hadn't pushed. I added a spoonful of sugar to my tea and stirred.

"And high school? Well, he was one of the most popular boys at Parkland. Always laughing. Always smiling. Even the teachers loved him. He was smart, respectful. All the girls adored him, but only one captured his heart."

It was a little difficult to resolve the Chase I knew, who was reserved and serious, with the Chase his mother described. And I didn't exactly care for her last comment.

"He could have dated anyone, but from freshman year through graduation, he only had eyes for Jennifer. Even though they went to different colleges, they were inseparable on vacations and breaks. Although I didn't exactly approve, he would drive out to State College to spend weekends with her at Penn State. But what can I say? They were in love."

Funny how a peanut butter and jelly sandwich could turn against me so quickly.

"Do you believe in soulmates, Rain?"

My body grew leaden. I couldn't open my mouth or lift my cup. The best I could do was a slight shrug of my shoulders.

Mrs. Holgate's smile from earlier had turned into more of a smirk. "Well, you would if you'd ever seen Chase and Jennifer together. I've never seen two people so in love. That doesn't just go away, dear. They will find their way back to each other. I've no doubt about that."

She dipped into her pocket and produced a wallet-sized photo of Chase and Jennifer, which was from the same shoot as the framed photo hanging in the hallway. Jennifer was beautiful, with long dark hair and bright-green eyes. Chase stood behind her, his arms wrapped around her shoulders, head tilted so that as Jennifer smiled at the camera, he smiled at her. And, yes, he looked like he loved her—very much.

"They make a beautiful couple," she said, slipping the photo back into her pocket. "And they'll make beautiful children someday." She leaned forward and touched my leaden hand across the table. Her fingers were thin and cold, and I wanted to shake them off, but I still couldn't move. "You need to face facts, dear. It's inevitable. They're soulmates. The longer the two of you stay together, the harder it's going to be for you when he realizes what a mistake he's made."

Mistake? I wasn't sure if she meant breaking up with Jennifer or being with me. Maybe both. I gave my head a shake, trying to clear away some of the hurt that had descended with her words.

"Mistake?" This time I said it out loud. "Do you think it's a mistake to break your engagement when you find your fiancée in bed with your best friend? Is that the mistake you're talking about, or am I the mistake?"

She reared back as if I'd slapped her, and I had a sinking feeling she had no idea why Chase and Jennifer had broken up. Too bad, bitch. I probably shouldn't have been the one to tell her, but I had every right to defend myself.

"I'm sure I don't know what you're talking about or where you heard that, but it's an ugly thing to say. That poor girl is heartbroken. She would've never done anything like that. Not all women have loose morals." She dropped her voice and leaned forward again. "I think you may have gotten your stories confused. Isn't it true that you're the one who was sleeping with someone else's fiancé? You think I don't know women like you? Women who just take what they want, not caring who suffers? A woman just like you, all flash and no substance, stole my husband and destroyed my family, practically ruined my boys' childhoods. If you think I'm going to let you destroy my son, think again. He's been hurt enough. You will never be good enough for him. And don't say I didn't warn you. When he finally sees you for what you are, he and Jennifer will find each other again, and you'll still be a two-bit whore looking for your next baby daddy."

I stood so quickly the chair toppled over. "Chase!"

Mrs. Holgate stood as well. "Don't be a fool."

Chase appeared in the doorway holding Izzy. "What's wrong? Are you okay?"

"I'm sorry. Can we go? I'm not feeling well."

"Yeah, sure." He set Izzy down and picked up the chair. "Can you go get the coats, sweetheart?"

"Are you okay, Mommy?"

"I am, sweetie. I'm really tired, and something has upset my tummy."

Chase put his hand on my arm and tried to lead me to sit down, but I shook him off. "Really, I just want to get home." I turned to his mother. "Thank you again for the gifts and dinner." It was all I could get out, and more than she deserved.

I met Izzy in the front hall, where she was holding up my leopard-print jacket—something a woman with no substance would wear. All flash. I bit back tears and was slipping it on when Mrs. Holgate emerged from the kitchen carrying a container of leftovers for Chase and a jar of homemade grape jelly for me and Izzy.

She leaned in to kiss my cheek, and I stiffened. "Remember what I said," she whispered. "Leave, or you'll be the one who gets hurt this time."

My legs threatened to give out. Even the attack I'd suffered from Preston's fiancée hadn't thrown me like this. In her way, Suzanne had every reason to hate me. I'd have hated me too if the shoe had been on the other foot. But this? This made no sense. The woman was either psychotic, or Chase's sister-in-law had really poisoned his mother against me.

Chase gave his mother a tight hug. "Thanks again for everything, Mom. I'm sorry we have to leave so abruptly, but we had a great time, right, Rain?"

My nod was met with another smirk over his shoulder.

"I hope you feel better, dear. Call me when you get home. You know I worry."

***

The ride home was quiet. Izzy fell asleep, and I pretended to. I couldn't talk to Chase about what had happened, not in the car, but I would as soon as we got home. His mother had no right to say the things she'd said to me, and I'd be a fool to tolerate it.

Before I could stop it, I burped. The damn grape jelly was burning a hole in my stomach.

"Excuse me." I shifted, trying to get comfortable.

"You all right?"

I glanced at Izzy, who was out like a light.

"I'll be fine. I need some Tums or something."

"I hope that's all it is."

"Yeah, me too. Look, Chase—"

"I gotta tell you, babe, I don't think I could be happier right now." He grabbed my hand and pulled it to his lips. "You making the effort with my mom. It means the world to me. I don't have much family left, just her and my brother, who's being a dick right now. But we'll work that shit out. Today was more than I could've hoped for. You and Izzy and my mom, you're the people I love most in this world, and to have you at odds—to be honest, that was kinda killing me."

I watched his face as he watched the road. He stole a quick glance, and when he saw me staring, he smiled. Scratch that. He was beaming. Fuck.

"If I haven't said it yet today, I'll say it now. I fucking love you, Rain. You have no idea how happy you've made me."

Right. "I love you too, babe."

And I did. So much. Which meant I would do everything I could to keep making him happy.

CHAPTER FORTY-FOUR

Rain

I unzipped my boot, slipped my foot into the sparkly silver flats, and frowned.

"What's wrong with those?" Diane asked. "They're cute."

I took a few steps and stopped in front of an endcap mirror at the local Payless. I turned from side to side. "They're so . . . flat."

"And pretty soon, you'll be too pregnant to gallop around wearing those stilts you call shoes. There has to be something here you like." She scoured the rack of size sevens, stopping at a pair of leopard-print ballet flats. "These are cute."

I held up a pair of gray faux suede peep-toe pumps with a one-inch platform. "Yeah, but these are cuter. And with the platform, the three-inch heel is probably only barely two inches."

She marched over and tugged the shoe out of my hand. "I know these are considered sensible shoes in Rainworld, but the rest of us would feel better if you stayed closer to earth for the duration of your pregnancy." She slipped the little suede cutie back onto the shelf next to its mate and handed me the leopard-print flats.

I dropped grudgingly onto the bench and slipped on the flats. At least the pattern was something I was comfortable with. "These are fine."

I boxed them up, grabbed the boring black ones as well, and headed to the register.

"It's not a death sentence, Rain. It's only another five months. After the baby comes, you can wear whatever you want."

I handed my credit card to the clerk. "I know. Do you mind if we run over to Macy's? Might as well pick up some mom jeans while we're out."

"Sounds good. Want me to carry that for you?" She pointed to my bag.

"I'm pregnant, not infirm."

"You're cranky is what you are."

I blew out a sharp breath. I was cranky, but there wasn't much I could do about it. When Chase proved to be so happy about his mother and me getting along, I didn't have the heart to tell him what she'd said to me in the kitchen when we were alone. I was afraid it would sound like I was trying to make trouble where there was none. Other than her short outburst when he told her I was pregnant, she'd recovered nicely and gone out of her way to be gracious to both Izzy and me.

Until we were alone, of course.

I didn't want to tell my mother or Diane either. They would have gone all vigilante justice on her, which was the last thing I needed. Instead, the entire conversation continued to gnaw at me like a worm in a bad apple. For Chase, I would swallow her insults and do whatever I could to change her mind about me. Let her see that I loved him and that he loved me, that I wasn't some slutty homewrecker. It was a long shot, but as long as he was under the impression that things were good, it was the best I could do.

That and to make sure I was never alone with her again, in case she really was psychotic.

Diane wrapped an arm around my waist. "How about after you get your stretchy pants, I take you for some ice cream?"

I laugh. "I'd prefer a margarita."

"Oh, we'll get one of those too, but I'll be the one drinking it. And on the way home, I'm stopping at the liquor store for two big bottles of tequila, one for me and one for Chase. We have five more months of cranky Rain, and neither of us should have to deal with that sober."

I rammed my shoulder into hers. "Funny."

"I try."

CHAPTER FORTY-FIVE

Chase

"What do you mean, no?"

"What do you mean, what do I mean?" Rain stared at me as if I'd lost my mind. "It means I won't marry you."

"I thought you loved me."

"I do love you. That doesn't mean I'll marry you. Besides, you're only asking because I'm pregnant."

"So what difference does that make? I love you. You love me. It's the logical next step. I don't see the problem here."

"I do."

I followed her from the bedroom into the kitchen.

"What?"

She reached into the refrigerator and pulled out the orange juice, frowned at it, then set it on the counter. "What, what?"

She was trying to drive me crazy. "You know what, what. What's the problem? We love each other. We're having a baby. I love Izzy too, but you already know that."

She reached for her vitamins, took one, then followed it with the OJ. I waited somewhat patiently while she rinsed the glass and set it in the dishwasher. "I do know that, and we both love you, but I'm still not going to marry you."

She snatched a banana from a basket on the table, peeling it as she walked out of the kitchen with me hot on her heels.

"Iz," she called, nearly plowing into Izzy as she turned the corner. "There you are. Are you ready to go?"

Izzy planted her hands on her hips and glared up at her mother. "Why won't you marry my daddy?"

Rain was suddenly at a loss for words, even the single-syllable ones she'd been lobbing at me. Her eyes sought mine, begging for help.

I folded my arms across my chest. "I got nothing."

"Thanks a lot," she muttered, handing me her banana.

She dropped to her knees and put her hands on Izzy's shoulders. "Sweetie, listen to me. I love Chase very, very much, and I don't need to marry him to prove it. We can still be a family. A piece of paper doesn't change that."

I groaned. Like a six-year-old could follow that bullshit piece of paper line.

Izzy stamped her foot. "But you said he could be my daddy." She swiveled toward me. "And you proposed, just like Prince Phillip and Princess Aurora." Her bottom lip popped out and her eyes filled with tears.

Fuck me.

I got on my knees beside Rain. "Iz, that doesn't change. I'm still going to be your daddy. Just because Mommy and I don't get married right away doesn't mean we won't get married someday. In the meantime, like she said, we're a family." Her sweet little face was breaking my heart. I tucked my finger under her chin and tipped her face up until our eyes met. "I promise you that no matter what, you will always be my daughter and I will always be your daddy, for as long as I live. Nothing will ever change that, okay?"

She wrapped her arms around my neck and buried her warm, wet cheek against my neck. I stood, holding her in my arms. "C'mon. I'll carry you out to the car and get you in your car seat, okay?"

Rain followed and waited until I'd finished buckling Izzy into her car seat.

"Am I meeting you at the Realtor's, or are you picking me up here?"

"Shit. I almost forgot. What time again?"

"We're supposed to be there at five."

"How about I call you later? If I can get out early enough, I'd like to grab a shower first."

"Okay." She tilted her head up, waiting for me to kiss her goodbye.

I did, but I captured her shoulders in my hands and held her in front of me.

"I meant what I said to Izzy in there. No matter what happens between us, I will be her father. I don't make promises I won't keep. And the same goes for loving you. I want to spend my life with you. That's also a promise I intend to keep."

She had already slipped on her sunglasses, so I couldn't see her eyes, but her lip quivered in a way that made me think she was about to cry. But all she did was nod. "I know, Chase. I believe you."

CHAPTER FORTY-SIX

Rain

"Are you sure?" Chase asked, standing in the doorway and looking out over the back yard.

"I am. This is the one. I can feel it. This is our house."

"It's not very big."

We'd looked at more houses than I could count, and I had begun to wonder if we'd end up staying in his apartment indefinitely. Some were too stark and modern. Others were too old, too expensive, too far from work.

But this house was perfect.

It wasn't big, just a dated ranch at the end of a dead-end street, but it had a big kitchen, a decent-sized living room, and three bedrooms. There was only one bathroom, and it didn't have a big tub, but the room was big enough that we could add one eventually. The back yard was fenced in, and it was a good size for kids to run around and play. It had a garage, which Chase had insisted on for my car and his bike.

"I love it, I really do," I said. "It needs some upgrades, but we can do that as we can afford it. There's even enough room if we want to add on someday, but honestly, I think it's perfect."

"What about the color?" he asked, wrinkling his nose.

"I'm not a fan of that harvest gold from the seventies, but we could paint it. Maybe blue or gray, with white trim and black shutters. And a red door."

He nodded. "I could see that. And where the patio is, I'd like to build you a sunroom with a glass ceiling, so you can have lots of plants and grow your herbs and things—but mostly so you can look up at the stars and talk to your dad all year round, just like you were doing the night I first kissed you."

I slipped my arms around his waist and lost myself in his eyes. "If I wasn't already falling in love with this house, that would have done it for me right there." I kissed him. "And if I hadn't already fallen in love with you, you would have swept me off my feet with that line. In fact, I might just swoon anyway." The intensity of his stare and that sexy half-grin wasn't helping me remain upright.

"Go ahead, I'll catch you."

He tucked a finger under my chin. "If we buy this house, will you promise to live here with me forever?"

I swallowed the lump in my throat. "I'll live here as long as you want me to."

"I want you forever. You know that. I want to marry you."

I closed my eyes and struggled to remain grounded. My emotions were getting the better of me with the pregnancy and having found our perfect house already had me close to tears. I wasn't sure if I could deal with this as well.

"Don't tell me it's too soon," he said. "It's been six months. We're buying a house. We're having a child together. Isn't that already a huge commitment?"

"It is. But marriage is different. I'm not ready, Chase. Not yet."

He sucked in a breath and closed his eyes, just as the Realtor came looking for us.

"Well, what do you think? Could this be your house?" she said.

Chase opened his eyes, and despite how happy we'd been just a minute earlier, there was a flash of sadness, maybe even disappointment, before he smiled again.

"Rain?"

I gave his hand a squeeze. "Yes. This is our house."

**

Chase was stretched out on the sofa in his apartment watching a movie while I sat on the floor trying to figure out how to paint my toenails. I grabbed hold of my foot and tried to pull it closer, but my belly kept getting in the way. I inched closer to the cabinet holding the television, propped my foot on the shelf, and bent as far as I could. My arms were about four inches too short. I lay on my back, spread my legs as wide as I could, bent my knee, and pulled my foot closer. I was able to paint my big toe, but in trying to get to the rest of them, I smeared nail polish all over my hand and my foot.

"Damn it!"

"Want me to do that for you?"

I rolled onto my side. "You know how to paint nails?"

"No, but it'll be easier for me than for you. You look like a contortionist. Not that I mind that in a woman, but I'm afraid you're going to hurt yourself. Or get nail polish all over the carpet."

"Okay. But you're going to have to help me up. I don't think I can do it by myself."

He pushed himself up from the sofa. "Way ahead of you, sweetheart."

After he removed the nail polish I'd smeared all over my foot, he sat on the coffee table with my foot in his lap and proceeded to paint my toenails my favorite Victoria's Secret pink. He was slow and methodical, and when he finished, there wasn't a smudge or a stray dab of pink to be seen.

I held up each foot, one at a time, because holding up both at once was no longer possible. "Nice job. If you decide you don't want to work with your brother any longer, you might be able to get a job at a nail salon."

"I might just do that." He sat alongside me and pulled my feet onto his lap. As if he weren't already the best boyfriend ever, he started massaging the soles of my feet. I moaned loudly, and he gave me a devilish smirk. "Do that again, and I'm carrying you off to bed."

"I can't help it, that feels so good. Damn."

I was practically mush by the time he was done. I wished I could spend the rest of my pregnancy on the couch with my feet in his lap.

He rubbed a hand gently up and down my shin. "Can I ask you something?"

I sighed loudly. "Fine, I'll rub your feet now."

He laughed. "Not what I was going to ask, but if you really want to, I suppose I can let you."

"I'd do anything for you."

He quirked an eyebrow at me. I waited while his eyes returned to the movie he'd been watching, and he kept rubbing my leg. When he did speak, he kept staring at the television.

"If I'd proposed to you the right way, on my knee with candles and all the romance you deserved, would you have said yes?"

I pulled myself into a sitting position and shimmied toward him until I could climb into his lap and straddle him. I gently tugged free the elastic holding his ponytail and ran my fingers through his hair. I held his head, resting my thumbs on either side of his face, tilting it until I could look deep into his beautiful blue-green eyes.

"It wouldn't have mattered. It's just too soon. When the time is right, it won't make a difference how you ask. The answer will be yes."

He lifted me off his lap and set me beside him, then rose and flicked off the television. "Good to know. That would've been pretty damn embarrassing if I'd been stupid enough to have asked you in public. I'm going to bed. I have to get up early."

I lay back on the sofa and stared up at the ceiling while he got ready for bed. When he finished in the bathroom, Izzy's door opened and her bed creaked. I pictured him sitting beside her, smoothing her curls, listening to her breathe. Soon he would lean forward, kiss her forehead, and then get up quietly, leaving her door open just a crack in case she cried out for us during the night.

It had been seven months, and I was more in love with Chase than ever. I tried to show him every day, in every way I could think of, but I couldn't marry him. Not because I didn't believe he loved me, because I did, and I knew I was hurting him every time I said no.

I wanted to spend the rest of my life with him. Desperately. But not if it meant hurting him in the end. Chase was loyal and steadfast when it came to me. I was afraid if things didn't improve with his family and how they treated me—for real, not just when he was watching—he might turn away from them. Permanently.

I couldn't do that to him. Or to them.

But I did have an idea. We were moving into our new house in two weeks. After we got settled, we'd throw a housewarming party. We would invite all of our friends and our families. This way, it wouldn't be awkward for any of us, and I wouldn't have to find myself alone with Lorraine or Mrs. Holgate. It might be a way to break the ice; let them see we were happy and that we wanted to include them in our lives.

Then, once things evened out with his family, I would be free to say yes.

CHAPTER FORTY-SEVEN

Rain

I stood in front of the full-length mirror Chase had installed on the closet door in our new bedroom and stared at my silhouette, one hand on top of my belly, the other pressing my dress tight against my body below my belly.

"I look like I swallowed a basketball."

Chase came up behind me and took in my reflection. "A little, maybe, but it's cute."

"Cute?" I pivoted so that I faced front. You could hardly tell I was pregnant if I came at you straight on. I did a one-eighty and strained to look over my shoulder. "How about my butt?"

Chase grabbed a cheek in either hand. "Perfect."

"Yeah, but is it bigger?"

He squeezed one side, then the other. "Feels the same to me."

"Oh, you." I gave him a gentle shove. I was eight months pregnant but I'd only gained fifteen pounds, all of it in my belly.

"You almost ready? Your mom just pulled up."

I plopped down on the bed and held out my foot. "Yeah. I just need you to buckle my sandals."

Chase knelt down in front of me and lifted my ankle. "You're wearing these?" He did a quick measure with his thumb and forefinger. "These are over three inches high. Shouldn't you be wearing flats?"

I made a pouty face. "I don't have any that match this dress. Could you just buckle my shoes? I promise I'll hang on to your big, strong arms whenever I'm walking." I batted my eyes at him. "Okay, big fella?"

He smirked. "Funny."

"C'mon. Don't you want me to look all sexy for you? This might be one of the last times we get to go out to dinner before the baby comes. Pretty soon, I'll be running around barefoot all day with spit-up in my hair."

"Nice. When you put it like that." He buckled my straps and then helped me stand.

And damn it if I didn't sway.

"Rain . . ."

"I'm fine. Chill. I've been wearing flats for so long that I need to get used to the altitude. Just give me a second."

I snatched my bag off the dresser and let Chase lead me from the bedroom.

"Don't you look pretty?" my mother said, giving me a kiss on the cheek. "Cute shoes. Are they new?"

"Ma!" My own mother had just outed me.

Chase looked down at my feet and then back up at me, and he knew I'd pulled one over on him. "You said you didn't have any shoes to match that dress. If you had to buy new ones, why didn't you buy shoes you could walk in?"

I was too pregnant and cranky for this discussion.

"First of all, the dress is black, Chase. I could wear any color with it, so that was a lie. Secondly, I hate flats. I only have four more weeks to go. Why would I want to buy another pair of shoes I'll never wear? And third, I can so walk in these." I ended my rant by sticking out my tongue. See? Cranky.

I draped a pashmina around my shoulders. "We're just having dinner at the Stagecoach, so we won't be late. I'll put Izzy to bed when we get home, so just have fun. Don't give her too much sugar though, okay?"

My mother folded her arms across her chest and glared. "I raised you, you know? And you turned out just fine, even though you're convinced all I fed you was sugar."

"I know you didn't, but you weren't a grandmother then."

Chase lifted Izzy so I could give her a kiss without bending.

"Love you. I'll see you when we get home."

"Bye, Iz. Be good for Mimi," Chase added, kissing her neck until she erupted with a fit of giggles before he put her down.

Just like he promised, Chase stayed glued to my elbow on the way to the car, then again into the restaurant and to the table.

"What are you going to do if I have to go to the bathroom, huh?" I asked with a grin.

"If you were worried about that, you should've worn sensible shoes."

I groaned. "I hate those two words used together. It's the stuff of nightmares: 'sensible shoes.' Blech."

He sipped his water and pointed to mine. "I guess you'd better abstain if you don't want me standing outside the bathroom stall."

"You mean bathroom door."

"I mean the stall door. If you think I'm letting you walk across a tile floor in high heels while you're eight months pregnant, you're sadly mistaken."

I would've laughed, but I knew he was serious. Which is why when I needed to pee halfway through dinner, I held it.

And held it.

By the time we were driving home, my eyeballs were floating.

"Can't you drive faster?" I wiggled in my seat. "I have to pee."

He didn't say anything, but I could tell he was trying not to laugh.

When we got stuck at the only red light in Millstone, I swiveled in my seat and lifted my leg so I could stick my foot in his lap.

"Unbuckle my shoe so I can get it off."

"Why?" he asked, fidgeting with the buckle while waiting for the light to change.

"So I can run into the house as soon as you pull in the driveway."

Fortunately it was a long light, and he had time to unbuckle both of my shoes. I kicked them off, refusing to sigh in relief even though I wanted to, because yes, they hurt. The moment he pulled into the driveway, I hopped out and scurried across the lawn.

"Be careful," he barked as I hopped over the short hedge along the sidewalk.

The front door was locked, and of course I didn't have my key. I pounded on the door with the palm of my hand. "Mom! Open up!"

The door swung open. "What the hell—"

"Move!" I pushed past her while trying to run and squeeze my legs together at the same time, just as two dozen people shouted "Surprise!"

"Oh, my god!" I waved and kept moving—that, or I would pee on my new carpet in front of a room full of people. "Can't talk."

I zipped down the hallway, hiking up my dress to get to my panties as I reached the bathroom door, hoping no one could see me from the living room. If anyone was hiding in the bathroom, they would be the one getting the surprise.

I collapsed onto the toilet just in time to hear another less hearty chorus of "surprise" for Chase and let my head drop into my hands.

What the hell was going on? If my mother hadn't answered the door, I might've thought we'd entered the wrong house.

I was washing my hands when Chase tapped on the door and stepped inside.

"What the hell is going on?" I asked.

"It's a surprise housewarming and baby shower."

"What? How?" We had invited everyone to a housewarming party for next weekend. I'd already made a lot of the food and frozen it, but we still had to finish painting the kitchen, and the baby's room wasn't done yet. I tried to remember if I'd made the bed.

"You didn't know anything about it? Sense anything?"

Did I? I searched my mind, but nothing was coming to me. I shook my head. "Nothing. I had no idea. That's so weird."

Chase looked as flustered as I felt.

Maybe pregnancy affected my psychic ability.

"Give me your hands," I said.

"What?"

I held my hands up, palms forward. "Like this. Give me your hands."

He held his hands up, and I pressed my palms to his, then closed my fingers over his. The vibration was still there, as strong as ever. "Well, that still works."

Chase was getting antsy. I guess he didn't like surprises any more than I did. "What are you talking about?"

"Nothing. I'll explain it later."

"Whatever, but we need to pull ourselves together and go out there. Everyone is waiting and wondering if you're sick."

"Who's here?"

"Everyone. Although I didn't see my family."

"I invited them for next week. Oh, my god. What if whoever threw this party didn't invite them?" That had been the reason for this whole housewarming thing in the first place, to get Chase's family here.

"Maybe I just didn't see them. If we stay in here much longer, people are either going to think you're in labor or that we snuck out the bathroom window."

The casement window was too narrow. Neither of us would have been able to escape through it. Which reminded me, we should put a bigger window in when we remodeled.

His sharp tone brought me back to the present. "Are you ready?"

"Not really, but I guess we don't have a choice."

It felt odd to be nervous walking down the hall in my own house, but I did. It didn't help to be greeted with another chorus of "Surprise!" when we entered the living room.

I saw my mother with some guy I didn't recognize, Diane and Wally, Bobby and Janelle, Dennis and the rest of the racing crew, Irena, Lynette and her new boyfriend, my Aunt Donna and Uncle Bob, and lots of other friends. I didn't, however, see Mrs. Holgate, Lorraine, or Dylan.

Two tables stood side by side, one piled with pastel-wrapped gifts and another with gift bags and wrapped boxes. We had specifically said no gifts on the invitations we sent out, but it seemed no one had listened. Why would they? It's not like any of them were actually attending that party anyway.

I was more than surprised. I was overwhelmed and I needed to sit down, but it seemed I was going to have to hug two dozen people first.

After the first few greetings, Chase interrupted. Whatever psychic abilities had deserted me must have flown over to him, because he'd totally read my mind.

"Hey, if you guys don't mind, Rain needs to sit. You can all pay her homage over here." He was teasing, but I recognized the tension in his jaw. He was upset. I just didn't know if it was because he disliked surprises that much or because his family wasn't here. I hoped to god they'd been invited. Then again, if they had been and they'd refused to come, that might be worse.

In the meantime, I was just grateful I could fake a smile.

CHAPTER FORTY-EIGHT

Rain

After opening what felt like a hundred gifts and eating the food I'd prepared and had frozen earlier for next week's party, I cornered Diane in the kitchen.

"Who's responsible for this?" I didn't want to sound like an ingrate, but it was hard to relax and enjoy myself when all I could think about was Chase's family. My limited psychic abilities may have deserted me, but I could tell just by looking at Chase that something was bothering him, and I knew what that something was.

Diane poured herself another margarita and licked some of the salt off the rim before she answered. "You're acting like we did something wrong. It was me, your mom, and Aunt Donna. Who else would it have been? Lorraine?"

She snorted.

"Sorry. I'm thankful, really. I just had no clue this time. I was really surprised."

She rolled her eyes and laughed. "I've surprised you before."

"No, you haven't."

"Um, your birthday? Remember?"

I shook my head and pushed her further into the kitchen where no one could hear us. I took her glass, licked the rim and took a mouthful of her margarita, and handed it back to her. "I knew. And wipe that horrified look off your face. One sip won't do anything, I don't have cooties, and you won't get pregnant from my germs."

She stared at her glass woefully, then shrugged and took another sip.

"Why didn't you invite Chase's family? You knew they were invited to the party next week?"

"We did invite them." She was practically spitting. "Lorraine emailed and said 'Sorry. Can't make it.' Four fucking words. And Chase's mother said she had been planning to attend the original event, but she already had plans this weekend. She said she would mail her gift."

I slumped against the counter. "Does Chase know?"

"I think Wally told him."

From where I stood, I could see Chase in the living room with Wally and some of his other friends. They were laughing and carrying on, but Chase wore his usual serious expression. He seemed distracted, unfocused—unhappy, even, despite the surprise our friends had given us.

"Give me another sip," I demanded, holding out my hand.

Diane pulled her arm back and almost sloshed half her margarita onto my clean kitchen floor. "I'll make you a virgin margarita."

"A virgin margarita isn't going to give me the fortitude to deal with that." I pointed at Chase. "Look at him. He's miserable. This is such a slap in his face, and it's my fault."

"How the hell is it your fault? I thought things went well when you guys went to visit his mother at Christmas."

"Christmas, Diane. That was five months ago, and we haven't seen her since. And as far as I know, things are still messed up between him and Dylan. Things only appeared to go well."

There was no one in the kitchen with us, but I didn't want to take any chances. I lowered my head close to Diane's ear and whispered. "His mother hates me. When she had me alone, she made it clear I wasn't right for Chase and that he and his ex-fiancée will eventually get back together."

Diane reeled back. "That fucking bitch. If I'd known, I never would've invited her."

I shook my head. "No, no, you had to. That was the only reason I wanted to have the housewarming in the first place. I thought I could get his family here with other people around so it wouldn't be awkward, and we could try and lay some groundwork to build some sort of relationship. If they could at least tolerate me, it would be better than this."

"Fuck them. They shouldn't have to be made to tolerate you. You're not someone who needs to be tolerated. You're one of the best people I know."

I didn't know how many margaritas Diane had ingested, but she was not only getting weepy, she was getting loud.

I plucked the glass from her hand, drained the last of it, and put it in the sink. Then I grabbed a Pepsi from the cooler. "Here. Drink this. You've had enough of the hard stuff. Don't tell anyone what I told you. Other than one little freak-out when he told her I was pregnant, Chase's mother was nothing but kind and friendly when he was in the room, so that's all he knows. I don't want him to know anything else. Understand? Don't you say one thing to Wally, because he'll tell Chase—and I swear, if he does, I'll tell Janelle it was you who spilled red wine on her new white couch at the twins' birthday party."

"You bitch! That wasn't me!"

"I don't care."

She narrowed her eyes but then stuck out her hand. "Deal."

I shook her hand. "And seriously, who gets a white couch with twin boys anyway?"

"I know, right? Even though I didn't spill the wine, I would've spilled something on it eventually."

I took the can of Pepsi from her and drank. I wasn't supposed to have caffeine either, but I needed a jolt of something to keep me going. All I wanted was to sneak off to my bedroom.

Diane yanked the can from my hand. "Can you get your own drink already?"

"I will," I said as Chase entered the kitchen for another Heineken from the cooler. "But first, I have to deal with this."

***

I sidled up to Chase, slipped my arm around his waist, and tucked my hand into the back pocket of his jeans. "How're you doing?"

His body swayed slightly, and when he smiled down at me, I could see he was drunk—or close to getting there.

He put his arm around me, resting his hand on my hip, and pulled me closer.

"I'm great. Some surprise, huh?" His tone was flat. Anyone hearing him might have thought he was ungrateful, but I knew differently, and it was killing me.

"Izzy's having fun," I said. She was sitting next to Janelle, telling her all the names we had chosen for her new baby brother or sister. "She should probably go to bed soon. I'll get her and—"

"I'll do it." He threw his head back and finished half the bottle, then set it on the new end table. I snatched it up before it could leave a ring. "I need a break from all this celebrating."

"Kiss me first," I said, wishing I could suck the sadness out of him somehow. It bothered me to see him like this. His pain was my pain, and it was deep.

"I'm only going to put Izzy to bed."

"I know. Kiss me anyway." I pulled him down, desperate to kiss the sadness off his face. When I caught his bottom lip in my teeth, he growled softly.

"Later," I promised. "You, me, and this basketball of a belly. I figured out a new way to get jiggy with it."

He let out a loud laugh. Success!

"You got it. I think I need to get a little jiggy." He kissed my forehead, then went to collect our daughter, smiling.

And for the first time since we'd walked into our house that night, my heart felt a little lighter.

CHAPTER FORTY-NINE

Rain

"What are you looking at?"

Diane came up behind me as I peeked out of her dining room window into the back yard. I smiled.

"Nothing." I smiled some more.

Chase was dropping off some old junker that Wally wanted for parts. I'd ridden over with him in the tow truck. As I stood at the window, he uncoiled the chains on the rollback. The wind was blowing, and he kept pushing his hair out of his face with his forearm. I couldn't hear what they were saying, but judging by the way he and Wally were laughing, I assumed there was some good-natured ribbing going on between them.

"Seriously," she asked, looking at the two of them and perhaps not finding Wally still as adorable as I found Chase. "What are you smiling at?"

I shrugged. "I don't know. I just like watching him, I guess."

Chase moved around to the front of the truck, pulled open the door, and climbed inside.

"If you like looking at him so much, why don't you just say yes? Then you can look at him anytime you want." She stared up at me and blinked her baby blues, then slowly raised her eyebrows in a silent and prolonged "Hmm?"

"Other than when he's at work or under that race car in your garage, I do get to look at him whenever I want. We don't need to be married for me to be able to look at him."

She let out an exaggerated sigh.

"Is he or is he not the best man you've ever known?"

"Yeah, but—"

"Does he or does he not treat you better than any man you've ever known?"

I nodded.

"Is he or is he not the best sex you've ever had?"

"Diane!" I laughed. "I never told you that."

"You don't have to. You're not the only one who can read minds, you know."

"Since when?"

"Baby, all I have to do is look at your face when you look at him. Jeez, even Wally can read your mind, and the only thing he reads is the TV Guide and the directions on the back of his Hot Pockets."

"Why do you still let him eat that crap?"

"Because I can't cook for him six times a day, and don't change the subject."

I shook my head and went back to spying out the window. All Chase was doing was unhooking a car from the rollback. It was probably something he did two or three times a day. I could even understand if he'd been shirtless, but it was May and he had on a T-shirt, thick work gloves, and steel-toed boots. But just watching him move, laughing, comfortable in his own skin—well, I could've watched him all day.

"Oh, my god. Please don't tell me it's Preston."

My heart leaped to my throat. "What?"

"Preston. Please don't tell me the reason you won't marry Chase is because of Preston, that you have some sick, misguided idea in your head that he'll be back."

I wanted to clamp my hand over her mouth. I shuddered. Call me superstitious, but I still believed in the Betelgeuse rule, and I didn't need what's his name appearing in Diane's dining room. Or anywhere else in my life. I hadn't heard from him in months, and I didn't want any reincarnations, thank you very much.

"Of course not," I said, horrified. "How could you think that?"

She settled her hands on her hips. "How? Because you're with a gorgeous man who worships the ground you walk on, whose baby your carrying, yet you refuse to marry him. Why wouldn't I think that? It's not like you've ever been clearheaded when it comes to Preston."

I cringed. Four times. She'd said his name four times. That couldn't be good.

"And I'll tell you another thing. I'm not the only one who thinks that." Her eyebrows inched upward.

"Who would think that?"

"No one's said anything to Chase, of course, at least not that I know of. But the guys talk, and you know Wally. He's an old lady in a forty-two extra long."

I faced the window again. The old Impala was parked outside Wally's garage. Chase was rewinding the chains. Of course there was a reason I wasn't marrying him: his family. I couldn't imagine willfully avoiding his mother for the rest of our lives.

My own mother would never have been this pigheaded about something. Even with Preston—oh my god, five times—but even with what's his name, she let me know she disapproved, yet she never threatened to disown me or turn her back on me.

Chase saw his brother five days a week, but their relationship was still strained. I could only imagine what Dylan and Lorraine had said when they learned I was having a baby.

I thoroughly believed that Dylan had tried to convince Chase it wasn't his. And if I was right, that would've made things that much worse between them, even though Chase knew Dylan could be right.

But the idea of Chase's thinking I wouldn't marry him because I was still in love with he who shall remain nameless? That I couldn't bear. That would destroy any chance we had for happiness.

Chase reached up to secure the chains. As he did, his shirt inched up, exposing the skin around his waist. I went weak in the knees.

When he saw me at the window, he grinned. Warm and tingly, it went straight through to my spine. When he and Wally began walking toward the house, I grabbed my purse.

"I'll talk to you tomorrow," I said, hoisting the strap over my shoulder. "We have to go."

Diane was dumping chips into a basket lined with a paper napkin.

"I thought you were staying. I made dip."

"You stirred onion soup mix into a container of sour cream."

"I had to rinse the spoon and put it in the dishwasher, didn't I?" She folded her arms and gave me a long look. "What's wrong?"

"Nothing. I just remembered something I need to do. I'll call you tomorrow." I beat a path out the door, cutting Chase and Wally off before they reached the house.

"What's wrong?" Chase asked as I came barreling through the door. I pulled it closed behind me.

"Diane has a headache, so we're going to take a rain check." I slipped my hand into his and started pulling him toward the truck.

"She was fine twenty minutes ago," Wally argued.

"It came on all of a sudden," I said. "You should go see if she needs anything."

He glanced up at his back door. "Yeah. Hey, I'm sorry about that."

"It's okay," I called over my shoulder.

Chase helped me into the cab and climbed in beside me. "That's too bad. I have to drop the truck off at the station, but we can stop at Blondie's if you want or go to a movie or something, since Izzy is spending the weekend at your mother's."

I shook my head. "I have a better idea. It might be a little crazy, but I hope you'll say yes."

"Does it involve one of your cravings? Other than a pitcher of margaritas, I'll get you anything you want."

"Is that a promise?" I held my arm across the console. He took it and kissed the back of my hand.

"You know it is."

"Good. Let's drop this off and head home."

Chase hadn't proposed to me in at least a month. It was possible that he'd gotten sick of asking or that he'd changed his mind, but I didn't think so.

It was time for me to worry about my own happiness, and to hell with anyone who wanted to stand in the way.

If he wasn't going to ask me to marry him again, then I'd just have to ask him.

And I knew the perfect place.

CHAPTER FIFTY

Rain

We hadn't been back to Cape May since Chase first brought me here to see the sunrise. But with it being such a special place for him and now me as well, it was the perfect place to take the next step.

I'd checked the weather report last night before we left. It called for clear, sunny skies in the mid-seventies, which meant we would have a perfect sunrise.

It didn't matter. Even if it had predicted rain, I would have hauled Chase out here, gotten down on my knees, and begged him to marry me. But this way was much better. Rain makes my hair frizz, and I wanted to look my best.

"I still can't believe you talked me into this," Chase said, grumbling as he helped me waddle over the dunes near the lighthouse. I had a towel tucked into my bag, as well as a bottle of Heineken. The stores had already closed when we left last night, so I couldn't get any champagne, which would have been festive. Of course, Chase wouldn't have let me have any, and honestly, he probably preferred the beer.

I planned to propose as soon as the sun broke the horizon. I wanted it to be perfect. I couldn't have come up with a better plan even if I'd had more than two hours to come up with one.

Trudging through the sand was wearing me out, and I was already winded. My flip-flops were slowing me down, and we should have been in place already.

"Stop," I said, trying to catch my breath. "Let me take my shoes off."

I could see the first threads of orange and pink stretching across the horizon and reflecting on the water. I kicked off my shoes and tried to pick them up, but my belly wouldn't allow me to bend.

Holding on to me with one hand, Chase snatched them up, and we kept walking.

I scanned the beach until I found the perfect spot, and we trudged toward it. I dropped my bag, which was a big mistake, because now I couldn't bend to pull out the towel.

"Could you hand me the bag?"

"You just put it down."

"I know, but I forgot I needed something."

He picked up the bag and peered inside. I snatched it from his hands before he saw the bottle of Heineken. "Hey! I have personal stuff in there."

Even in the dim light, which was growing brighter by the second, I could tell he wasn't too happy with me. This might all blow up spectacularly in my face.

"I just want everything perfect. And I don't want to miss the sunrise."

"We could've been here a lot earlier if you hadn't needed to put on a full face of makeup. It's the beach. No one cares."

"Don't be grumpy. I want this to be a special day for us."

He looked out over the ocean, then back at me.

"I do too. I'm sorry. I guess I'm just a little stressed out."

"Why? This is your favorite place, right? You should be unstressing."

"I'm not sure that's a word."

"Well, it should be."

The first rays of brilliant orange broke the horizon. I grabbed hold of his arms and tried to lower myself to my knees, which wasn't easy, especially with Chase trying to pull me back up.

"Stop," I said. Struggling against him was useless; he was insanely strong. He pulled me back to my feet.

The sun continued to rise.

"I want to get down on the sand."

"Let me get the towel."

"Forget the towel. Just help me get down!"

Ignoring me, he pulled the towel closer and smoothed it out. Then he sat and held his arms out to help me down.

"No. You get up. I need to go down."

He looked at me like I was crazy. "I can't sit on your towel?"

"No. You stand."

Grumbling and cursing under his breath, he stood. Not expecting much help from him at this point, I grabbed onto his belt loops and began lowering myself, tugging his pants down along with me.

"What the hell are you doing?" He grabbed my wrist just as my knees hit the towel. So much for a lifetime of squats. Where were they when I needed them?

Apparently my little exercise had given him the completely wrong impression.

"Are you kidding? We can't do that here. Someone might see us. If you wanted to do that on the beach, we should have gotten here while it was still dark."

Oh, for crying out loud. Did he think that was the only reason a woman would be on her knees? Although, other than scrubbing the floor, I couldn't think of any.

"That's not what I was about to do."

"Well, then what are you doing besides missing the sunrise?"

A strange, uncomfortable feeling came over me, and I held onto his leg a little tighter. He was so tall I was having trouble seeing his face, given how close I was to him.

"Can you come down here?"

"You just yelled at me to stand up."

"I know. Could you just humor me?"

He dropped down onto his knees in front of me. "What?"

This could go down as one of the worst proposals of all time. I tried to regain my focus.

"Chase, I love you very much. I should've known the first night we met when we shook hands, but I was too stubborn. And I should've known the night of my birthday when you kissed me, because I had never in my life been kissed like that. And I should've known the first time you brought me here to see the sunrise.

"But that's when I started to know. And from then on, it just kept growing. Each day, I think I can't possibly love you more, but I'm always wrong, because with each new day, my love for you gro—oh, shit."

Panic flashed across his face. He gripped my shoulders. "What?"

I shook my head. "Nothing. I'm just uncomfortable."

"Then sit. Why are you kneeling?"

I shifted my weight a bit, trying to relieve some of the pressure on my legs. "I'm fine. Where was I?"

"I have no idea. I think you were telling me how much you love me."

"Right. I do. More than I ever believed it was possible to love someone."

"You're squeezing my hand really hard. Are you all right?"

I sucked in a lungful of ocean air and nodded vigorously. "Yep. Fine. I just need a moment."

"Okay. While you're catching your breath, can I say something?"

"Yeah, go ahead."

He settled a hand on my hip, and when his eyes met mine, they were shiny. "I'm not sure where you were going with all that a moment ago, but I've been in love with you for just as long."

He opened his hand, and in it lay a diamond ring. A simple round solitaire that had to be far too expensive. The most perfect ring I'd ever seen.

"Will you marry me?"

I gave him a shove and blinked back the tears that had sprung to my eyes. "Damn it, Chase. I was trying to propose."

He looked dubious. "Seriously? That was what you were doing?"

Nodding, I wiped at the stray tears that tracked down my cheeks and held my arms up for him to help me to my feet. Then I held out a shaky hand, and he slipped the ring on my finger, which hummed and sparked at his touch.

And then he kissed me, and the electricity coursing through me a moment earlier was nothing compared to what his lips were doing to me now.

When we stopped to take a breath, I told him I'd brought him a Heineken to celebrate.

"It's not even six o'clock in the morning." He kissed me again. "How about we go back to the room, celebrate another way, and then I'll drink that Heineken?"

"We can't."

"Sure we can."

"No, we can't. We have to go."

"Why?"

"Because my water just broke."

CHAPTER FIFTY-ONE

Chase

My arm supported Rain's back. Her hand gripped mine, and I raised her into a sitting position. The grunts and groans coming from her barely sounded human, and the louder she cried out, the harder my gut twisted.

Why would any woman in her right mind want to give birth?

"Okay, stop," Dr. Hart ordered. "Good girl. One or two more good pushes and we'll have ourselves a baby."

I lowered Rain gently against the pillow. Strands of damp hair clung to her face. I brushed them out of the way and kissed her forehead. "You're doing great, babe. Really. And if you never want me to touch you again after this, I'll understand."

She laughed. It was weak, but it was still a laugh. "Let's see how it goes, and I'll get back to you on that." She squeezed my fingers. It was a far cry from the punishing grip of just a few moments earlier.

We'd made it to the hospital in record time—thanks to the early morning hour and the fact that we were heading away from the shore, not toward it. Rain had been calm the entire way, and had only started the breathing exercises we'd learned as we neared the hospital.

The pressure on my hand intensified.

"Again," she said through gritted teeth.

I wished there was a deep-breathing exercise to calm my racing heart.

I helped her into a sitting position. "C'mon, baby. You're almost there."

"Make it count, Rain," Dr. Hart said.

I didn't think she was strong enough to break any of the bones in my hand, but the way she was gripping me, I wouldn't have been surprised if she had cracked one or two. She grunted and her body sagged against my arm.

"I see hair," Dr. Hart said.

I didn't move, not wanting to let her go, until Rain tilted her face toward me. I'd never seen her look more exhausted or more beautiful. I leaned forward, trying to peek over the top of Rain's knee, but before I could actually see anything, she grabbed my hand.

"Are you ready to push again?" the nurse standing on the other side of the bed asked.

Rain nodded as I scrambled back into position.

"Deep breath now, and push," Dr. Hart said.

"C'mon, baby, you can do it. Push."

"Good girl, Rain," the doctor said. "Keep pushing. Deep breath. And push, push, push."

The nurse continued the chant, repeating what the doctor had started. I held my breath in sympathy as Rain pushed until her face turned beet red, and I thought she might burst a blood vessel. She released her breath in a rush of air and slumped back. I heard a low mewl, then a much stronger, much louder cry that sounded like it was being played on tightly strung rubber bands.

"It's a boy!" Dr. Hart stood and placed our tiny, wriggling son on Rain's chest. His pale lavender skin was about two sizes too big. His face was pink, but the more he howled, the pinker he became, until he was almost red. What little hair I could make out was wet and blond and plastered to the top of his head. A nurse briskly rubbed a soft blanket over his skin, cleaning him.

Rain smiled up at me, her eyes brimming. "What do you think, Daddy?"

"Can I touch him?"

Her laugh competed with the robust vocalizations of the baby she held tightly in her arms. "He's yours. You can touch him whenever you want."

I eyed the nurse to make sure. When she nodded, I trailed a finger from his shoulder to his tiny, flailing wrist. I'd never felt anything quite as soft, and I worried that my calloused, overworked hands would scratch him. My mind leaped back to high school English and reading Steinbeck's Of Mice and Men. Maybe I should do like Curley, and wear gloves with Vaseline at night to soften my hands so that I wouldn't hurt him.

"Do you want to cut the cord, Chase?" Dr. Hart asked, lifting the long white rope that connected my son to his mother.

I took a deep breath. I'd done my reading, paid attention in birthing class, but I still wanted to be one hundred percent sure it wouldn't hurt him.

"He won't feel this, right?"

Dr. Hart held out the surgical scissors. "Not a chance. Don't worry."

My knees and my hands were shaking, and it took two tries to get through the cord, but I did it.

"What do you think?" Rain asked.

My grin stretched so wide, it almost hurt. "I think I'm in love." I kissed her. Then I kissed my son.

My son.

Fuck biology. As far as I was concerned, this was my son, whether we shared DNA or not. I was here when he took his first breath, and he'd be my son until I took my last. I swallowed the lump that had crept into my throat and blinked back tears.

He'd been here less than ten minutes, and not only had he grabbed hold of my heart with that tiny fist, he'd turned me into a wuss.

"Name?" the nurse asked.

We had discussed it, but Rain wanted me to have the final say. I'd give her one last chance to change her mind, but without me even opening my mouth, she shook her head and gave me a tired smile. I didn't even have to think about it.

"Zachary Storm Holgate."

My son.

CHAPTER FIFTY-TWO

Chase

As far as deliveries go, Dr. Hart said everything went great. Even Rain said it was a lot easier than Izzy's birth. But seeing her in so much pain and then pushing a tiny human out of her body nearly did me in.

It was still fucking amazing. I was officially a father, as of 3:12 that morning. I had a son, Zachery Storm Holgate. No hyphen. I chose Storm to be his middle name to honor her parents. I had no desire to honor my father, and despite how my mother had seemed to accept Rain and the pregnancy after a disastrous start at Christmas, she thrived on sowing seeds of doubt whenever we'd speak, which was becoming less and less often. I wasn't even sure I wanted to call her.

I was exhausted, but ecstatic, and I didn't want anything to ruin this day for me.

I checked my shirt pocket to make sure Rain's ring was there. She'd worn it for all of about four hours yesterday. By the time we packed up and checked out of the hotel, then drove to the hospital, she had to take it off in case they needed to put her under anesthesia. As long as she'd be putting it back on. That's all that mattered.

After Rain was back in her room and resting, she sent me home. I took a shower and then slept for a few hours. When I woke, I made all the necessary phone calls. The only reason I called my brother was to tell him I'd be taking the day off and all of next week because Rain had delivered our son. He congratulated me and I thanked him, but there was still an awful lot of damage between us that needed to be repaired.

Today wasn't the day to think about any of that.

I climbed out of my truck, grabbed the flowers I'd picked up from the market—the brightest mixed bunch they had—and jogged across the parking lot, excited to see my future wife and my new son.

I couldn't stop grinning, my heart was so full. From Rain not only finally agreeing to marry me, but actually attempting to propose—I laughed out loud at the thought of yesterday's sunrise debacle—to Zac's arrival, I hadn't stopped smiling for the last twenty-four hours. It wouldn't have surprised me if I'd been smiling in my sleep.

When the elevator reached the third floor, I hurried down the hall so fast I nearly ran into one of the nurses exiting Rain's room.

"How's she doing?" I asked, wishing she'd step aside and let me in.

"She fell asleep a little while ago. I think she expected you earlier."

Damn it. "Yeah, I overslept. I guess yesterday caught up with me. Is the baby back in the nursery?"

She nodded. "He was fussy and kept her awake most of the night, so she agreed to let us take him for a while to give her a little break. I can bring him back if you want. I was just dropping off a delivery of flowers for her."

She looked at the supermarket bunch I carried in my hand.

"Those are nice too."

"Do you have something I can put these in? I wasn't thinking when I picked them up."

"I'm sure I can find something."

When she finally moved out of the way, I entered the room. Rain was curled on her side, one hand tucked under her chin. It was amazing how much I'd missed her in such a short amount of time. With her and Izzy both out of the house, it had been too quiet.

The flowers the nurse had been talking about were sitting on a low shelf in front of the window. Roses. At least three dozen red roses, arranged in a deep red vase.

I set my paltry flowers on the tray table next to the bed, and although it was wrong, I tore the card from the arrangement and opened the envelope.

Congratulations. Can't wait to meet him. Love you xxx ooo.

It wasn't signed, but it didn't matter. I knew who had sent them. I crushed the card in my hand and lifted the arrangement off the shelf. On my way out, I dropped my flowers into the water pitcher on the tray.

"Mr. Holgate," the nurse called after me. "I found you a vase."

I waved her off and kept walking until I reached the elevator. Outside the hospital, I dumped the roses in the first trash bin I came to.

Then I climbed in my truck, and I drove.

***

Thank you for reading Miss February! I hope you love Chase and Rain. Find out what happens next when their story concludes in Mrs. February!

Is it possible to find your happily ever after if the past keeps coming back to haunt you?

It took three years, but Rain and Chase finally exchanged vows on a sandy beach as the sun rose over the Atlantic Ocean.

Happiness was theirs. But when jealousy and indiscretion threaten to unravel their tightly knit union, Rain finds herself fighting an elusive adversary—and losing.

At first blinded by love, Chase begins to encounter triggers that set him up for a fall. Opening his eyes to the truth is painful, but if he's to survive, it's his only option. Even if it hurts like hell.

Past experiences and present interference have a tendency to distort things, so what we think we see, might not really be true at all.

Sometimes you just need to close your eyes in order to hear what your heart has been telling you all along.

And then let it lead you home.

Find Mrs. February now on Amazon and free in Kindle Unlimited!

NOTE TO READERS

Reviews are important to independent authors. If you decide to leave a review after you've read this book, please email me a link to your review at authorkarencimms@gmail.com and I'll send you a special bookmark as a thank you.

Want to listen to the Miss February playlist? You can find it by clicking here.

Find the Pinterest board for Miss February by clicking here.

Acknowledgements

It's normal for books to go through revisions and rewrites, some more than others, and Miss February is no exception. In fact, she kind of kicked my ass. I honestly don't know how I could have gotten through it all without my PA, Jenn Holter. Jenn helped me focus on what I needed to do and stay focused. She became my cheerleader, my coach, a hard taskmaster, and an honest reader who wasn't afraid to tell me she if didn't like something. She even sent me little exercises to help me breathe when I had myself so wound up that I couldn't think straight.

I don't know what I would've done without you, Jenn. Don't ever leave me!

Andrew Biernat, thank you for your positive messages. While I was struggling to finish the rewrite, I told Andrew I needed motivation, and boy, did he pick up the ball and run with it. Andrew, you are sweet, and smart, and you have a big, beautiful heart. I can't wait to see you on the cover of my book later this year.

Lori Ryser, what would I do without you? Like my previous books, Lori has been the very last set of eyes to scan and correct any errors or inconsistencies. If anyone finds a mistake, I guarantee it's something I did after she looked at it.

Thank you to my line editor, Lisa Poisso. My books shine because of you. I'm so lucky to have found you.

To my son, Garrett, thank you for another great cover. I know I drove you crazy, but I love it. And to Lisa Hopstock and Marissa Miller, thank you for the time you put into the original cover. Even though we didn't end up going that way, you guys did a wonderful job.

Kerry Palumbo, thank you for your friendship, your love, and your support. And thank you again for helping make my back cover copy stand out.

Jade Eby, thank you for your beautiful formatting and interior design of my books. I'm always thrilled once you've worked your magic.

Dennis Massone, thank you for your expertise on everything from what Chase would be doing in the pits before a race, to what he'd wash his hands with, to the excitement of driving a modified stock car. I named the driver of No. 57 after you. Stephanie Harris and Stacy Mendoza, thank you for your help with my other car questions. That part of the story will appear in Mrs. February.

My dear friend Diane Lane Stone—like Dennis, I've known you since junior high school. You read this book when it was nothing but ideas and scattered, random chapters. You encouraged me to keep writing, so I did. Thank you. And thank you for inspiring Rain's feisty best friend.

To one of my dearest friends, Ione Connolly. Thank you for driving me around the old neighborhoods so I could visit and photograph some of my old haunts which are used as settings in this book. Every time we're together, I feel like I'm sixteen again. We need to do it more often.

To my lovely daughter-in-law, Olka Cimms, thank you for translating Irena's words into Polish and helping make her a far more interesting character.

Thank you to my beta readers, Ann Travis and Lydia Fasteland. I can always count on you both to give me clear, detailed, honest feedback. And thanks to the very earliest readers, Tyra Hattersley and Rhonda Donaldson. You helped me take a hard look at where Miss February was going and change that direction.

Sandy Barg, you are amazing. You read and reread, and then read again. Not only that, you have championed me on Facebook, sharing teasers and connecting me with other authors. If I thanked you a thousand times, it still wouldn't be enough.

Whitney Barbetti, you laugh when I call you my mentor, but seriously, you are my guiding star. If it weren't for you, very few people would know my name or have read my books. Someday I'm going to hug you—super hard. Thank you a zillion times over for all you've done for me.

Jena Camp at Indie Girl Promotions, thank you for the fabulous teasers and graphics, and everything you've done for me as well, through this book and my last ones. You're the best.

Nick Denmon, thank you again for your beautiful words and for allowing me to use them as my epigraph for Miss February. You touch my heart, always.

To the members of my fan group, the VIP Room, I love you guys. You've lifted me up when I needed it, made me laugh, gave me support, and we can't forget Sandy's "Good Morning" posts, (which help us all wake up with a smile!)

Thank you to all of the bloggers who have shared my work. Where would we indie authors be without you?

And lastly, to my husband, Jim. You put up with so much so that I can lock myself away in the attic and write. Thank you for everything you do for me. I would be lost without you.

Turn the page for an exclusive sneak peek of

MRS. FEBRUARY
Book Two in Karen Cimms'
Calendar Girl Duet
Available on Amazon and free in Kindle Unlimited

Mrs. February

Rain

It had been a long, wonderful day. The best day.

We'd had to be on the beach in time to start the ceremony at six o'clock sharp so that we could be pronounced husband and wife at exactly 6:13 a.m., just as the sun rose. That had been my crazy idea, but even three years later, the memory of Chase sharing the sunrise with me was still one of my favorites. Our family and friends may not have liked getting up that early, but Chase had loved the idea. And I loved him.

I'd made him wait long enough to accept his marriage proposal, and then even longer to finally set a date. When he told me his mother was wondering what we were waiting for, I was shocked. Finally, his family had accepted me. When I told him I wanted to get married at sunrise on the beach in Cape May, he insisted on August 15. We only had two weeks to plan, but we pulled it off.

And although we'd been living together for three years, after everyone headed home after the breakfast reception, we spent almost the entire day in our suite at the Grand, behaving exactly as newlyweds should.

I was exhausted—happy, but exhausted. We had an early dinner, and by the time we got back to our room, we could barely keep our eyes open.

So why was Chase waking me when it was still dark outside?

I growled and pulled the covers over my head.

"C'mon, babe. Wake up. It's still our wedding day, and there's one more thing we need to do."

I forced an eye open. "Are you kidding me? We did that. A lot."

Tugging at the covers, he laughed. "Not that. Something else. You need to get up and put your dress on."

The bastard flicked the light on next to my head. The clock read 11:25.

"I'm tired. Can't we do it in the morning?"

"No. It has to be tonight."

I rolled onto my back and squinted up at him. He was already dressed and holding up my wedding gown.

"It's a good thing you're cute."

"Cute? That's all? Earlier you said I was handsome and sexy." He pulled the covers off the rest of the way and lay my dress across the bed. "Now all I am is cute?"

"When I've been up since four in the morning, there are plenty of other names I'd like to call you, and none of them are 'cute.'"

He chuckled. "Now, now."

Grudgingly, I pushed myself up, wriggled to the edge of the bed, and held my arms up over my head. If he wanted me to get dressed, then he was going to have to get me there himself.

After dropping the dress over my head, he tugged me to my feet, spun me gently, and raised the zipper on the strapless gown.

I yawned loudly. "Where are we going?" If he expected me to put on makeup at this hour, he was going to be woefully disappointed.

"Not far."

I located my strappy silver sandals in the corner of the room.

"Nope. Flip-flops are fine."

Too tired to argue, I slipped my feet into the white rubber thongs I'd worn to the beach earlier.

We stepped off the elevator a few minutes later into a near-empty lobby. "I should just make you carry me. Then I could go back to sleep."

"If you insist." He scooped me up as if I weighed nothing and set out across the lobby toward the front doors.

"The parking lot is that way," I said, pointing to the right, but he kept on walking.

We crossed Beach Avenue heading toward the ocean. The farther we got from the hotel, the darker it became. There was no moon, and the stars above us seemed endless. When we were as close to the surf as we could get, Chase set me down. He pulled a large beach towel from the tote he'd slung over his shoulder before we left, spread it out on the sand, and pulled his iPhone from the pocket of his chinos.

Moments later, the piano intro to "My Future Days" by Pearl Jam, his favorite band, filled the space around us.

Goosebumps sprang up along my arms. It could've been from the breeze blowing off the ocean, but I'd bet anything it was the romantic mood my new husband was creating in front of me. "What are you doing?"

"Shh." He held out his arms, and I stepped into them. "I loved everything about today except one thing—we didn't have a first dance. I didn't want us to miss that."

The air was cool against my skin, but inside, I was soft and warm and gooey as a toasted marshmallow. I circled my arms around his neck, and he pressed a palm against my lower back. I'd never felt happier or more content.

There on the beach of Cape May where we'd been married eighteen hours earlier, we danced in the dark—me in my wedding gown and Chase in his white shirt and chinos, serenaded by Eddie Vedder.

Life was perfect.

The song ended but we still moved together to the rhythm of the pounding surf, invisible to all but the stars winking at us overhead.

I lifted my head, wanting to tell Chase for at least the twentieth time that day how much I loved him, when a star shot across the sky.

"Oh my god! Did you see that?"

His low chuckle told me that in fact, he had.

Moments later, I saw another.

He led me to the towel he'd set out earlier and pulled me down beside him. When he lay down, I did the same, resting my head against his shoulder just as another star tracked across the heavens.

"When you said you wanted to be married here, I remembered an article I'd read about how bright the Perseids meteor shower would be this year because of the new moon," he said. "I couldn't control the weather, but at least I could set the stage. I wanted you to feel close to your father today, even though he wasn't here to give you away."

The sky above turned watery, and I blinked back the burn of the tears filling my eyes. I rolled over so I could see his face.

"My dad didn't have to give me away, Chase. You already have my heart. I gave my whole self to you long ago. Today just made it official." I pressed my hand into his. "But thank you. You have no idea what this means to me."

Another flash of light streaked across the sky.

My father had taught me all about the Perseids when I was a little girl. They got their name because they look like they're flying out of the constellation Perseus, an ancient hero from Greek mythology. I knew we weren't really seeing stars but bits of comet dust disintegrating in the earth's atmosphere. I may not have been the best student, especially after Dad died, but I've never forgotten lying in the back yard with him, studying the constellations. And tonight, thanks to the wonderful man lying beside me, I felt closer to him than I had since he'd left us.

My eyes followed a speck of comet dust across the sky. I'd never seen so many shooting stars at one time. And that just confirmed it: I believed with all my heart that my father would have approved of my husband.

"I wouldn't have thought it possible, but you've made this day even more special." I waved my arm in a wide arc. "You've given me everything, from the sunrise to the all the stars in the heavens."

He propped himself up on one elbow, his face hovering over mine. His hand skirted across my hips until he found my hand on the other side.

"Thank you for becoming my wife." Soft, warm lips touched my forehead. "Just promise to love me forever, because that's what I plan to do, Rain. Love you until the end of time."

He kissed me before I could answer, but silently, I promised. I couldn't imagine there would ever be a time that we would give each other anything less than forever.

Find Mrs. February now on Amazon and free in Kindle Unlimited!

ABOUT THE AUTHOR

Karen Cimms is a writer, editor, and music lover. She was born and raised in New Jersey and still thinks of the Garden State as home. She currently lives in Northeast Pennsylvania, although her heart is usually in Maine.

Want to connect with Karen? Sign up for her newsletter and follow her on the following social media platforms:

www.karencimms.com
Facebook: www.facebook.com/KarenCimms
Instagram: www.instagram.com/karen_cimms/
TikTok: www.tiktok.com/@karencimms

ALSO BY KAREN CIMMS

Of Love and Madness Series

At This Moment

We All Fall Down

All I Ever Wanted

Better Man

You're All I Want for Christmas (a holiday novella)

Calendar Girl Duet

Miss February

Mrs. February

Gravel Hill Boys

Forever and Always

Never Say Never (Coming late Spring of 2023)

Standalone Books

Love, Lies, and Lattes (formerly Broadway Beans)

www.ingramcontent.com/pod-product-compliance
Lightning Source LLC
Chambersburg PA
CBHW060306260626
47160CB00007B/2516